Put to sleep

The chief of the Ithaca Police Department stepped forward and leaned into a microphone. He was familiar to anyone who had lived and worked in the area as long as I had—a good man, the scuttlebutt had it, and an honest one. His manner was direct, uncompromising, and succinct:

"Veterinarian Benjamin Grazley of the Canandaigua Equine Clinic was forty-six years old. He had been traveling north on Route 96 and stopped at a gas station in the town of Covert. He was shot to death at approximately 7:15 A.M.

"He left a widow and two children."

A cacophony of shouts erupted from the mass of reporters, but Rita herself shouted the word that the entire room had feared to hear . . .

Sniper.

Hemlock Falls Mysteries by Claudia Bishop

A TASTE FOR MURDER

A DASH OF DEATH

A PINCH OF POISON

MURDER WELL-DONE

DEATH DINES OUT

A TOUCH OF THE GRAPE

A STEAK IN MURDER

MARINADE FOR MURDER

JUST DESSERTS

FRIED BY JURY

A PUREE OF POISON

BURIED BY BREAKFAST

A DINNER TO DIE FOR

The Casebooks of Dr. McKenzie Mysteries by Claudia Bishop

THE CASE OF THE ROASTED ONION

The Case of the
ROASTED
ONION

CLAUDIA BISHOP

BERKLEY PRIME CRIME, NEW YORK

THE BERKLEY PUBLISHING GROUP
Published by the Penguin Group
Penguin Group (USA) Inc.
375 Hudson Street, New York, New York 10014, USA
Penguin Group (Canada), 90 Eglinton Avenue East, Suite 700, Toronto, Ontario M4P 2Y3, Canada
(a division of Pearson Penguin Canada Inc.)
Penguin Books Ltd., 80 Strand, London WC2R 0RL, England
Penguin Group Ireland, 25 St. Stephen's Green, Dublin 2, Ireland (a division of Penguin Books Ltd.)
Penguin Group (Australia), 250 Camberwell Road, Camberwell, Victoria 3124, Australia
(a division of Pearson Australia Group Pty. Ltd.)
Penguin Books India Pvt. Ltd., 11 Community Centre, Panchsheel Park, New Delhi—110 017, India
Penguin Group (NZ), Cnr. Airborne and Rosedale Roads, Albany, Auckland 1310, New Zealand
(a division of Pearson New Zealand Ltd.)
Penguin Books (South Africa) (Pty.) Ltd., 24 Sturdee Avenue, Rosebank, Johannesburg 2196, South Africa

Penguin Books Ltd., Registered Offices: 80 Strand, London WC2R 0RL, England

This is a work of fiction. Names, characters, places, and incidents either are the product of the author's imagination or are used fictitiously, and any resemblance to actual persons, living or dead, business establishments, events, or locales is entirely coincidental. The publisher does not have any control over and does not assume any responsibility for author or third-party websites or their content.

THE CASE OF THE ROASTED ONION

A Berkley Prime Crime Book / published by arrangement with the author

PRINTING HISTORY
Berkley Prime Crime mass-market edition / September 2006

Copyright © 2006 by Mary Stanton.
Cover art by Mary Ann Lasher.
Cover design by Annette Fiore.
Interior text design by Kristin del Rosario.

ISBN: 0-425-21223-8

BERKLEY® PRIME CRIME
Berkley Prime Crime Books are published by The Berkley Publishing Group,
a division of Penguin Group (USA) Inc.,
375 Hudson Street, New York, New York 10014.
The name BERKLEY PRIME CRIME and the BERKLEY PRIME CRIME design are trademarks belonging to Penguin Group (USA) Inc.

PRINTED IN THE UNITED STATES OF AMERICA

10 9 8 7 6 5 4 3 2 1

For my sisters
Whit Hairston and Cynthia Whitaker, Esquire

Cast of Characters

At McKenzie Veterinary Practice, Inc.

Austin McKenzie a retired veterinarian
Madeline McKenzie his wife
Joe Turnblad the McKenzies' assistant, a second-year vet
 student
Allegra Fulbright the McKenzies' assistant, a college senior

At the *Summersville Sentinel*

Rita Santelli the publisher
Nigel Fish a reporter

Citizens of Summersville

Victor Bergland a professor of veterinary science
Thelma Bergland his wife
Lila Gernsback a horsewoman
Nora and Jennifer Longworth horsewomen
Orville DeGroote a farmer
Ingrid DeGroote his daughter
Simon Provost chief of detectives, Summersville

Colleen   a waitress, the Monrovian Embassy
Manfred Schmitt   owner, cook, the Monrovian Embassy
Brewster McClellan   a venture capitalist
Marina McClellan   his wife
Stephanie McClellan   their daughter
Diana North   a veterinarian, large-animal practice
Greg D'Andrea   a veterinarian, small-animal practice
Jerry Coughlin   a veterinarian, a research scientist
Ben Grazley   a veterinarian, racetrack practice
Phillip Sullivan   a lawyer

And Friends

Lincoln   a collie
Miss Odie   a cat
Andrew   a Quarterhorse
Pony   a Shetland pony
Blackie   a Labrador puppy
Juno   an Akita cross

Prologue

❧❧

LARKY Schumacher upended the stainless steel bucket onto the gravel drive and let the iodine solution splash over his rubber boots. He slung the empty bucket and sopping sponges into the cargo hold of his Ford Expedition and pulled the hatch shut. "It'd be a good idea to leave those bandages on the foreleg alone until I see the horse again," he said. He was a big man, with strong hands and the weathered complexion that characterizes most large-animal veterinarians. The sullen sixteen-year-old slouched in front of him shrugged and tucked her hands into her breeches pockets. "Whatever," she said. The insolence in the tone made Larky's palm itch. He stood still a moment, took a breath, and relaxed. His kids had been this age once. Although not this truculent. Never this truculent.

Larky let his gaze drift over the lush green pastures and the artfully silvered three-bar fences of the McClellan estate. He fixed on a double-oxer jump planted smack in the middle of the riding arena and stood frowning at it. "Stephanie," he said, deliberately not looking at her, "you're pretty sure you can't tell me how Beecher got those sores on his neck?"

"How should I know!" she flared. "Lice, probably. Too many sparrows in the barn. And if you've got sparrows, you've got lice. Everybody knows that. All I know is Beecher'd scratch himself bald if I didn't tie him down."

He glanced briefly at her, then looked away. "We've agreed that he'll be turned out until the wounds on his neck dry up. You aren't going to tie him down anymore."

Stephanie narrowed her eyes. Two spots of color burned high on her cheekbones. Her thin back was rigid. "All that sun will bleach his coat. We're going to be riding at Earlsdown in three weeks. That is, if you're a good enough vet to get that lump on his cannon bone healed up. His coat'll be a mess."

"Put a turnout sheet on him, then," Larky said. "Just get him outside. I don't," he repeated, without emphasis, "want him tied down anymore."

"Fine."

"And you'll turn him out as soon as I leave?"

"I said I would, all right? Let me alone!"

After nearly twenty years in the horse business, Larky knew when to give it up. He nodded. "Okay. Your father wanted me to give the Angus their spring shots. I'll go do that now, unless you'd like a hand turning Beecher out."

She stared him down.

Larky slid into the driver's seat and drove the short distance to the small cowshed that held Brewster McClellan's prize Angus bull and heifer. Stephanie watched him haul his black bag out of the backseat, her face impassive. Suddenly, she took off toward the huge Italianate house that burdened the rise behind the riding arena. So poor Beecher wasn't going to get turned out after all. He shook his head. Going back to confront her was counterproductive. She'd blow up, run to her father, and he'd lose a wealthy client before he even started. He was already on thin ice with her mother, who'd been frantically insistent that he come and see the horse this morning. The hell with it. He'd take care of the cows and shove off.

It took him longer than it needed to. Someone had opened the double doors leading to the turnout paddock and the cattle roamed at large in the big fenced area. Neither Samson nor Delilah was interested in getting a quick dose of antitoxin. But he wasn't in a rush, and the morning was a gold-and-blue celebration of life, and Larky took a moment to scratch the big bull between the ears before he packed up to leave.

Behind the wheel of the Expedition, Larky looked at his watch. Still early. He was due to meet the farrier at the Greenbrier stables at nine, which meant there'd be enough time to go into Summersville for a latte at the new Starbucks. He turned north on Route 15 and took the next left onto SR 41.

This was a quieter, pleasanter way into town. The woods ran right up to the road and filtered the sunlight into gold and shadow. He let Stephanie and her worrisome behavior drift away in the clear air. Driving always relaxed him, and he was looking forward to the coffee and the interesting task ahead at the stable. So he almost passed by the pitiful huddle on the shoulder. But a woeful yip made caught his attention. He pulled under the shade of a large oak. A puppy lay on the pavement, forelegs sprawled unnaturally wide. Larky got out of the van, crouched down at a prudent distance from the pup and made soothing noises. The puppy's shape and size suggested a four- to five-month-old black Lab. But its coat—or rather, her coat, he noticed as the pup struggled to sit up—was a curious mixture of brown and cream. Some Akita in there, maybe.

He straightened up to walk over and pick the pup up, confidant that she wouldn't bite. The last he knew of life was that the puppy was glad to see him.

One

❧❧

As I record this case and mull over subsequent events, I confess that at the time this story begins, I had no presentiment of the gruesome murders to come, or of my role in apprehending the killer. If I had, would events turned out differently?

I will never know.

There were those who were surprised when I embarked upon a career as an investigating detective. After forty years as a veterinarian and a scholar, I was a bit bemused myself. My dear wife was not. I have never, Madeline said, refused a ditch or fence, no matter how wide or high, and who better, she asked, to rise to the challenge of a horse-based homicide than Austin Oliver McKenzie?

Who, indeed?

It began appropriately enough, with the announcement of a murder.

That April morning began like many others at our farm in upstate New York. At seven o'clock, after my usual visit to the barns to feed the stock, I sat in our comfortable kitchen with Madeline at my side, my dog Lincoln at my feet, and the cat Odie asleep on the woodstove hearth. I was both peaceful and content. I consumed my oatmeal as I leafed through the previous day's mail: advertisements, bills, offers for credit cards, bills, several more bills, and free copies of a publication called *Cows Today*.

There was also one first-class letter.

I glanced at the return address and tossed it on the discard pile. Madeline reached over and picked it up curiously.

"Merely junk, my dear." I peered over my spectacles at Madeline, for twenty years the delight of my heart.

"Open it first, sweetie." Madeline's tones were calm and affectionate, as they always are, but her sapphire gaze was penetrating. She could not fail to note that the return address was styled:

Organizing Committee Earlsdown Three-Day Event

"The last time I let you throw out unopened mail, three checks went missing." She dropped the letter on top of the New York State Electric & Gas bill and resumed her meal. She swallowed her slice of ham and reached for a second piece. I, too, reached for the ham, and then withdrew my hand at Madeline's regretful shake of the head.

I sliced my small piece of fat-free turkey into four neat quarters and contemplated the pattern the squares made on the Fiesta ware. I did not begrudge Madeline her second slice of Honey Baked Ham. Her enthusiasm for the delicacies of the table insures the voluptuousness of her magnificent figure. I did, however, mildly resent the fact that at five feet, nine inches, and a fighting weight of one hundred and fifty pounds, Honey Baked Ham was forbidden *me*. But we are all slaves to the double helix and the genes contained therein. My father Hiram suffered from high cholesterol, too.

"So, are you going to open it?" Madeline eyed the creamy envelope I had moved back to the discard pile. "Part of that looks like an invitation."

"It does, indeed."

Madeline's sapphire blue eyes fastened on mine reproachfully. She spooned scrambled eggs onto her biscuits and ladled gravy over the whole. I sighed, picked up the silver letter opener given to me by the grateful owner of a champion bull I had saved from an attack of brucellosis, and opened the damned thing.

Madeline waited, her fork suspended.

I read both the invitation and the accompanying letter. "The letter is signed by someone who styles himself Brewster McClellan."

"Austin, he either *is* Brewster McClellan or he isn't."

"It *is* Brewster McClellan and I don't want to have anything to do with him."

"What does he want?"

"It's a request for my services as Veterinarian Delegate at the Earlsdown Three-Day Event in late March. I shall decline."

Madeline evinced mild surprise. "The horse show where poor Jerry Coughlin got kicked out of the veterinary business last year?"

"He wasn't kicked out, Madeline. The local show committee issued a letter of censure. Coughlin hasn't recovered yet. I hear he's doing some poorly paid research for a small start-up company. It's a shame."

"I remember now," Madeline said soberly. "What a mess." She twiddled a bit of hair, a habit of hers when puzzled. "So they want us to attend this year. Hm. I thought Larky Schumacher had that gig all sewed up."

The phone rang. I ignored it. There is a great deal I dislike about some technology: the combustion engine, television, and air-conditioning rank high among my pet peeves. (Xerox copiers, on the other hand, are useful pieces of equipment, as are computers.) But the chief object of my opprobrium is the telephone. It is nosy, intrusive, and when you answer the damn thing, it's generally someone you don't want to hear from in the first place. It rang again. Madeline smiled at me. I snatched the receiver from the cradle and shouted, "McKenzie." (I have discovered that this method of response sometimes results in the other party hanging up.)

"Austin, you crazy son of a bitch. How are you?"

I sat back in my chair and regarded the Agway calendar hanging on the wall over the kitchen sink. Today's date was marked "harvest winter wheat." Harvesting winter wheat would have been highly preferable to talking to Victor Bergland on the telephone. If I'd had any to harvest. "Hello, Victor. And how is the graduate school progressing?"

"Without you, you mean? We're thriving. Ho. Ho. Ho." Victor Bergland is an acquaintance of many years. He succeeded me as department chair of Bovine Science at my retirement. He is a bushy-bearded fellow with an ego as big as his belly. If I owned a ram with his temperament, I would sell it to someone I didn't like.

I let a repelling silence elapse.

"Wanted to know what you think about Schumacher."

I glanced at the invitation in Madeline's hand. "What about Larky Schumacher?"

"You're kidding me. You haven't heard? He's dead."

I sat up. "Dead?"

Madeline gasped.

"As a doornail." Victor has never been noted for his inspired locutions. "Shot to death on State Road Forty-one, just off of Fifteen. He was headed into town after a barn call at the McClellan's place. Stopped the van for some reason, got out, and pow! Right in the back of the neck. Coroner says he died instantly."

"When did this happen?"

"Yesterday morning. It was all over the evening news, Austin. You don't get out much, do you?"

"My lord. This is terrible. What happened?"

I could almost hear Victor's shrug over the telephone. "Nobody seems to know for sure. Folks down at the Monrovian Embassy think it's a sniper."

The Embassy, as our local diner is known to its habitués, is a hotbed of gossip and misinformation. I lunch there as often as possible. And even, if not under Madeline's affectionate eye, take an occasional cholesterol-laden breakfast there.

"Myself"—Victor's voice broke into my thoughts—"I think he just stepped out of the van to take a leak. Wound was from a thirty-double-ought-six. So for my money, it was some out-of-season hunter from Syracuse or Rochester. Idiots come up here with those shotguns and think they can pot away at deer any time of year."

This did, indeed, seem a more likely source of Larky's death than a sniper. Victor said he would let us know the date and time of the funeral and I hung up. We would attend, of course. Neither Madeline nor I had known him well, but he was one of our own.

Madeline was as horrified as I when I explained the time and nature of Larky's death.

"I suppose that explains the invitation," Madeline said soberly.

"It doesn't explain why the invitation is here now," I responded. "Less than twenty-four hours have lapsed since Larky's death."

"It's awfully late for the committee to get in touch with anyone. This is Wednesday. The show starts in ten days. I suppose the show committee had to act fast." Madeline's tone was dubious.

"Perhaps. But it seems very odd to me." I reflected for a moment, to no purpose. The timing was suspect. There was no doubt about it. "In any event, I shall turn the invitation down."

Madeline examined the contents of the letter. She picked up the piece of cream pasteboard invitation first. Her auburn eyebrows raised a trifle. "This is for the Hunt Ball. Worth its weight in gold to the horsy crowd. Hmph and hmph again." She set it aside without interest. Madeline holds no brief for the glamorous life of the upper reaches of the equestrian community, of which the annual horse show at Earlsdown is a prime example. She is far happier in rubber boots and barn jacket than an evening gown. She is beautiful in both.

Then she read the letter. She made a face, folded it into a paper airplane and tossed it at me. It skidded off my head and landed on my lap. She drank half of her cranberry juice at a gulp and set the glass down with a thump.

"Austin!"

I know that tone of loving exasperation well. I turned around in my chair and gazed out the expanse of window to the lawn beyond. There had been a frost the night before. It had not been kind to the early tulips. They wanted deadheading. And the daffodils were blooming in berserk fashion around the fishpond at the bottom of the lawn. The bulbs needed to be separated, or we would be awash in stunted, ill-nourished blooms in no time.

"Austin?" Madeline's mellow contralto is hard to ignore. But I continued my perusal of the flowers, compiling a mental list of gardening tasks.

Madeline is five feet, ten inches tall and generously proportioned. She rose to her full height, placed herself between the windows and my abstracted gaze, and shouted, *"Hey!"*

That particular tone of voice meant business. Even the dog

knew it. Lincoln rose from his place at my feet and stood at her side, his plumey tail wagging, his eye reproachfully on me. He is a sable-and-white collie. The sight of these two creatures standing side by side is very pleasing. The mahogany of Lincoln's coat matches Madeline's hair; both are silky, thick, and luxuriant.

She waved her hand vigorously. The invitation flapped like a semaphore. "McClellan's offering us fifteen grand! Just to show up at Earlsdown for a week!"

"I refuse to do any consulting work for a man named after a saddle."

"*Plus* expenses and a week at a really fabulous show." Did I mention that the cream of Madeline's skin intensifies to peach with emotion? "We could use the break, don't you think? I think we've been getting into a bit of a rut, myself."

I ignored the implied aspersion on my character. My habits of discipline and consistency in no way make me a fuddy-duddy. "Our current routine has nothing to do with it. McClellan's notoriously ill-tempered. Not only that, I believe him to be duplicitous. And I can't imagine who would name him to the Organizing Committee. Perhaps he stole the letterhead from Les Whyte's secretary."

Madeline blinked at me. "Holy crow. You really don't like this guy. Have you ever met him? I'm pretty sure I haven't."

I frowned. "I haven't actually met him, no. But I know of him, and none of it is good. He owned the animal that Jerry Coughlin was alleged to have killed last year. His daughter competed on it. More to the point, he was the one that brought the charges against Coughlin when the horse died. Admittedly, he backed off after the investigation was complete. Even so, the man's trouble."

Madeline frowned. "I remember that. It was a pure mess and a tragedy to boot. But I thought they decided that it was negligence, not intentional. As for this guy McClellan, it's not like you, Austin, to pass judgment without having actually met him."

It was clear that Madeline was not about to let up on the character of the odious McClellan. Whom, I admit, I knew as odious only by repute. One of Madeline's sterling qualities is her sense of fair play, so I conceded, albeit reluctantly, "True. For all I know, the man is of excellent character and merely stupid about horses. There are any numbers of people like that in the show world. Nonetheless, Coughlin was forced out in the middle of show week, just like that." I snapped my fingers. "And his reputation blackened without real proof. The horse was named Faraway, I believe."

Madeline had not been listening attentively. She plucked the note from my lap and smoothed it on the table. "Earlsdown's held at the Lodi show grounds, and Lodi's not far away. Less than forty-five miles from here."

"I was not referring to the horse show venue, but to the name of the horse." I paused. "Coughlin was apparently treating it for exhaustion when it died." Three-day events are notoriously hard on the animals. Riders whose only concern is a win can ride their mounts to an ugly death if not stopped by competent veterinary advice. The horse had colicked from exhaustion. Coughlin had administered a higher dosage of adrenaline than the animal could handle. It had died of a heart attack. "Not to mention the fact that I don't want to spend a week dressed in a blazer and tie talking to halfwits like Victor Bergland."

Her fiery blue gaze softened. "Oh, sweetie. I know how much you think you hate horse shows . . ."

I loathe, detest, and despise horse shows. Not all horse shows. Just the professional circuit in general and Earlsdown in particular. For some reason, this particular A-circuit event is rife with even more venom, spite, and malice than is the norm. And that's just the officious volunteers who monitor the parking lot. The entrants and their attendants are worse.

". . . and Earlsdown especially, after you got that parking ticket last year. But once we get there, you end up loving it. Just like me." She paused, twiddling her hair in earnest. "Sweetie? We should really think about accepting McClellan's offer."

My protest was mild, but firm. "We can't just pick up and leave for a week, my dear. I have patients and clients to consider. And what about Lincoln and Odie?"

Lincoln barked in apparent protest. Madeline bent and patted him in an approving way. Upon hearing the bark, Odie roused herself from her warm perch on the stove, yawned, and directed a baleful look at the collie. Those who engage in anthropomorphism might have thought the dog agreed with Madeline and that the cat agreed with me. Not true. Odie generally places herself on the opposite side of any disagreement between the dog and myself, as a matter of principle. This renders all Odie's protests moot. But it did seem as if I were being outvoted.

"Lodi's an easy drive from here, and we can all travel together in the unit. It's why we *got* the unit, remember? So we could take the guys with us." Madeline referred to our RV, an elderly forty-five-foot motor home that she has transformed into a model of comfort.

"And what about our patients?" I said icily. "And who will feed and care for the stock in the barn?"

She shrugged. "Call Victor. He can handle any real emergencies. He's a vet himself . . ."

I snorted.

". . . Well, he is, sweetie, and a good one, too, or he never would have taken over your old position after you retired. Anyhow, he must have one or two hungry second-year students hanging around that would love to stay here and do barn chores. A good one can handle any routine stuff that might come up."

"And my newspaper column? Do you expect a second-year veterinary student to handle that?"

I am, of course, *that* Dr. McKenzie. My advice column to importunate pet owners is a weekly feature in the *Summersville Sentinel.* My editor is Rita Santelli, a woman of charm but little editorial discernment. She is constantly revising my advice to my readers. She claims it is both rude and blunt.

Madeline nudged my hand to gain my attention. "Take advantage of the miracle of wireless technology, Austin. Rita can e-mail your letters to you. You can write the column from your laptop. You won't even have to leave the RV. Besides . . ." Two dimples appeared in Madeline's cheeks. "Rita might even whoop it up a little if you did the column by e-mail instead of going down there in person every week. Not," she added hastily, "that she doesn't enjoy your little

chats together." She reached across the table and patted my
hand again. "E-mail's faster, too. Goodness knows we both
have enough to do around here. And Rita would like it."

Madeline, as usual, had an excellent point.

As I have mentioned, Rita's position at the *Summersville
Sentinel* is that of editor. Normally, I walk down to the *Sentinel* offices once a week to collect the written solicitations for
my advice and to discuss the lamentable state of previous
week's edition with the *Sentinel* staff. Rita had suggested the
e-mail option more than once, averring that it took far less
time to scan the material into her computer than it did to
soothe the staff back into productivity after my visits.

Madeline picked up the letter. " 'Course, we don't want to
forget that McClellan's offering fifteen thousand dollars, either. For a week's work. Good grief, Austin."

I adjusted my spectacles onto my nose with a firm hand.
"We have never been for sale, my dear."

"Well. You decide what's best."

There was so much more my beloved refused to say. We
did indeed need the money.

Madeline sighed a little wistfully, then came over, wrapped
her arms around my neck and kissed my cheek. I kissed her
back. Lincoln shoved his muzzle under my hand and the
damned cat, seeing what I believe to be known as a group hug
in progress, jumped onto the table and butted her head against
my forearm. The cat also took the opportunity to nibble at the
ham. Without another word, Madeline smiled radiantly at us
all and went to the sink to wash the dishes.

I know my wife well. She'd rather eat a rat than point the
finger of blame. I certainly do not deserve Madeline. A more
forgiving and patient spouse would be hard to find. I deserved
whatever opprobrium she refused to fling my way.

I see I must digress. Many months ago, I had taken a large
loan against my comfortable retirement income and invested
in Enblad, the same Enblad whose CEO now languishes in a
minimum-security prison, and whose CFO is living a gilded
life on a tropical island that has no extradition agreement with
the United States of America.

Facing financial ruin, I immediately opened a large-animal

practice, of course. One must pay one's bills. But the practice was taking time to build. And I must admit adjusting to the daily lot of a practicing veterinarian's existence was taking longer than I'd hoped. The academic life had softened me. It had been many years since I'd stood in an unheated barn at ten degrees below zero, with my right arm thrust three-quarters up the hind end of a heifer.

"We're going to manage just fine without that check. Don't think another thing about it." She filled the sink with hot, soapy water and began to wash the dishes. "Well, if you don't want to go to Earlsdown, then that's that."

"I do not," I said firmly.

She began to hum an old country and western tune titled, I believe, "You Done Stomped on My Heart (and Smashed That Sucker Flat)." After a moment, she broke off to ask, "Did you look at today's call schedule?"

We had a call schedule? I was pleased. My practice seemed to be picking up. "No, I have not. We have farm calls today?"

"Quite a few. I put the list in the truck. Orville DeGroote called while you were in the shower. He said that big gelding of his daughter's is starting a couple of abscesses."

"Oh," I said. The gelding was a kicker. And a biter.

"So I'll go with you today on your rounds. That bugger's a real handful"—she meant the abscessed gelding, although DeGroote himself was no walk in the park—"and I can twitch him for you."

This was true. The bugger in question—a seventeen-hand Quarterhorse with a vile temper—had taken a nice chunk out of my forearm the last time I had floated his teeth. And he was prone to foot abscess, which required boring a hole in the sole of the hoof with a lethally sharp curette, a procedure to which many equines object. One of Madeline's many talents is a dab hand with a twitch; neither bovine nor equine objects to being led around by the nose when the alternative is a painful pinch to the snoot.

"And since we're going to be out on farm calls today, anyway, I'll give Bill VanDerPlanck a call. He wanted his bull calves castrated and we might as well do it now. No time like the present."

Like most cost-conscious farmers VanDerPlanck refused to pay for anesthetic for routine farm operations such as castration and cleaning up abscesses. Well, if castration of a few lively bull calves loomed, so be it.

I cleared my throat. "And how many calves did VanDerPlanck grow this year? I seem to have forgotten."

"Twenty-three," Madeline said sunnily. "And you know it's no use waiting until the last minute for castrations. I'll bet those boys are running two hundred pounds each already."

I considered the effort required to castrate twenty-three two-hundred-pound bull calves, each with an understandable objection to having their balls cut off.

Madeline turned to look at me. Her gaze was limpid. "Other than the bull calves and the abscess, we don't have a whole lot on for the next ten days or so, except for some Coggins tests for the folks headed down to Earlsdown."

The Coggins test requires a blood draw and an annoying wait for the results from the Department of Agriculture's testing facility in Utica. Horses in New York State can't be trucked without a current Coggins. Horse owners headed for a show always wait until the last minute to see if the Coggins is current. It never is. They call you at one in the morning ten days before the show to get the serum sample drawn. Then they call you at two in the morning the day before the show wanting to know where the certificate is. I sighed. The week ahead of me was not challenging. Drawing Coggins test was dull. Castrating bull calves was dull and dangerous.

I tapped Brewster McClellan's note with an idle finger. He had appended his cell phone number.

"Perhaps a week at Earlsdown would offer some entertainment for you, my dear."

"We'd have a terrific time," she said promptly.

"I suppose," I said, "I could call Victor back. He himself might welcome a chance at a locum tenens."

"Get him off his chubby little keister for a week," Madeline said encouragingly. "You'll be doing him a favor."

I chuckled a little. It would indeed do my old rival good to wade knee-deep in cow manure for a week or two. And if I didn't find time to castrate VanDerPlanck's bull calves this week, they'd be over three hundred pounds by the time Victor put nippers in hand. Ha!

On the other hand—even the considerable satisfaction of one-upping Victor Bergland wouldn't compensate for the sheer bloody-mindedness of the people at Earlsdown.

I continued to mull.

Madeline stood at the sink, humming the refrain from "These Boots Were Made for Walking" as she rinsed the dishes.

The consulting fee would relieve some of my current financial difficulties. No question about that. I glanced at the pile of bills, which remained unopened, and then at Madeline, elbow-deep in sudsy water. Perhaps there would be sufficient funds left over for a dishwasher.

"Hm," I said. I resettled my spectacles with no small degree of irritation. A week away from home, exhausted horses, and frantic riders, to boot. But the alternative was worse. "You may indeed have come up with a workable solution, my dear."

"Nail down McClellan first, Austin. Then give Victor a shout." She abandoned the dishes to come and give my hand a warm squeeze. She added, with military fervor, "Hoo-rah, sarge!"

"Hoo-rah," I responded, glumly. So I repaired to the office to arrange what was to become an unexpected foray into the investigation of a crime.

Two

❧❧

LINCOLN accompanied me out the door and down to the barn from which the McKenzie Veterinary Practice, Inc., offers its services. After I had accepted the tenured position of full professor of veterinary science at the Cornell College of Agriculture and Life Sciences more than forty years ago, I purchased a small, thirty-acre farm called Sunny Skies, some ten miles from the university in a community called Summersville. The house had been in a state of disrepair. The lawn and gardens had been even more neglected. But the twelve-stall barn had been in mint condition and the pastures fenced in sturdy oak. It was a veritable Eden for the animal members of my family. After my marriage—which had been a big, fat surprise to my colleagues at Cornell, who had thought me a committed bachelor at fifty—the house, the lawn, and the gardens bloomed under Madeline's efficient and loving care. The barn, the attached office, lavatory, and small operating room, were under my dominion; they were mint when I bought the place and they remain mint to this day.

I trod briskly down the graveled path that led from the house to the barn. We had fed the animals just before dawn, of course, but the morning had not yet offered me the opportunity to perform my daily check on the progress of the spring plantings. The vegetable gardens to my right were raked over, mulched, and ready for seedlings as soon as the weather warmed. The flowerbeds to my left were already a riot of narcissi and jonquils, although the scented croci were already past their prime. I would have to find time to deadhead them later today.

At the end of the gravel path, the turnout paddocks form a

U around the barn. The pastures were that new and tender green that is spring's best harbinger. I paused to look at my barn: twelve stalls at right angles to a large indoor arena. The sunlight—pale gold and without heat—gave the illusion that the silvered oak structure was immersed in a huge transparent bowl of light.

My big chestnut Quarterhorse Andrew grazed in the small area of these paddocks set aside especially for him. His pasture buddy is a brown-and-white Shetland named Pony; she was not, at this moment, in view. Andrew raised his head at my approach and gave a hope-filled whicker. "No carrots," I said firmly. "I am headed into the office." Pony, who had been hiding just behind Andrew's tail, peered around his hindquarters, directed a snort of contempt at me, and gave Lincoln a cool appraising look. The dog, in turn, looked up at me, his ears tuliped forward in a question.

"Undoubtedly," I agreed, "Pony is planning more mischief. Ignore her." Pony is a smart, sneaky troublemaker with a most unhorselike sense of humor. I rattled the gravity latch at Andrew's gate to be sure that all was secure. Pony is a notorious escape artist, even when the place she is escaping to—the highway that runs past our farm—is far less desirable than the place she is escaping from—a pasture with shade trees and quite a nice pond in the middle.

The shrill sound of a ringing phone dispelled my curiosity about Pony's plans for the day and forced me to the office. I flung the door open and entered.

"Austin? You there?"

"I'm here, Victor."

"So you've finally decided to get some help out there."

"I beg your pardon?"

"I just talked to Madeline. She called me to see if I'd call you. Guess she wants me take over the practice for the week, assuming you've got any clients for that practice of yours. She said you two are off to Earlsdown?"

"The invitation was in *today*'s mail," I said meaningfully.

"So Madeline said."

I have never cared for the lubricious vocal overtones that strike my ear whenever Victor refers to my wife. On the other hand, the old burke is so jealous he can't help himself, so let him slobber away if he has to. I pressed on. "But Schumacher died yesterday morning. The invitation's arrival today seems . . . precipitate."

"What? Oh. You think they asked you because Schumacher's dead? They asked you because Schumacher begged off."

"Begged off?" This was most peculiar. For almost any practicing vet interested in horses, an invitation to Earlsdown was the best visibility possible.

"That's what I hear. Anyhow, about coverage for your patients, such as they are. I can't take the time to come over and set you straight myself, and I told Madeline that. So she said you'd be looking for some help to take care of things while you're away."

"I may be, yes. For a week or two."

"Madeline thought maybe longer than that. Maybe part time. Anyhoo"—a term I despise—"I've got a candidate in mind. And I can post a notice on the job board, too. Too bad you can't afford a full-time assistant. Can't be all that easy, running a practice at your age. How many clients have you picked up, anyway?"

I decided not to answer this. Victor has a lot in common with ovines, a species easily distracted. He even looks like a sheep, if the light is right. I suspect it's why he grew the beard.

"And how is Thelma?" I asked politely, changing the subject to nettle him. Thelma is Victor's wife of many years. She has a voice that would not only shatter glass, but rout the entire violin section of the New York Philharmonic at first screech. And she has a jaw like a mandrill monkey.

"Thelma's fine," Victor said curtly.

"I understand that her mother lives with you now?" My tones were dulcet.

I had met Thelma's mother, too. She had, if it's possible, an even louder, ruder voice than her daughter's. And I hadn't forgotten the ill-temper shared by mother and daughter alike.

"Yeah," Victor said. "Yeah, the old bat's settled right in."

The gloom in his voice was noticeable. "I'm so sorry," I said, gleefully.

"I'll bet you are." Then, in a most ramlike manner, he rounded back to the task at hand. "I think I can scrounge up a couple of candidates for you. I mean, it's not like you have a whole carload of work out there. Ho. Ho. Ho."

Ho. Ho. Ho.

"What d'ya want, that I should send them around?"

"Perhaps. I have yet to accept the invitation to Earlsdown. Why don't I let you know sometime this afternoon?"

"Whatever. Madeline said the consulting gig includes the Hunt Ball, too."

The degree of envy in Victor's voice was regrettably satisfactory.

"I have to confess that the thought of Madeline in a ball gown was one of the reasons I'm considering this offer," I said.

Did I mention that Thelma is shaped like an artichoke? There was a short silence, in which both of us, I presume, imagined Madeline in full fig. I relented. "However, we will probably not attend. She is far happier in jeans and boots."

There was a short silence. Thelma is an enthusiastic shopper.

"Well, you watch your ass out there in Lodi," Victor said. "I've heard rumors about McClellan. He's got a rep. Mean bastard."

"Yes. I was about to call you to inquire about him. You met him during the course of the drug investigation last year?"

"Yeah. Jerry Coughlin asked me to review the necropsy results independently. Horse died of an overdose of adrenaline, no question about it. Only question was, was it the right thing to do in the first place?"

"I recall all of that, Victor."

"I'm sure Jerry would have asked you if I hadn't been available," Victor said. "Thing is, prescribing adrenaline for the colic's about as effective as a roasted onion up its butt."

This homely and highly ineffective nineteenth-century remedy for colic has a peculiar fascination for Victor. I don't know why.

"'Course, there's probably a lot more of those cockeyed remedies that you ran into in the old days, eh, McKenzie? Ha ha ha ha."

"And how is Coughlin doing these days?"

"Chickens," Victor said flatly.

"Chickens?"

"Doing avian flu virus research for the CDC and a little research for some start-up company. Only work he could get. Plus, you know, that divorce of his was pretty ugly. Talk was that's how come he OD'd the horse. Didn't have his mind on the job at hand. Anyhow—his practice hasn't recovered yet from the flapdoodle. Might not, even though his license was reinstated a couple months ago. And McClellan was the guy that engineered the suspension. Keep your nose clean, McKenzie. Or you'll be out on your butt, too. That it, then? Cheerio! Keep those onions nice and hot. Ha ha ha ha."

Ha ha ha ha.

I concluded the conversation with Victor by dropping the phone back into the cradle. Then I dialed the number of Brewster McClellan's cell phone. The subsequent conversation almost put me in a temper for the rest of the day.

I have said that I find technology an obstacle to a serene and happy life. The fruit of technology I find most loathsome is the cell phone. McClellan picked up after an irritatingly high number of rings. He was in the bath, or the barn, or a bar, for all I knew. Wherever he was, the ambient noise made it impossible to conduct a civil conversation. I concluded, between the squawks, shrieks, shouts, and profanity, that McClellan wished to stop at the clinic this evening at seven to conduct our business transaction in person. There was a contract to be signed and a check to be delivered. I also concluded that Mr. McClellan's grammar needed a good swift kick in the dangling participle, but I let that pass me by—as I have had to do so often in these grammatically benighted times.

I noted our departure dates for Lodi on the calendar, and then went into the main part of the barn to check on the orphaned calf we were attempting to wean. I replenished the nursing bottle we'd rigged on the creep feeder, just as Madeline came through the barn doors down the aisle. She was wearing her Summersville All-Stars baseball jacket against the chill of the spring air and her green Wellington boots. I paused in my work to admire the pink in her cheeks and the sparkle in her eye. She joined me at the pen, her shoulder comfortably snugged next to mine.

"What do you think?" she asked, casting a maternal eye over the little fellow. He was a Red Angus, a breed of which I am particularly fond.

"Another week and he'll be able to ingest a mash." I stepped back from the pen. His weight was improving. "But for the moment, we'll need to continue bottle-feeding every four hours."

Madeline sighed. "That's going to put a hole in the day. We'll have to come back early afternoon to give him another bottle. Right now, we've got to get on the road, Austin. Tyler Simpson just called. One of his dairy cows tangled herself up in some barbed wire and tore off a couple of her teats. We'll have to put off the VanDerPlancks and the castration and get over to Simpson's before the poor heifer bleeds to death. And I called the thingummies . . ."

"The DeGrootes."

"Whatever, about the gelding and told them we'd be there right after we leave the Simpsons, but that's not going to work if we have to come back here, so I'll tell them we'll see him tomorrow." She drew breath. "Whew! Come on, sweetie. I've got the truck loaded and ready to go."

So the three of us—we travel nowhere without the redoubtable Lincoln—spent the next few hours in surgery. And since Simpson is a conscientious fellow ("Might just as well save myself the cost of another farm call and get them spring shots over with right now.") we vaccinated the entire forty-cow dairy herd against brucellosis, bovine encephalitis, tuberculosis, and what is popularly known as "milk fever."

We were therefore somewhat behind time when we returned to our clinic.

I pulled the Bronco into the drive and frowned. Andrew's pasture was empty of either horse or pony. A battered Ford Escort was parked next to the barn that hadn't been there when we had left. Worse yet, the air was silent, save for the twittering of the songbirds building nests in the apple trees. Madeline, busy with her calculator, was unaware of these ill omens.

"You know, Austin, even with the volume discount we're giving regular farm customers, we're going to do better than break even this month." She caught my expression and dropped her voice to a whisper. "What's wrong?"

I laid a warning hand on her arm. "Do you hear anything?" I whispered in return.

"I hear you. What else am I listening for?"

"The sound of a hungry calf."

Madeline frowned. "You're right! It's an hour past his bottle time. And I don't hear as much as a squeak."

"And look," I pointed through the windshield. The twenty-foot-high sliding doors that are the entrance to the barn proper were opened all the way. When we had departed that morning, I had left them halfway closed against the chill of the air.

Madeline's eyes grew large. "A burglar!"

I smiled. "There is not much to burgle in the barn, Madeline. To be accurate, I fear we are looking at a rustler. With the current price of beef as high as it is, I am not at all surprised."

Madeline's creamy brow furrowed. "That doesn't seem likely, Austin. You've been reading too much Louis L'Amour, maybe."

I let this pass. "Stay here," I said sternly.

Lincoln and I slipped noiselessly out of the truck. I closed the door softly. I avoided the noisy crunch of the graveled path and tiptoed down the grass verge to the sliding doors, Lincoln ranging at my side. I felt Madeline behind me.

We keep a tire iron in the toolbox in the rear of the truck. It was there no longer. Madeline brandished it with a cheerful grin. I nodded approval. I also appropriated it. My wife is nothing if not forward thinking, but she is inclined to the impetuous.

The three of us approached the barn door in silence. I snapped my fingers at Lincoln and dropped my left hand, palm down. He dropped immediately into a sit. I briefly considered snapping my fingers at Madeline; instead, I drew her to my side.

We flattened ourselves either side of the open doors, I on the right, Madeline on the left. My tire iron was at the ready. I peered around the edge to the barn's interior.

I don't care for dark barns. In fact, I actively disapprove of dark barns. As a result, one of my first decisions when I purchased Sunny Skies was to place clear Plexiglas strips under the entire roofline to let the sunshine in. That precaution has served me well for many years, and it served me well now. I had a daylight-clear view of the interior. My farm tools and horse tack are usually neatly lined in their appropriate racks against the walls, hay bales and sawdust bags stacked tidily underneath. The equipment was lined up no longer. Our two saddles were askew on the pegs. The bridles hung in a tangled mess. Hay had been scattered all across the floor. And a neat pile of horse manure sat in the middle of the aisle where no horse manure had been before. I drew back and raised an eyebrow in Madeline's direction. The disruption was clearly the work of Pony. She had done it before.

It did not explain the presence of the Ford Escort. Nor the silence of the calf.

My barn has five working stalls of sturdy oak on either side of an eight-foot-wide aisle. I'd converted the sixth stall on each side into a feed room and a small animal pen, respectively. The animal pen contained the orphaned calf. I peered into the barn again. And I immediately saw the rustler.

He—or perhaps it was she—was bent over the calf's pen, milk bottle in hand. I leaped forward, just as Madeline collared me and hauled me back. Years of farming our thirty acres have given my wife a healthy arm. I stumbled into her pillowy side and righted myself. She wrenched the tire iron from my grasp and flung it to the ground. "My dear!" I protested. "The rustler!"

"That's no rustler." And indeed, his attention attracted by our little contretemps, the young man who turned to face us had no trace of burglarious intent in his face. His garb immediately proclaimed him a student. He was wearing jeans, L.L. Bean leather outdoor boots, a gray sweatshirt with the Cornell logo where a breast pocket ought to be, and most of the contents of the milk bottle. More significant than his clothing as a sign of his benign intent, Lincoln rose to his feet and proceeded into the barn, tail wagging happily.

The young man patted my dog, then stuck out a milk-covered hand as we approached. "Dr. McKenzie? I'm Joe

Turnblad. I'm a second-year at Cornell. Dr. Bergland suggested that I drop by to see you today. I must say, sir, it's an honor to meet you. Your work on bovine back fat is a byword at the university, sir. A byword."

A job applicant, then. And possibly a suck-up. I ignored the proffered handshake.

He glanced down at himself with a rueful grin. "Sorry about the mess, sir. When I drove in, I heard the calf crying . . ."

"Bawling," I said. "Calves do not cry, they bawl."

"Uh. Yeah. Bawling, and when I came in to see if there was anything wrong, I saw . . . well, the place looked like a tornado hit it. What happened, do you think?"

"Pony staged a jail break," I said. I craned my neck to look beyond him to the recesses of the indoor arena. A familiar squeal floated through the air. "I knew she had something in mind this morning."

"Yeah. Well, I tried to put everything back into place, and the milk bottle'd fallen off the feeder . . ."

"The bottle was removed by an outside agency," I said coldly. "To wit, the Shetland. I fastened the bottle to the feeder myself. When I affix a bottle to a feeder, it does not fall off on its own."

". . . And the little guy here seemed pretty hungry, so I . . ."

"You are too hasty, young man. Hold yourself one moment, please." I looked at my dog, pushed my palm forward in the direction of the indoor arena, and whistled. Lincoln emitted an obedient "woof " and trotted down the aisle to the indoor arena. He turned right and disappeared.

". . . Tried to feed him myself," the young man continued. "But he kept spitting it up."

"You need to keep the bottle at an angle," Madeline said kindly. "Otherwise calves'll spit that stuff all over you." She laughed. "I'm Madeline McKenzie, by the way."

"Joe Turnblad," he said again, with a smile composed equally of anxiety and conscious charm. "I'm second-year at the vet school. If you could just explain to your dad . . ."

There was a short, and on my part, markedly chilly silence.

"My *wife*," I said, stressing the noun with some humor, "need not explain a thing, young man. And even a second-year ought to know better than to feed an animal about which he knows nothing. What if the calf had been on medication?"

Mr. Turnblad blushed. "Sorry. You're absolutely right, of course."

Lincoln reappeared at the far opening to the indoor arena, looked at me, and barked once. I nodded and whistled.

Madeline grabbed the young man by the sleeve of his milk-sodden sweatshirt and pulled him against the wall. Pony burst out of the arena and clattered down the aisle, brushy tail twitching, the dog at her heels. Every few paces, she squealed and kicked out with her hind legs. Lincoln loped along behind her and dodged the kicks with aplomb. Andrew followed at a more plodding pace, ears forward, and a look of mild anxiety in his brown eyes. The three of us followed dog, pony, and horse out of the barn. Lincoln herded the two animals to the paddock gate, nosed it open, and drove them in. I followed at a more sedate pace, and secured the chain. Lincoln wriggled under the fence and lay flat on the grass, panting happily. He is a dog that takes pride in a job well done.

"I think we need a padlock," Madeline said. "Honestly. I know you don't approve of anything but a quick-release, Austin, but that Pony is just a constant pain in the butt." She smiled at Joe Turnblad. "She's amazing. She's a regular Houdini."

I didn't respond. I kept one eye on Andrew. Then I turned to Mr. Turnblad. "Well, Mr. Turnblad?"

"Sir?"

"It is obvious that you are here to apply for the locum tenens. What do you see?"

He followed my gaze. Andrew stood with his head down. His flanks heaved. His nostrils flared and he blew noisily in and out.

"May I, sir?" Mr. Turnblad nodded at the stethoscope I keep in my jacket pocket. I withdrew it and handed it over. He looped it around his neck and (rather nimbly) climbed the fence. Keeping a wary eye on Pony, he walked up to Andrew and applied the correct end of the 'scope just behind Andrew's elbow. He listened intently for a moment. Pony sidled next to him, extended her neck, and drew her lips back, exposing long yellow teeth. They were, I noted, in need of floating. Beside me, I felt Madeline draw breath. I closed my hand over hers in warning. Mr. Turnblad continued his examination unaware, his left elbow millimeters from Pony's teeth. She chomped. Mr. Turnblad jumped a foot. He shouted and rubbed his elbow. There was, I was pleased to see, little or no animus in his demeanor, and he did not attempt retaliation. Pony snorted, backed up, blinked at him in her deceptively innocent way, and started to graze.

Mr. Turnblad straightened up and folded the stethoscope into his pocket. He put two fingers under Andrew's lower jaw and concentrated on his watch. Andrew turned his head and nibbled lightly at Mr. Turnblad's cheek. Mr. Turnblad stroked the horse in return. He then exited the pasture the same way he'd entered.

"His pulse rate's sixty-five. That's pretty rapid. And he's sweating some. Unless he's been racing pretty hard, that's not normal. The heartbeat's definitely irregular. There's a cardiac condition of some kind. But that's all I know, sir." He smiled, suddenly adding, "Except that he's a very nice guy."

"Andrew's a sweetheart," Madeline said.

"You wouldn't know much more without an ECG to confirm a diagnosis," I said. "He has atrial fibrillation."

"That's a shame. You've tried to convert him?"

"Twice." I cleared my throat. "It didn't take." All three of us looked at the old boy, who stood patiently in the sun, waiting for the captured bird in his chest to settle. "He was born here, and here's where he'll stay," I said. "What are your thoughts on that, young man?"

Mr. Turnblad drew his breath in between his teeth. "Well. I guess . . ."

"Guesses are not good enough."

"Okay. Then I'll tell you straight out. You owe animals a good life and a good death. If he starts to lose weight, if his lungs fill up, if he has trouble breathing, if he can't stand for more than an hour or so at a time, then it's time to put him down. Before that?" He leaned on the fence and looked at the peaceful scene. Andrew moved to Pony's side, his breathing calmer now, and began to graze. "Before that, I'd say old Andrew has it pretty good."

I was forced to let the sloppy locution pass, not out of tenderness for Joe Turnblad's feelings, but because a small red sports car sped smartly down the drive and pulled up in a spray of gravel.

"Nice car," Joe said, for it was a Mercedes 450SL, I believe, and then, "Whoa," a command not directed at Andrew, but to the very pretty girl who unfolded herself out of it. She was slender, with hair the color of Hershey bars.

"We've missed lunch," I said to Madeline. "If this goes on much later, we're going to miss dinner."

"There's a low-fat turkey sandwich in my purse, if you can't stand to wait." Then, to the young lady, she said, "Hi."

"Hi!" She wore a pair of fawn-colored breeches and a greenish-brown sweater that matched the color of her eyes. She smiled prettily at Madeline, and said, "Dr. McKenzie?"

Madeline smiled back. I was aware that some silent message passed between them. Had the young lady been a filly new to the herd, I would have said that the message was to acknowledge the lead mare. I cleared my throat. "I am Dr. McKenzie."

"How do you do, sir." She extended her hand and I shook it. There were calluses on her palm. "I'm Allegra Fulbright. Dr. Bergland posted a message at school. You're looking for an assistant? Well, sir, I'm your woman."

"I'm Joe Turnblad," the young man said. "And Dr. Bergland spoke personally to me. And shouldn't have you called for an appointment?"

Allegra ignored Mr. Turnblad. I tugged at my mustache. Newcomers to the herd spend a certain amount of time kicking the bejesus out of lower-ranking horses until the new hierarchy is established.

"You're a veterinary student, dear?" Madeline asked.

"Yes." An attractive pink suffused her cheeks. "That is, I will be in the fall. I'm, um, sort of pre-vet, right now."

"*Pre*-vet," Joe said, in an "ain't it wonderful" tone of voice. "So what's your pre-vet major? Sociology?"

"Music," she said. "With a major in voice. But I've had a lot of experience with horses."

"Music," Joe said. The scorn is his voice was palpable.

"This is a farm practice, Miss Foolbright. It's not limited to horses. As a matter of fact . . ."

"It's Fulbright," she responded testily.

"Have you had a lot of experience with cows?"

Miss Fulbright smiled: "As a matter of fact, I have."

"On daddy's estate, I bet."

I waited with interest. A filly will show her teeth, squeal, and pin her ears back before she actually whirls and smacks the victim a good one. But no such activity was forthcoming. Allegra did not kick young Joe in the shins.

"Yes. Black Angus, as a matter of fact. We raised them for show."

"What about hogs? Chickens? Sheep? You show those, too?"

"Dr. Bergland said that Sunny Skies was a . . . a new practice, and it was limited to cows and horses."

I noted the ellipses. I wondered just what else that old goat Bergland had said and I opened my mouth to inquire.

I was forestalled by my spouse.

"That's it, everybody," she said briskly. "Into the house for lunch."

Three

~~~~

MADELINE has long maintained that good food will stop just about any kind of squabble right in its tracks, if the offer is made quickly enough. Lunch that day would have diverted Eliot Spitzer from a lawsuit: Zweigle's hot dogs and Madeline's homemade cashew chili with sweet onions and shaved aged cheddar.

I, of course, was doomed to cantaloupe, turkey, and fat-free cottage cheese. When Madeline saw the polite way Allegra Fulbright took little, nibbling bites of her chili, she gave her cantaloupe and turkey and fat-free cottage cheese, too. It was no wonder the child looked thin.

Everybody settled down to eat, and both applicants reclaimed their manners.

"You have an absolutely amazing home, Mrs. McKenzie," Allegra said. She cut her cantaloupe into small squares that wouldn't keep a fruit fly alive, much less a one-hundred-and-zero-pound "almost-pre-vet student." "The colors are just amazing."

Madeline receives that comment from a lot of people who see our house for the first time. She smiled warmly.

Joe swallowed his chili in three huge gulps, all the while rolling his eyes in apparent disdain. This may have been a reaction to Allegra's sucking up. Or perhaps he didn't like the chili. Which would mean more leftovers for me. The prospect of a midnight scavenge into leftovers cheered me considerably, and I reconciled myself quite happily to the turkey. But when Madeline nodded at the stove to tell Joe he could obtain more, if he desired, he shot up like a hungry owl after a shrew. So I suppose it was Allegra that was giving him mental indigestion, and not Madeline's chili. I half rose from my chair to follow Joe's example. Madeline stuck her foot out to prevent this. I sat back down rather suddenly.

Madeline continued to smile warmly at Allegra; "I do like a lot of color in my house. That peachy sherbet color on the walls scared the painter half to death. If Austin hadn't spayed his cat for free, I don't think he would have done it."

"Sunburn," Joe said through his second hot dog. "It looks just like a sunburn." He shrugged at Allegra's scowl. "*I* like it."

"It's a beautiful color," Allegra crossly. "You know very well I think it's gorgeous, too."

"And how would I know that? Amazing, you said. Like, 'what an amazing baby,' when it's the ugliest kid you've ever seen, or 'what an amazing haircut,' when it sucks, or . . ."

"I wanted a pinkly sort of brown," Madeline said, loudly, in an apparent effort to keep the squabble from blowing up into a gully washer. "Or maybe a browny sort of pink. Whatever you call it, it turned out rather well, I think."

All four of us interrupted the meal to gaze about the room. Our farmhouse is old, and the rooms are small, with high ceilings. There is a comfortable saddle-colored sectional against the south and west walls. A brick fireplace occupies the north. The kitchen is on the east end. Our large, old mahogany table is right in the middle. Madeline had chosen whitish drapes for the windows in some heavy fabric and liberated several old Oriental rugs from the local estate sales when we first married. The rugs covered the pine floors. All in all, it was quite a cozy room.

"This must have been two rooms in the old days, though," Allegra said. "If those crown moldings are authentic, this house must date from the mid-1800s. And those old houses were nothing but lots of little rooms. To conserve heat," she added.

"I suppose you're used to twelve thousand square feet of McMansion?" Joe said. The young man achieved quite a creditable sneer through his mouthful of chili. "Or, nope, let me guess. You live where the Foolbrights have lived for the last three hundred years in an authentic Greek Revival that hasn't been touched by the wrecker's ball."

Allegra gave him a look that would have taken the fur from the cat, if she'd been in its way. I judged it prudent to intervene. "Three." I set my knife and fork crosswise on my plate. "It was three rooms, not two. And Madeline took the walls out with a sledgehammer. We didn't need a wrecking ball."

"You took the walls down, yourself, Mrs. McKenzie?" Allegra asked.

"I did indeed."

"Madeline is capable of anything," I said, with justifiable pride.

Madeline rose from the table. "Now," she said briskly, "You three need to talk about the job here. I'll just take care of these dishes. You all go right on ahead." She began to clear the dishes from the table.

"Certainly, Mrs. McKenzie," Allegra said, just as briskly. "Joe, is it?"

Joe looked startled at the sound of his name.

"Joe, you're not going to just sit there and let Mrs. McKenzie do all the dishes herself, are you?"

"Oh! Sorry!" And the poor kid blushed sunburn pink. "Please, let me, Mrs. McKenzie. And thank you for the lunch. It was great." He jumped to his feet, grabbed the Fiesta ware right out of Madeline's hands, and set to work at the sink.

Allegra, of course, having neatly diverted the competition, pulled a crisp white folder from her Hermès briefcase, set her résumé before me and got down to business.

"Swarthmore," I said, after reading through her vita, "with a junior year abroad in France."

"Yes," she said eagerly. "So if any of your clients are bilingual, I'm ready to roll."

I looked over the rim of my spectacles at her. There were very few cow-owning Parisians in Summersville, New York.

"I've got a little Spanish, too," she added, as if confessing. "Just enough to get by."

"And your bachelor's degree is in voice?"

"Yes, sir. But you'll notice that I've spent most summers since I was thirteen on the A circuit. I've just had tons of experience with horses. Dogs, too."

The A circuit was hunter-jumper territory. One needed a

great deal of money to subsidize seven years of activity in that arena.

"And I see you have some eventing experience."

"Yes, sir. At Earlsdown. Last year." Her voice was subdued. I glanced up. Her cheeks were flushed. She straightened her chin and her eyes met mine. "I had to withdraw my horse."

"Happens to the best of us," I said mildly. I resumed my perusal of the paper. She had not listed her parents, nor a residence address other than her dorm at Cornell. I found that a bit curious. But after forty years in the classroom, little surprises me about students.

I enclosed the résumé into its folder. "Thank you, my dear. Perhaps you could relieve Mr. Turnblad at the sink."

Joe dried his hands on his jeans, flopped, rather than sat, into the chair opposite me, and pulled a single sheet of paper from his shirt pocket.

I knew that Madeline would be prejudiced in favor of the young man. He was young, strong, and able to handle all the arduous tasks that she thought I couldn't do anymore. Hah! We would see about that. Joe was definitely wet behind the ears as far as practical experience with large animals. Any farm kid would have been way ahead of Pony and her big, blunt teeth. On the other hand, he did have a sound academic background. And his thoughts about owing an animal a good life and a good death were congruent with Madeline's and my beliefs. Not only that, Joe had *not* smacked Pony up the side of the head when she'd bitten him. A smack is a logical reflex action under those circumstances, and it wouldn't have accomplished a thing. Except to annoy me considerably.

I regarded him over my spectacles, a tactic that has disconcerted the most unruffled student in the past. He was taller than I and probably weighed less, despite the muscle in his hands and forearms. He shifted a little nervously, and a cup and saucer that had remained on the table fell to the floor and chipped. Madeline's Fiesta ware is pumpkin colored. The chip was pretty obvious. Joe turned scarlet. "Sorry, Dr. McKenzie. That must have been one of a set. Just let me know where you got it and I'll get Mrs. McKenzie another one." He picked the cup up and attempted to mash the chip back into place.

"Really, Dr. McKenzie. At least let me pay for a replacement. Or I can muck out for you for a couple of days."

The young man was serious. Did he think I hadn't seen what was in the back of his car? A sleeping bag. A cardboard box of peanut butter, dried soup, and a ten-pound bag of pancake flour. Two boxes of vet texts. He was living rough—in central New York winters—and too proud to forget about a chipped cup. I had little doubt he didn't have the money to replace it and mucking out it would have to be.

On the other hand . . .

I continued my unwavering stare. What if he had dropped the cup on purpose? The obligation to work would certainly give him an edge over Allegra. Well, well.

"Mucking out it is. I always appreciate a hand with the manure," I said. I unfolded his résumé and dropped my gaze to the paper. "About your undergrad degree?"

"Columbia. Biochemistry."

"You're from New York, then? That's where your parents are now?"

"I grew up in the Bronx. With my grandmother. She died a few years ago." He glanced back over his shoulder. Allegra had both hands in the air and was talking to Madeline nineteen to the dozen, as my own grandmother used to say. Madeline looked a little bemused.

I turned my attention back to young Joe. He was what, twenty-two? Maybe twenty-four. He would have grown up before the Bronx part of New York became gentrified. So he'd grown up poor, undoubtedly, which might explain the chip on his shoulder as far as Allegra Fulbright was concerned. It might also explain his evasiveness. "Not too many farms around the Bronx when you were growing up," I said.

"You mean how did a city kid like me get interested in being a vet? No, sir. There weren't too many farms in my neighborhood." He grinned suddenly. "I got to the library a lot, though. You ever read Larry McMurtry? *Lonesome Dove*? Or the book by Jim Kjelgaard, *Big Red*?"

I had to smile back. "Indeed I have."

"And there was an animal clinic down the street from Harriet's place."

"Harriet? You called your grandmother Harriet?"

"Her choice." He shrugged. "Anyhow, I worked there summers when I was a kid. Just sweeping out, cleaning the cages. Stuff like that."

A small-animal practice in the city. And a city pound. From that to Cornell and its sweeping acres. Hm.

Before I had a chance to delve into the matter further, Allegra called out from her post by the window and said, "Somebody's headed into the yard."

I rose and looked out the window myself, Madeline at my side. A large stock truck bounced down the lane toward the clinic. Orville DeGroote was at the wheel. There was a horse loaded in back. Then—because he was Orville DeGroote and a cranky so-and-so—he laid his hand on the horn as if we were an English village being invaded by Messerschmitts and he was an air warden. "It's Orville and that horse of his, Madeline," I said.

Madeline clapped her hands together. "Excellent! This is a typical case for our clinic. Orville couldn't have brought that horse at a better time." She slipped her hand in mine. "If both of them give you a hand with the horse, Austin, you'll have a chance to see them in action. It's perfect!"

Madeline is usually right. It was with a great deal of satisfaction that I shepherded my flock into the yard to greet the test patient. The choice Madeline and I faced was a difficult one: two appealing youngsters, both ready to learn. One position available. Like Solomon before me, I must be both judicious and wise. It's fortunate that I am a man particularly suited to the challenge.

DeGroote pulled up his battered, ill-kempt stock trailer with a shriek of brakes badly in need of pads. He left the motor idling—an annoyance related to diesel engines to which I have never accustomed myself—and eyed me through the smeary windshield with the manner of a captive baboon.

He jerked his thumb at his passenger. His oldest daughter jumped out of the truck and trotted obediently around to the rear of the trailer. DeGroote stuck his head out of the driver's window, spat a wad of tobacco onto my neatly mown grass, and said, "Figured I save myself cost of a barn call if I bring the horse to you instead of t'other way round. So you can't stick a farm call on the bill, doc. Understood?"

"I've mentioned my PITA charge before, DeGroote," I said icily. The Pain In The Ass surcharge for recalcitrant or unpleasant clients is a useful innovation when dealing with such as DeGroote. He has even paid it, on occasion.

He thrust open the driver's door and descended with a grunt. DeGroote and his entire brood are as blond as golden retrievers. The sons and daughters have some of the amiability of that happy breed; the old man does not. He wore green overalls with smears of cow manure down the bib, a billed John Deere cap, and a mutinous expression. "Ingrid was complainin' so much about that durn horse and the lameness, I brought it over myself." He nodded respectfully to Madeline, blushed in Allegra's direction, and assessed young Turnblad with a speculative glance. Then he leaned against the side of the truck and spat another wad of tobacco juice onto my lawn. "Well, get to it, doc. Time's money."

I walked to the back of the trailer, trailed by my dog and my wife. Joe Turnblad, after a moment's hesitation, came with us. Madeline smiled encouragingly at Allegra, who slipped between Joe and me with a determined air.

Ingrid, for such is DeGroote's eldest daughter's name, backed her reluctant gelding off the truck and onto the gravel. It was a sorry excuse for a horse. Swaybacked, ewe-necked, cow-hocked behind, and pigeon-toed in front, the god of horses had not missed one conformation flaw in the design of this particular animal. Its coat was an uninspiring shade of liver and it had a small, mean eye.

Ingrid patted its sweaty neck and looked at me with hope-filled eyes. They were the same washed-out blue as her father's. "What do you think, Dr. McKenzie? He pulled up lame for sure this morning. He's been a little off all week. But I had a heck of a time getting him out of his stall this morning."

Allegra patted his neck, too. "He's beautifully groomed," she said with great tact. Either that, or she didn't know a horse from a donkey. "You must love him very much. You did just the right thing in bringing him to us."

Ingrid gave her a grateful look.

Mindful of DeGroote's impatient grunt, I said, "Ingrid. Will you walk him up and down the drive, please?"

She tugged at the lead line, and the poor beast stumbled forward. He was limping heavily on the right fore. And his gait was not so much a stumble as a combination hop and scramble. I held my hand up. "Stop." I raised one eyebrow at Joe Turnblad. "Do you have an opinion?"

He smiled at the girl. "What's his name, Ingrid?"

"Sultan," she said. She turned pink and looked at her feet.

Joe patted Sultan on the neck. The horse jerked back and glared at him. Then he stood directly in front of the animal and bent forward to pick up the left fore.

"Wrong foot," Allegra said pleasantly.

So she did know a horse from a donkey.

Joe's chin jutted. He dropped the left fore and picked up the right.

"Wrong stance, too," Allegra said. "Watch it. Unless you want to get kicked." She was wrong about the kick, though. Sultan was a biter. He leaned forward and sank his teeth into Joe's shoulder. Oh, dear. The poor boy's second assault by equine—and the day wasn't over yet.

Joe jumped back and the horse let go. As I had noted before, Joe displayed no animus toward the horse, a point that counted heavily in his favor.

A little instruction would not be amiss at this point. I moved to Sultan's right flank. "Always approach a horse from the side. If you are investigating a possible wound, approach the afflicted area with the same degree of circumspection."

Splat! DeGroote's third wad of tobacco landed neatly on top of the second. "I'm not payin' you by the word, am I, doc?"

I ignored him and addressed my student. "Slide your hand down the shoulder, down the forearm, and over the hoof. Then tap," I struck Sultan's ankle with my knuckles, "and lift when the horse moves forward." I kept the upturned hoof between my knees and brushed away the straw accumulated there. There it was, the dark, bruised spot on the sole that indicated the site of the abscess. Sultan reared, and I dropped the hoof. I felt Madeline's warm hand on my arm. "I think we can leave this to the youngsters, Austin."

I took a deep breath, more to taste the morning air than anything else, of course. "I'm fine, my dear." I looked from Joe to Allegra and back again. "I assume one of you, at least, has some questions?"

"Is he pastured with other horses?" Joe asked. "Could be a kick."

"It's not a kick," Allegra said. "Sultan's a Quarterhorse. And he's got the typical Quarterhorse hoof, which is to say, it's too small for his size." She patted Sultan's sweaty flank. "Did you just put him out on grass, Ingrid? We may be looking at a case of founder."

This was a good question. An oversupply of spring grass can founder many a horse. It is a common complaint in the months when the grass is lush.

"Laminitis hits both feet at once," Joe with the certainty of one who had thoroughly read the text. "The lameness comes from a kick to the shoulder."

"None of that's right," Allegra responded, with the wisdom born of experience. "And besides, the sore is in the hoof, not the shoulder. You can see it just from the way he's holding it up."

Young Allegra was right on the money. It can be difficult to pinpoint the source of a lameness, but Sultan was, indeed, sore in the hoof. There is no substitute for the experienced eye.

"Well, he hasn't foundered," Joe said with certainty, "And if it's navicular, it's an atypical case."

There is no substitute for the well read, either. Joe was also right on the money.

"Then, maybe it's a stone bruise?" Allegra said. Even my un-intuitive ear picked up her uncertainty.

"Nope," Joe said. "Navicular, possibly."

I decided it would be wise to intervene before Allegra clobbered her rival with the nearest blunt instrument. "Allegra is closest to the proper diagnosis, Joe. Pick up the hoof and examine the sole, young lady."

She did so. "I was right, I think. See? There's the bruise, right there."

"There's heat in the ankle," Joe said, as he bent next to her. Joe's hair, I noticed, was the color of a Hershey bar, too. It had been a long while since Madeline had included sweets in my diet. "You don't get heat in the ankle with a stone bruise."

"Correct again," I said. "Drop the hoof, back off, and we will proceed." I raised an eyebrow in Madeline's direction. "My dear? The twitch?"

Madeline went to the van, retrieved the disinfectant kit and bucket, the twitch, and the farrier tools. She set these at my side. She then applied the twitch expertly to Sultan's muzzle and spoke softly into his ear.

Sultan sneered at me. But he stood angrily in place while I selected a short, curved scalpel from my kit. Then I stood with my back to the horse, picked up the affected hoof and wedged it between my knees. I cut quickly into the discolored area of the sole. Pus spurted from the cut and ran freely over the hoof walls. I felt Sultan relax as the painful pressure was alleviated. I even felt a grateful puff of air in my ear. The poor fellow felt better, and wanted to let me know it.

"Behold the abscess," I said. I continued to hold the foot aloft. "And what is the next step?"

"Pack it with antibiotic and wrap the hoof," Joe said.

"Soak it first, fool," Allegra said.

They glared at each other. Madeline handed me the squeeze bottle of Betadine and I splashed the hoof cavity generously. "Soaking in a solution of Betadine and warm water is indicated, certainly," I said as I straightened up. "But Ingrid will want to take the horse home, first." My wife, already anticipating my next move, handed me gauze, Vetrap, and a roll of duct tape. "No veterinary practice should be without duct tape," I instructed. "You will note, Mr. Turnblad, that I stuff the hoof cavity with sterile gauze, then contain the pad of gauze thusly . . ." I wrapped a roll of Vetrap around the hoof and pad, then swathed the whole shebang with duct tape. "As you see Mr. Turnblad, Miss Fulbright, the hoof is protected from detritus, but the abscess is allowed to drain into the gauze pad. Ingrid? When you return home, you should indeed soak Sultan's hoof. Miss Fulbright, could you share with us the procedure for caring for the abscess, please?"

Allegra smiled triumphantly at Joe and said rather pertly, "Are you sure you wouldn't like to tell us, Mr. Turnbald?"

"Turn-blad," he said, with a slight grinding of teeth. "And you're right, Miss Fulbright, I haven't a clue."

"Hmmm. Well. I'm sure you'll get to wound care one of these years. In the meantime, there's no substitute for hands-on experience, right, Mrs. McKenzie?"

Allegra gave Ingrid succinct instructions on the length of time needed to soak the hoof, the ratio of Betadine to water for the solution, and the number of times the procedure should be repeated each week. I handed Joe a vial of antibiotic and a syringe; he injected the horse handily, and the treatment was over.

"He should be ready now, Mrs. McKenzie," Joe said. He clapped the horse on the neck.

Madeline released the twitch and rubbed Sultan's muzzle to restore the circulation. The horse placed his chin on her shoulder. He rolled a cross and baleful eye at Joe, the source of the painful needle. Then he heaved such an enormous sigh of disgust that a chuckle went around the assembled observers.

"You're all right, Sultan," Madeline soothed him. She smiled at our two candidates for employment. "And you're all right, too." She winked. "It's just that sometimes you're the bug, and sometimes you're the windshield."

Four

THE DeGrootes were billed and then dispatched. Allegra and Joe stood somewhat uncertainly in the middle of the barnyard. They carefully avoided looking at one another. They even more carefully avoided looking at me.

I myself was not sure what to do next. Clearly, our candidates were evenly divided. Just as clearly, neither alone would suit. Joe lacked practical large-animal experience; Allegra the theoretical. We did not have sufficient funds to hire both.

King Solomon's position was not, as I now recall, an enviable one. Particularly as it pertained to babies. Which is what these two children looked like to me.

"Austin," Madeline said decisively. "Stop chewing your mustache."

"My dear?"

"Why don't you let Joe give you a hand in the barn." This was not a question. "It's almost time for evening chores. Allegra? I could use a hand with dinner. And I want you to see the rest of the house. Let's save the chat about the job until after we eat."

I tried to recall to whom King Solomon was married. I could not. Whoever recorded those biblical events could not have been as luckily wed as I am, or the individual would have not failed to note the role of his queen in the successful management of the state of Israel.

"Excellent suggestions, my dear. Mr. Turnblad? If you will follow me."

It took some time to acquaint Joe with the evening clinic routine, not because it was onerous, but because the young man was full of questions. We generally stable Pony and Andrew at night in the spring, and he was full of admiration at Lincoln's expertise in rounding up Pony and getting her into her stall. He expressed a desire to know more of the work involved in Obedience and Herding trials. I taught him the rudiments of calf handling as he successfully (this time) set up the feeder for the little Red Angus. And his experience with the care of small animals surprised me. He was quite competent with the two cats recovering from spaying procedures, and the marbled black-and-gray part Labrador puppy, whose hip I'd pinned after discovering him on the verge of Route 15 the day before, a victim of a careless driver.

"Saw a lot of broken hips and legs in the clinic in New York City," Joe said, as he probed the surgery site with the right degree of gentleness. "Feels like it's knitting fairly well. I see you have a portable X-ray? That's great to have on hand in cases like this, sir. So is the rest of that stuff."

He nodded at the small array of diagnostic machines that lined the far wall. My clinic itself is modest; one might even say minimal. I had obtained most of my machinery as Cornell auctioned it off as obsolete. Victor Bergland had barely been able to conceal his derision when he attended the opening-day ceremonies. No such snobbery characterized Joe's response.

"A clinical chemistry analyzer, too. Stocks for the large animals, operating table, lots of lights, and portable anesthesiology equipment . . ." He grinned. "We could have used a lot of this at the shelter where I worked as a kid. What more could you want?"

"A larger patient load, perhaps," I admitted.

"An assistant could free your time up to attend to more patients, sir."

"Hmph." I eased the Lab pup back into its cage and hardened my heart to its whimpers. Lincoln touched his nose to the Lab's in reassurance, and I eased the wire door closed. "Madeline will be expecting us for dinner."

It was chilly as we crossed the yard to the house. The temperature had dropped significantly, as it will in central New York in early spring, and we came through the back door to be greeted by warmth and the delicious scent of coq au vin. I disencumbered myself of my waterproof boots and looked at my home with happiness.

After Madeline's sledgehammer assault on the interior walls of the farmhouse, our kitchen became a large, expansive space suitable to accommodate any numbers of students, friends, colleagues, and neighbors. The usual appliances occupy one end, our large mahogany table the other, and the woodstove sits benignly in between. The site is one to which Lincoln and I always repair with pleasure.

But the air was unusually fraught on this early evening. Even Lincoln seemed to feel it. He curled on his thick bed by the stove, stuck his nose under his tail, and watched us all with interest.

Allegra greeted me with deference. She fondled Lincoln's ears with delight. She smiled at Joe with a snarl that demonstrated the whiteness of her eyeteeth. Joe offered Allegra a more artful insult by ignoring her—a beta dog often behaves as if a new and unwelcome member of the pack does not exist. Madeline tells me there is nothing more infuriating to a woman. As if any man or woman could ignore my splendid wife! In any event, Allegra's putative hackles were much in evidence. I was not unaware of the reasons for this dissension, of course. I greeted my wife with a kiss and a regretful sigh.

"You were a long time, Austin."

"Joe was most interested in the surgery. He has a swift and sure hand with injections."

"And you noticed how good Allegra was with Sultan?"

We exchanged significant glances.

"I have yet to arrive at a recommendation. What are your thoughts?"

"We'll talk about it after supper."

While the two candidates assisted Madeline in the final preparation for our meal, I sat at the kitchen table and placed the résumés side by side. Young Joe was a scholarship student, albeit tuition only. He had worked full time throughout his undergraduate career.

The part of Connecticut from which Allegra hailed implied that she needed no financial assistance other than that provided by her wealthy father, as did the lower echelons of her academic career: the Chapin School; Swarthmore; and a year abroad in France. And now Cornell.

"Hm," I said. Allegra glanced my way and chopped onions with an increased feverishness. Joe uncorked a bottle of Australian Shiraz with a spuriously unconcerned air.

Madeline set a plate of carrots, celery, and a no-fat yogurt dip in front of me. She threw her arm around my shoulder. We read along together while the youngsters shuffled nervously around the room.

Joe hailed from the Bronx. Since high school, his summer jobs had been with the Bronx division of the ASPCA and a small-animal clinic not far from the home of his grandmother. Hence his expertise with small animals. I was sadly familiar with the duties allocated part-time workers in such places. He would have seen a great deal of the nastier side of human nature, and even more of animal suffering. "Brave man," I murmured.

"Some wine before dinner, sir?" Joe set a very full glass of the red at my right elbow. Allegra nipped in like a herder after an errant weanling, replaced the glass with one half full, and removed the glass to my left, which is, of course, the proper way to serve wine, no matter how informal the occasion. Joe retreated to the stove in a sulk.

I laid the top sheets of both résumés aside and reviewed the sections relating to personal pursuits. Allegra had competed successfully on the three-day event circuit for the past several years, a recreational pursuit that demands thousands of dollars. She had competed last year at Earlsdown itself. Joe listed his hobby as hiking—an excellent sport—that requires nothing more than the cost of a good pair of boots. Allegra spent a fair amount of time singing with various theater groups.

I chewed celery with little enthusiasm. A difficult choice, indeed. Madeline bent to my ear and whispered, "What's up?"

"Could we perhaps make our decision based on need?"

"Allegra's left her family. She wouldn't tell me why." Madeline dipped a carrot into the yogurt and thrust it between my teeth. "She's stony broke. So's Joe. The stony broke part, at least."

I reflected for some moments, to no avail.

Allegra responded to Madeline's request to set the table with nervous alacrity. By the time the table was laid and we were seated, Madeline had reminded me twice to stop chewing my mustache. To forestall any potentially uncomfortable discussion at dinner, I spoke at length on the media's almost willful misrepresentation of Creutzfeldt-Jakob Disease, to the enlightenment of both young hopefuls, I believe.

With the service of coffee and sherbet at the conclusion of the meal, conversation slowed, stalled, and languished into silence.

The silence was broken by the shrill of the front doorbell.

"I'll get it," Joe and Allegra said simultaneously.

Madeline shook her head. "Sit down, kids. It can't be a patient. Nobody ever comes to the front door. Austin will get it. Who is it, Austin?" The question was delivered in the apparent belief that I could see through three inches of solid oak.

"I have no idea," I responded, somewhat testily. "It's after seven o'clock and all know that we keep early hours. Trick-or-treaters, perhaps?"

"It's April," Madeline said, as if that explained everything.

The bell shrilled again.

I remembered then, that trick-or-treaters show up in November so Madeline had indeed explained everything. "Girl Scouts," I said, with a certain degree of hope. "Is it cookie time? Oh, damn. Of course. It's after seven, is it not? That's who it is."

"That's who who is?" Madeline asked.

The bell shrilled a third time. Allegra and Joe exchanged a glance, seemed to come to some agreement, then rose and went to the front door together. When they returned, they were accompanied by Brewster McClellan and a thin woman I took to be his wife.

"This gentleman says he has an appointment," Allegra said.

I nodded. "He does. It slipped my mind with the crush of activities this afternoon." I rose and offered my hand, "Mr. McClellan?"

"You McKenzie?" he barked.

I eyed him with disfavor. He was big, snub-nosed, and pugnacious, resembling nothing so much as a Rottweiler, without that breed's generally amiable expression. His color was unhealthily high. His wife was thin and expensively blond. She wore breeches, paddock boots, and a faultlessly white shirt. She was unlit by any sort of passion. Dim. She was dim, like a shrouded lamp. She, I felt some sympathy for. "You are Mrs. McClellan?"

"Marina," she said, in a quiet way. She extended her hand. The nails were well kept and colorless.

"Please sit down." I waited until she settled on a chair like a bony sparrow. I turned to McClellan himself. "I am Austin McKenzie. And this is my wife. The young lady at your left is Allegra Fulbright. The young man at your right is Mr. Joe Turnblad." Mindful of my duties as host, however reluctant a host I might be, I gestured toward a kitchen chair. "Please sit down."

"Why don't we all sit right in the living room?" Madeline swept McClellan efficiently before her as she spoke. "Joe, you and Allegra sit there by the fireplace. You settle right into your recliner, Austin. And I'll put you here, Mr. McClellan." She shoved him onto the leather couch. "I'll be happy to get us all some coffee. Marina, would you mind giving me a hand?"

McClellan seemed momentarily confused, a frequent state of mind when Madeline is in full cry. He scratched his head vigorously, and then shrugged himself out of his checked sports coat. "I wouldn't say no to a Scotch-rocks," he said, although I had volunteered no such thing. I went to the sideboard and prepared a drink. McClellan stared rudely in Allegra's direction. "Your name's familiar. I think I know your father."

Allegra bit her lip and stuck her chin out in what was now becoming a familiar gesture of defiance. "I doubt it," she said coolly, "I'm Dr. McKenzie's assistant."

Joe sat up as if stung. I believe I looked puzzled. I certainly felt it. Madeline would not have made the job offer without consulting me. She knew I never would have made an offer without consulting her.

McClellan remained oblivious to the undercurrents. "That isn't it." McClellan squinted at her.

I handed him his drink; he accepted it without taking his eyes from Allegra. He snapped his fingers. "Show ring. That's it. Last year at Earlsdown. If you're a Fulbright, then you were Sam Fulbright's daughter."

Allegra nodded stiffly. I pondered that "were."

"The Wall Street guy," McClellan went on, knocking back a slug of liquor that would have felled the redoubtable Pony. "Old Sam. Yeah." McClellan's somewhat bleary gaze shifted to Joe. "Now you, sonny. I haven't seen you before, have I? Or have I."

"*I'm* Dr. McKenzie's assistant," Joe said. I continued to remain confused.

McClellan's bloodshot baby blues shifted back to me. "You have two assistants, McKenzie? I heard the private vet business wasn't that good this close to Cornell. I have it on the best authority that you were on your uppers."

I loathe that particular cliché.

"The heck we are," Allegra said, indignantly. "We have to beat off new customers with a stick, don't we, Dr. McKenzie? Whoever told you we were broke?"

Victor Bergland, that's who. The old goat. But I remained aloof.

"Busy enough for two full-time assistants?" McClellan demanded skeptically. I had no idea why the man sounded so incredulous. I am, after all, the world's most notable expert on bovine back fat.

"Although Joe and I aren't exactly full-time assistants," Allegra said, with a hesitant glance at me. "We've agreed to share the job. Right, Joe?"

Joe glowered at her. She stared back, her chin at that same challenging angle. Madeline swept in from the kitchen, a tray of coffees in her hands, Marina trailing behind like a lost dinghy. Madeline set the tray on the coffee table and looked expectantly at me. "Did I hear that right, Austin? The children have agreed to job share?"

McClellan yawned, jiggled his left knee, drained his Scotch, and demanded another. I ignored the request and remained lost in thought.

"So we job share?" Joe asked Allegra slowly. "Is that what you're saying?"

"Seems like the best plan to me. That is," Allegra said, with a sudden, anxious look at Madeline, "if that's okay with you."

"It's brilliant." Then Madeline smiled. Joe smiled, because Madeline in full beam is impossible to resist. Everyone was smiling but McClellan and me. I wasn't smiling because I was struck with the obvious suitability of the arrangement and I rarely smile when I marvel. McClellan wasn't smiling because I had yet to refill his Scotch. I did so, and Joe asked me, with some degree of trepidation, how much assistants got paid these days.

I named a figure that created an instant, if momentary, alliance between Joe and Allegra, and a snort of approval from McClellan. We could not, I knew, afford any more than that. The poor pay might work in our favor, though: the look of consternation that passed between our two new assistants augured for a possible rapprochement in the future.

"You'll live in, of course," Madeline said. "That pay wouldn't keep a cat in kibble. And you both need fattening up."

"We will?" Joe asked, dazed.

"Of course you will," Madeline said firmly. "The job includes room and board, doesn't it, my dear?"

"Of course," I said, somewhat absentmindedly. I was watching Marina McClellan. She drifted around the room in an aimless way. Every time McClellan made an idle movement, she twitched like a startled deer.

"I'd like the guest room upstairs, please," Allegra said instantly. (This with the air of claiming "dibs!") Then, to the clearly uninterested Marina McClellan. "The guest suite! It's gorgeous. It looks like something out of the Inn at Hemlock Falls."

A look of recognition crossed McClellan's frog-like features. He was obviously in a tax bracket to have had more than a passing acquaintance with that local luxury spot.

"I like the room off the operating room better, anyway." Joe settled back in his chair and crossed his hands behind his neck.

"I missed that," Allegra said thoughtfully. "Does it have a tub or a shower?"

"Can we get to the point, here?" McClellan demanded, with, I must admit, some justification.

"Absolutely," Madeline said. "We'll just leave you to discuss it. I'm going to go ahead and get the children settled. Marina, come with us. I'll show you the rest of the house." She leaped to her feet. Her ebullience warmed my heart. Madeline is the happiest of women, but when she is *very* happy the air positively shimmers about her, as it was shimmering now. "And Brewster?" her voice floated past as they all went the back door. "You shouldn't have any more Scotch. There's decaf on the stove. You don't want to aggravate your blood pressure."

"What the hell is she on about, my blood pressure?" McClellan said uneasily.

"My wife is rarely wrong in such matters," I said. "You should consider having it checked."

"Yeah. Well. Whatever. So. You understand that Schumacher thought he wouldn't have the time to give his full attention to the veterinary committee. He recommended you as a sub, as a matter of fact." He tapped his fingers restlessly on his knee. His eyes wandered over the room, settling anywhere but on mine. "Myself, I was thinking that we'd be able to talk him back on board, but then someone shot the poor bastard. So I guess you're it."

"Perhaps," I said dryly.

"You've vetted three-day events before, right?"

This didn't require an answer, unless McClellan were a boob or a phony. I recalled my initial suspicions that he had swiped the Organizing Committee's letterhead and was merely posing as the head.

The Committee is the only body that may issue an invitation to a prospective Veterinary Delegate. The Delegate is the head of a four-member Veterinary Commission consisting of an Examining Veterinarian, an Associate Veterinarian, and last, one poor soul at the bottom rung of the ladder trying to get sufficient show experience to move up. This vet gets stuck with all the drug testing. Not only are Delegates required to have prior experience at Two- and Three-day events, but most have a certificate from a specialized training course. Any member of the committee would know that most training certificates in central New York have been signed by Professor Austin Oliver McKenzie, Department of Equine Sciences, and Chair of Bovine Sciences, Cornell University.

"You are new to the Organizing Committee, I take it?" I asked, somewhat coldly.

"Yes. First time this year." He showed me a lot of teeth. "Very grateful to be honored, of course."

I wondered, cynically, how much the honor had cost him. Spots on Organizing Committees were usually allocated to the old-line dedicated horsemen, the professional, or the proficient. McClellan struck me as none of these.

"My daughter's had the eventing bug for a couple of years now and I guess it's been pretty obvious how much I care about it myself. So when it looked like there might be a chance for me to participate, well, I was just lucky, I guess."

This was delivered with all the charm of a stream of Mazola. Lucky? Bushwah. Somebody somewhere had allowed a back to be scratched.

"Anyhow, the committee would like to extend its thanks for your agreement to participate at this late date."

This speech had all the appeal of a telemarketer's memorized spiel.

"I brought the contract."

He thrust a sheaf of legal-sized paper at me. I began to read. McClellan proceeded to talk to me while I read, a habit I find intensely annoying.

"Too bad about Larky. He was a pretty good cowman and a good man with horses. I hear you're something of an expert with cattle?"

I grunted and turned the page.

"And not bad at horses, either. I want you to come and take a look at Steph's horse tomorrow morning. Schumacher had a look at him yesterday, just before he got knocked off, so of course, he won't be back."

The man must have been knocking back Scotches before he came. I sighed. There was a check attached to the contracts, made out to McKenzie Veterinary Practice, Inc. Fifteen thousand dollars. I sighed again. Then I signed all three copies, removed the check, and returned two contracts to him.

"So you'll be at my stables tomorrow morning to take a look at the horse?"

"What's wrong with him?"

"Bruise on the cannon bone." He shifted from one buttock to the other. "And a kind of skin condition."

"What sort of skin condition?"

"Not sure."

"Eleven o'clock, then," I agreed. I looked at my watch. "And now that our business is concluded, I'm afraid I must excuse myself. I have some duties in the barn to attend to."

I heard the back door open. McClellan's gaze sharpened. Madeline came into the living room first, carrying a duffle bag and dragging a suitcase on wheels. Allegra followed with two tote bags, a hanging suitcase, and what used to be called a train case, but probably isn't anymore. Joe brought up the rear staggering under the weight of a CD player, three cardboard boxes, and a large canvas duffle. Lincoln danced around them all, plumey tail wagging. The effect was quite paradelike. Marina edged in after them, then sat at the farthest end of the couch from her husband.

Madeline noticed the check I held, made a swift, graceful detour, plucked the check from my hand, gave me a cheerfully cheeky kiss, and proceeded on up the stairs.

They left quite a silence in their wake.

"Is she eventing at Earlsdown?" McClellan asked. His voice was truculent.

I raised an eyebrow. "Neither Madeline nor I have evented for some years."

"I meant the kid. The girl."

"Miss Fulbright? I have no idea. I doubt it. She's a student at Cornell. She has said nothing about any current plans to ride. I doubt that she has a horse. Why?"

"Nothing. But I haven't heard much good about her, if she's the same Allegra Fulbright that was at Earlsdown last year."

Marina made a small movement, perhaps in protest.

"It would seem unlikely that there are two Allegra Fulbrights," I said. "It seems equally unlikely that my assistant behaved in an untoward way."

McClellan grinned unpleasantly, showing artificially white teeth. "Doesn't matter. Stephanie's got a hell of a horse this year. She ought to take the lot. You'll see the animal I bought her to compete this year tomorrow. A beauty. Cost me all of eighty thousand. Worth every dime, or it'd better be. Not that eighty's chump change, right, doc?" He drained his coffee and set the cup on the coffee table with a crash. "You any good with horses?"

I didn't dignify this with an answer.

"Anything happens to that horse, my little girl Stephanie'd have a screaming fit."

"Stephanie is your daughter?"

"Great little rider. You've probably heard about her."

"I can't say that I have. I did hear about the horse she rode last year. It died, I believe, under unexplained circumstances."

His eyes narrowed. "So it did, doc. So it did. Shame, too. At least the bastard was insured. But accidents happen, right?"

I gave McClellan a pretty good glare of my own. "Rarely. Preparation, precaution, and prudence all mitigate against accidents, in my experience."

He laughed, leaned forward, and slapped my knee in an offensively jovial manner. "Right you are, doc. And they say lightning never strikes twice in the same place. Another Scotch-rocks for the road, 'kay? I've got to be getting back."

I rose to my feet. "I'm afraid we're out of Scotch, McClellan. I'll see you to your car."

Marina followed me to the door. "Thank your wife for me, Dr. McKenzie," she said stiffly. "And remind her that we're having a meeting of the Veterinary Committee at our home tomorrow night. Do you know the other members, by the way? Diana North and Greg D'Andrea. And Ben Grazley." She frowned into the collar of her coat. "We used Dr. Grazley as a vet for a while. Steph didn't get along with him. Anyhow, Brewster thinks it's a good time to get everybody on the same page. Or so he said." I held her coat while she shrugged herself into it. "About eight o'clock, then?"

Between the call to look at the horse in the morning and the dinner party the following night, I'd be spending far too much time with the dismal McClellans. And I generally loathe large dinner parties. On the other hand, it would be an opportune time to meet the other members of the committee. And perhaps Madeline would wear the peacock-blue caftan I'd purchased for her last birthday.

I opened the front door to usher Marina outside. McClellan shoved his way out between us and headed toward his automobile, a Lincoln Continental.

It was a frosty night. Marina wrapped her scarf around her throat and I started to walk with her to the car.

"Terrible thing about Dr. Schumacher," she said, with an uneasy, sideways glance. "Getting shot like that. People think it's a sniper. The very idea scares me to death." She shivered and drew her coat more closely about her. "I think they're right. It's one of those crazy, drugged-up kids from the ghettos in Syracuse."

"Syracuse doesn't have any ghettos," I pointed out, with some asperity. "And as for snipers . . ."

A large hornet whizzed past my right ear and buried itself in the Continental's shiny black flank. I leaned forward to examine it with some interest.

It was a bullet hole.

Marina flung herself into the car and began to scream.

Five

~∞~

CHIEF of detectives Simon Provost looked like a greeter at Wal-Mart. I have not had a great deal to do with the police in my lifetime, although Madeline and I remain firmly committed to Dick Wolf's entire oeuvre, from the original *Law & Order* to *Law & Order: Trial by Jury* (the latter a highly underrated show, I might add) so I was intensely curious about the process of criminal investigation. I was taken aback to discover that Detective Provost was by nature a cheerful soul, with the eager helpfulness of that same Wal-Mart employee.

"I have to tell you, doc," he said, as we both examined the neat round hole in the Lincoln's passenger door. "This business of guns in the hands of any Charlie that wants to walk in and buy one is getting me down some." He sighed and rocked back on his heels. "You wouldn't have a screwdriver handy, would you?"

"I'll get it," Joe offered. "Is there one in the van, Dr. McKenzie?"

"I'll go ask Maddy," Allegra said. "She'll know where one is." The two of them took off toward the house at a fast jog, their speed increasing as they tried to get ahead of one another. Madeline was inside with Marina McClellan, who had seemed unable to stop shrieking. Simon Provost had arrived alone, in a Ford Escort somewhat the worse for the amazing number of miles on it, the remains of a meatloaf dinner evident on his shirtfront.

"I want to know how come you haven't called the goddamn FBI," McClellan said. He had helped himself to more of my twelve-year-old Scotch, which hadn't done his diction any good.

"Gonna have to call a squad car to get the two of them home," he said to me. "Or do you think that Mrs. McClellan can drive?"

I shook my head. "I doubt it. Although she is in my wife's extremely capable hands."

"Nice woman, your wife." He poked at the bullet hole with his thumb. To McClellan, whose inquiries about the absence of the FBI were becoming increasingly repetitive (and highly annoying), he said, "Not their jurisdiction," and then suggested that McClellan go to the house and ask for a cup of coffee. Which he did.

A short, not unpleasant silence fell between Provost and me. The night was misty, with the promise of a late and unwelcome snow in the air. Provost had arrived within ten minutes of Joe's phone call to the local police station. He was followed by a squad car containing two eager recruits. Provost immediately dispatched the two, armed with powerful flashlights, to the woods directly opposite the drive. I could hear them thrashing about in the shrubbery now. Searching for clues, I supposed, although what they expected to find in the dark, I couldn't begin to guess. I cast a skeptical look in the direction of the bumps and crashes. "Have to be thorough," Provost said cheerfully.

"You followed the same procedure at the scene of the Dr. Schumacher's death?"

"Yeah," he said, wearily. "Don't expect to find much. But you never know."

"And did you find anything of import in the brush there?" I asked with a fair degree of curiosity.

"Not in the brush, no. The only thing we found near the body was blood and hair from some roadkill. And the blood from the doc, of course."

"A deer, I suppose," I said.

"Hah?"

"I said the blood and hair were undoubtedly from a deer. It's spring. The bucks are in rut. They aren't road smart at the best times, and the rut makes them stupid."

"No, it wasn't a deer. Lab said it was some kind of mottled black-and-brown dog hair. Mighta been two dogs fighting, for all I know." He rummaged in his jacket pocket and brought out a clear plastic baggie filled with clotted fur. "Here. I picked up a pile of it." He chuckled. "Maybe you can tell me what kind of dog it came from, doc."

I took the package gingerly. "Perhaps I can."

He looked up at the sound of running feet. "Ah. Here she is. Thanks, kid." Allegra had come racing back with a fistful of screwdrivers. Joe loped up behind her. Provost selected a squat, thick Phillips head, opened the car door, and began to remove the inside panel.

"Want a hand?" Joe offered.

Provost squinted up at him. "You know your way around a quarter panel, kid?"

"Worked summers in a body shop."

Provost eased himself out of the seat. "Be my guest."

"You're after the bullet?"

"That I am, kid. You find it, don't touch it. Just holler."

We removed a short distance from the car. I was brooding on the dog hair. Surely . . . but, no. The Lab puppy had been found on Route 15. I tugged at my mustache. I patted my anorak pocket, where I had placed the packet for safekeeping. I would know soon enough. Finally, I asked, "Have you found similarities between this case and the death of Dr. Schumacher?"

Provost sucked his teeth. "Now, what makes you think there should be?"

I forbore to answer. It was blindingly obvious: two gunshots at occupied vehicles within a space of forty-eight hours?

Provost's voice had a chilly edge. "People start thinking there's connections between things, they're going to be thinking things like 'sniper' and 'terrorist' and that's not the kind of words I want rolling around Summersville like so many grenades with the pin half off." Provost looked at me, his muddy brown eyes shrewd, his gaze assessing. "And we don't want any kind of panic now, do we? 'Specially over what's gonna turn out to be a couple of hunting accidents."

"Found it!" Joe's voice was excited. Provost nipped to the car. He and Joe placed the inside quarter panel on the grass.

The car was parked closely enough to the house to benefit

from the kitchen lights. "I see it!" Allegra said. "It's still in the side of the door. And it's all flattened."

"This kind of car's pretty well built," Joe said.

"Should hold up to a thirty-mile-an-hour collision," Provost agreed. He withdrew a digital camera from his jacket pocket and took a few carefully angled photographs. Then he pried the bullet from the car door and examined it in his palm. "Much less the shell from a thirty-ought-six," he muttered. "Huh!"

I cleared my throat. "Out-of-season hunters, again?" I inquired, somewhat sarcastically.

"Might be."

"Lieutenant?" The younger of the two recruits emerged from the brush somewhat the worse for wear. "Came up with squat, sir."

"Kind of dark, maybe," Provost said. "Okay, guys. We'll try again in the morning. Franklin? You get that kid to help you get the door to the Lincoln reassembled and then follow Wilson, here. You," he said to Wilson, as the second policeman emerged from the brush, "get Mr. and Mrs. McClellan home. Then you can both knock off for the night."

I watched as the two young men went off to accomplish their respective tasks. To Provost, who seemed to be willing to stand there all night in contemplation of his big, flat feet, I said, "Were you looking for anything in particular, detective?"

He squinted at me. "Now, what's got you all in a tear, doc?"

"Forgive the asperity," I said with asperity, "but it looks as there's a problem burgeoning here."

"Burgeoning?" Provost's eyebrows rose toward his scalp. "There's nothing burgeoning here but your imagination, doc. We got some kid loose with his dad's shotgun, is all. And the last thing I need is some amateur Columbo trying to stir things up."

He zipped his jacket closed and moved off toward his car. "Good night to you, sir."

"Good night, detective."

* * *

"WHICH I meant sarcastically," I observed to my beloved an hour or so later as we prepared for bed. "It is a mark of the unimaginative to refer to anyone offering professional support to an investigation as a 'Columbo.'"

"Do you really think there's a sniper on the loose?" Madeline said. She emerged from our bathroom fresh from the shower, trailing the scent of lavender, adrift in a swathe of chiffon.

"A sniper? Of course not." I frowned. "Now, a murderer? Perhaps. I told you, did I not? The fur on the roadside where Schumacher was found appears to be an exact match for the Lab pup's."

"Brrr. Murder. It sounds horrible." She jumped into bed and snugged against my shoulder. "Let's not talk about it. It's been one heck of a day, Austin. I need to let my mind curl up and settle down."

I put my arm around her and we sat back against the pillows. "I take it the youngsters have bunked in?"

"I made up the AeroBed for Joe in your office. We can look for a more permanent bed for him tomorrow. Lila will have something I can borrow. And Ally's in the guest room."

"You inferred that there had been a disagreement between Allegra and her father," I said after a moment.

Madeline nodded. "She didn't say much else, poor child. But I'll find out sooner or later." She gave a sigh of content. "It's going to be a riot to have them in the house, Austin. I miss having students around. It's been the only clunker about this retirement thing."

There was another, highly significant downside to my retirement that this pearl among women would never mention: the lack of a regular paycheck. I smoothed a tendril of her hair behind her ear.

She rubbed her cheek against mine. "You aren't really grouchy about getting back into the consulting racket, are you, Austin?"

"As long as you're happy, my dear."

"I'm always happy," she said. Madeline is prone to statements of simple truth. "And as soon as everybody hears you're back on board as a show vet, we're going to be getting

a lot of calls." Her gaze drifted to the dresser, where the check
from the Earlsdown account sat propped against the mirror.
"And what with the kids here to take up the bull work in the
practice, things are going to work out perfectly." She yawned.
"What a strange day it's been, Austin. What do you suppose is
going to happen next?"

I kissed her.

"Now, *this*," she said a few moments later, "is exactly what
I hoped was going to happen next."

Six

≈

I gazed rather dubiously at the substantial remains of my oatmeal. It was nine o'clock in the morning and I'd lingered over breakfast, reluctant to ingest any more of what Madeline styled a "heart-healthy" meal.

I eat oatmeal six days a week, generally without complaint in the rush to complete my day. But Joe had taken care of morning chores before he'd left for an early morning class at Cornell. Allegra was tending to routine duties in the clinic. My morning hours stretched before me, unhampered by appointments or the necessity to pitch manure or eat my oatmeal so quickly that I didn't taste it. Now that I had time to eat it at my leisure, I wanted eggs, bacon, and potatoes. I hate oatmeal. When the phone rang, I picked up the receiver with some anticipation. Any diversion would be beneficial.

It was Victor.

"You hear about Benny Grazley, Austin? Shot dead as a doornail," Victor breathed heavily into the phone. "Stopped for gas on his way to a farm call this morning and blam! Guy was only sixty-two years, for Pete's sake."

Astonishment kept me momentarily mute.

"Austin? You with me, here?"

"Where? How? When?"

"About seven this morning, from what I hear. He stopped at the Citgo station on Fifteen. On the way to a farm call at the McClellans. Got out to fuel up and blam!"

There was considerable background noise on the phone. I took the receiver from my ear, frowned at it, and replaced it. "Where are you? What's all the noise?"

"I'm at the Embassy, of course. The whole town's here and

they're up in arms, let me tell you. They're calling this guy the Summersville Sniper. There's talk of bringing out the National Guard." Victor snorted derisively into the phone. "Idiots. But it's a helluva thing, Austin."

"He had children, didn't he? And a wife?" I'd met Benny several times over the course of the years, but our paths rarely crossed. My regret was for the man taken before his time and his mourning family, rather than that of a more personal grief. And my shock over the murder was profound. "Madeline and I will send our respects."

"Yep. Sixty-two years old," Victor repeated. "The prime of life."

Victor, it need hardly be said, had just turned sixty-two.

I was terribly confused. What was happening to our veterinarians?

The huskiness of Victor's breathing increased. "Austin?"

"I am still here, Victor."

"Talk down here at the Embassy is that someone took a potshot at *you* last night. That true?"

Speculations of several kinds whirled through my mind. Were the shootings random, the work of a conscienceless sniper? Too many facts mitigated against it. Three veterinarians had been shot at. Two veterinarians were dead. All three had some connection with McClellan. And there was the fur from the puppy three miles where the puppy had been found. And the dog couldn't have dragged itself three feet, much less three miles.

Had someone taken a potshot at me, personally? Nonsense. It would be hard to find a fellow less inoffensive than I. So McClellan had to be the target of some strange conspiracy. Possibly.

"Austin?"

"I am still here, Victor. As to your question, all I can say is that I was in vicinity of a shotgun shell last night, yes. Was it aimed at me, personally? I doubt it. At my profession? Doubtful." I chuckled. "I may be wrong; perhaps someone is out to shoot all of the veterinarians in Tompkins County."

Victor did not find this as ludicrous as I; he hung up the phone with an abrupt squeal.

I drummed my fingers on the tabletop. This case—for it was at this juncture that I began to think of this as a case—had features, but no form. Bodies, but no rationale. Facts. I needed facts. The vet tech at Benny Grazley's clinic was a former student. If I could reach her, perhaps she could tell me something of Grazley's last hours. Clarissa something. That was her name.

With luck, Clarissa would answer the phone herself.

I was, however, frustrated in my initial attempts to reach Benny Grazley's clinic. Busy signals have a great deal in common with that common household pest, the fly, that is, the buzzing creates a substantial amount of annoyance in the hapless listener. When someone finally answered the phone and a male voice said rudely, "Yeah?!" I was not at my most benign.

"What do you mean, 'yeah?' " I demanded in return, "Is this the Grazley clinic?"

"Who is this?"

I have a favorite reply to this obnoxious query, and I used it: "Who is *this*?"

"State your business, please, sir."

Anything less courteous than the tone of voice in which this was delivered cannot be imagined. "My business," I said with no small degree of asperity, "is with Clarissa Markham. And unless you are she, *my* business is none of *your* business."

Whoever it was put his hand over the receiver. A new voice came on the line. Male, calm and cheerful. "This is Simon Provost. Can I help you?"

Simon Provost. Wal-Mart Man. The lieutenant.

I hung up.

I was considering my options as Madeline and Lincoln came in the back door. She greeted me with her usual affectionate embrace and said, "Ally's a Georgia peach, Austin. I can't think how our clinic got along without her."

"I didn't feel particularly overburdened before, did you?"

"Of course not, sweetie. But seven days a week, four weeks a month, fifty-two weeks a year was getting a bit much for you. And me," she added, with suspicious haste. "Just think of all the things this will free you for, while Ally and I work around here." She smiled happily. "Guess what? You know how I haven't had time to get to the patient files and transfer them to the computer? Well, you know how I really, really didn't want to? Know what Ally's doing right now?"

The question was rhetorical. I made no answer, but merely smiled back at her. The fresh air had made her complexion glow and her hair escaped in auburn tendrils from the knot on top of her head. Madeline thought she was fooling me about why she wanted two strong young people to take over the more onerous chores in our practice. The signs of worry I had seen in her lately, around her eyes and her full-lipped mouth were gone.

My news about Benny Grazley would surely bring them back. "I had a phone call while you were out."

"Hang on a minute. I'll get us both a cup of coffee and you can tell me all about it."

Madeline shrugged herself out of her worn Burberry jacket and draped it on the brass coat stand. She kicked off her green rubber boots and headed toward the coffeepot. "You made a fresh pot. Hooray." She poured herself a cup, refilled mine, and settled at the table, facing me.

"Brace yourself, my dear. There's been another shooting."

By the time I finished recounting the facts as I knew them, her face was pale. "This is just awful. Just awful. What can we do? A sniper in Summersville. I just can't believe it."

"I don't believe it myself."

"But what else could it be?"

I frowned. "I'm not sure," I admitted. "But I confess to having some fairly wild thoughts about conspiracy and murder."

Madeline's eyes narrowed. "You're feverish," she declared. She reached across the table to feel my forehead.

"I am not feverish. You know that little part-Lab pup in the clinic?"

"Of course," she said a bit impatiently, "the one we picked up day before yesterday. The one you thought was a cruelty case. With the funny marbled coat."

There is a dark side to humankind. And one of the darkest corners is the abuse of animals. I had indeed thought the little pup an abuse case. The X-rays looked very much as if someone had struck both forelegs with the proverbial blunt instrument—perhaps a baseball bat.

"One of the items in evidence at the scene of Schumacher's killing is a clump of dog hair. Marbled dog hair."

A number of emotions chased across Madeline's face. Disgust prevailed.

"You mean," she said slowly, "someone could have broken the pup's legs, left it on the side of the road where Larky would be sure to see it, and waited for him to get out of the van and help her. *And then shot him to death?!*"

"It's possible."

"It's horrible! What ever made you think such a thing?!"

"Because we found the pup on Route Fifteen. Larky was shot on State Route Forty-one. And my dear, you saw for yourself. There is no way on earth that pup could have dragged herself a good three miles. The murderer—I should say the putative murderer—took the puppy away."

Madeline put her palm over her mouth and murmured, "My word, my word."

"So," I said briskly, "if there is a purpose behind these shootings, as I am beginning to suspect there must be, we need some information. And I'd like you to get it for me. I'd like you to call the Grazley Clinic and ask for Clari Markham. Remember her?"

"Clarissa? Of course, she works as a vet tech for Grazley. Certainly, my dear. But . . ."

"Why can't I get the information myself? Simon Provost is fielding phone calls, that's why."

"Oh." Madeline bit her lip to keep from smiling. "I see."

"I fail to find anything humorous in my refusal to speak to that idiot Provost."

"You always did hate to be kicked in your dignity," Madeline said sunnily. "All right, let me have the number."

Clarissa was a gold mine of information. Someone purporting to be Mrs. McClellan had called the clinic service at six, demanding Grazley's services for an emergency. Apparently delighted at the prospect of reclaiming one of his wealthiest clients, Grazley hadn't questioned the call, but taken off in his Jeep almost immediately. He had called back to the clinic twenty minutes later, complaining that he was almost out of fuel.

"And Clari says that she was *certain* the Jeep had been gassed up the night before. Apparently Grazley was a fanatic about being able to take off at a minute's notice."

I reached under the table to the bookshelf that forms the base of our kitchen counter and retrieved my Tompkins County map. I found Swansea Road, the location of Grazley's clinic, and traced the route to the Citgo on Faulkner Road.

"There was only one route he could take to reach Fifteen," I observed. "And the Citgo is the only gas station along that stretch. Someone could have drained the tank, made the call, and then . . . waited."

"So somebody set him up," Madeline said in a hushed voice.

"Possibly, Madeline. Possibly. We are very far from a clear understanding of the parameters of this case."

"Good heavens, Austin. What are we going to do now?"

"I would like to know a bit more about why Benny Grazley was headed to the McClellan farm. McClellan made quite a point of telling me he'd fired him. And an equally loud point about my visit to the horse this morning." I glanced at the kitchen clock. "It's close to eleven, already. I'll keep that appointment. And I'll see about getting some answers to those questions."

"Austin?"

"Yes, my dear?"

"Be careful."

THE McClellans had invested an enormous amount of money in real estate. The house sat on the crest of a hill, facing a sweep of acreage to the south. What I could see of it was stuccoed. Pink stucco. And a great deal of it. The barn and pastures were four hundred yards west of the house itself. The entrance to the whole place was off Route Fifteen. I pulled the Bronco in and came to a halt. Lincoln, anticipating my departure from the truck, leaped over the back of the front seat, and settled at my side.

"We have a choice," I said to the dog. "A right turn takes us to the barns. The left to the house." I leaned forward and peered through the windshield. "Which is precisely the color of Pepto-Bismol."

Lincoln put his paw on my right knee.

"The barns, then."

I proceeded slowly down the asphalted drive. The facility was impressive. I'd seen such a spread for sale, complete, in a recent edition of *Farming Today*. The barn roof was constructed of bronze architectural shingles. A cupola with a jumping horse weathervane held pride of place at the peak. It was a Morton building, with pale oak siding. The high-peaked stable appeared to have eight stalls, each with a fenced paddock leading from the double Dutch doors. The entryway would be the tack room and, possibly, quarters for stable hands. A long building with a much lower roof was attached to the west end. An indoor arena, then, and a fine one. There was a dressage-sized outdoor arena, as well. A slender young girl rode a big chestnut stallion around the perimeter. She held him in an extended trot. He moved very nicely. Long legs, with a lot of bone, and a fine set of hindquarters taut with muscle. His left foreleg was braced with Vetrap, but I saw no evidence of a limp. I narrowed my eyes against the sun. His mane seemed to be chopped in an irregular fashion. Strange oddity on a show horse.

Two vehicles sat in the circular drive outside the barn entrance. One, a sporty Cadillac van, had been hastily parked. The driver's door was open. The other, a silver Hummer, blocked the entrance. The Hummer was purchased, no doubt, to navigate the sand dunes and desert stretches of upstate New York. There was no sign of the shot-up Lincoln Continental. In the shop for repairs, I assumed.

I parked next to the outdoor arena. As soon as I left the Bronco, Lincoln immediately appropriated the driver's seat. The girl, who was too thin, was intent on her ride. I set my carryall down, negotiated my way around the Hummer, and stuck my head in the half-open door just in time to see Brewster McClellan strike his wife. It was an openhanded blow, and petulant. "Goddamn it, Marina!"

"Do not," I said loudly, "do that again." I glanced outside. The girl rode on, oblivious. I stepped into the short hallway and shut the door. McClellan gaped at me, his face congested with anger.

"Dr. McKenzie?" Mrs. McClellan said. "Uh. Hello." Her face was as expressionless as it had been last night. Madeline had informed me the botulinum toxin is used to achieve this effect. The slap had left no mark on her complexion. She bit her lip, cast a scared glance at her husband under lowered brows, and slipped out, shutting the door noiselessly behind her.

"Dr. McKenzie," McClellan said. He stretched his mouth in a grin. "Little late, aren't you?"

Never apologize. Never explain. Particularly to bullies. I merely regarded him over my spectacles. McClellan made a show of looking at his watch. He wore a blue striped dress shirt and a suit. His watch was a gold Rolex. "Gotta run, doc. I'm meeting in town with the mayor." His glance slid sideways. "Sorry you had to see that little incident with Rini." He gave me a man-to-man grin. "Bet you've got the same problem, doc. Women going nuts with the credit cards."

"No," I said, "I do not."

"It's not that we can't afford it. Just that Rini's got a bit of a problem that way. And she hides it. Goes nuts for clothes and makeup and then doesn't tell me. 'Kay? I don't like surprises. Took me off guard, is all." McClellan hunched his shoulders.

It is a curious fact that the guilty overexplain themselves. Moreover, I didn't believe a word of it. Marina McClellan wore the same clothes she'd worn the night before; breeches, a worn sweater, and ancient woolen socks under her paddock boots. The only difference was her shirt, which today was a pale pink instead of white. And frankly, she had the sort of pale, washed-out complexion that could do with a bit of makeup. No, Marina McClellan was not a spendthrift. Not on herself, at any rate.

McClellan exhaled heartily. "Right. Well. Steph is outside with the horse. You go ahead and do what you gotta do. And send the bill in to me. Don't worry about the cost."

I followed him out the door. Stephanie and her horse were at the gate to the paddock, near Marina. All four of us, and I include the horse, watched as McClellan roared away in the Hummer.

I turned and went to the arena. I got my first look at the

horse close up. His mane was choppy because he had a series of small, scabbed-over wounds just where the hair of the mane grew from the neck. They started midway and went down to the nape.

"Steph," Marina said in her soft, nervous voice, "this is Dr. McKenzie."

"Hi."

The greeting was as flat and monotonous as my morning oatmeal. The girl was about fifteen or sixteen. Her hair and complexion were lusterless. She wore a long-sleeved flannel shirt, a shaggy vest, and breeches. I looked at her nails. They were bitten to the quick. The bed of her right thumbnail was rimmed with dried blood.

I said nothing about this, but merely asked: "Shall we see about Beecher, then?"

She dropped off the horse and stood holding him by the reins. I stepped back and, as is my wont with any new animal, looked him over from head to tail.

Beecher was a Swedish Warmblood, which is say, a light draft horse. Almost all of that splendid breed are chestnuts, and this fellow was no exception. He was a lovely, sunlight brown with a white snip on his muzzle. He had an exceptionally mild and kind eye. I looked at how his legs set into that broad, muscular body. "He's a wonderful animal," I said. "Just wonderful. You're eventing him?"

No answer.

"Steph," her mother prompted.

"Yeah, I'm eventing him. At Earlsdown. If that crappy leg of his is in shape."

"I saw you working him when I drove in. He looked sound enough to me. Did you say Dr. Grazley had taken a look at him recently?"

Stephanie made a disdainful noise. Marina said, "We weren't all that satisfied with the way he'd been treating Beecher. So Brewster fired him."

"He was an idiot," Stephanie said flatly.

"But he looked at him initially."

"Way back when this first started, yeah. But Daddy wouldn't let him within a mile of the place, now."

"So no one called him to come out and see to Beecher this morning."

"You crazy?"

"Stephanie," Marina protested.

Stephanie rolled her wad of gum from one cheek to the other. "Last vet to take a look at Beecher was Dr. Schumacher. He put the bandage on. And I was supposed to run the hose over the leg a couple of times a day."

I looked at her. "And have you?"

She shrugged. "I've been busy. And like you say, he's not gimpy now."

I bent down and unrolled the Vetrap from Beecher's right fore. A healed cut ran from the cornet band about halfway to the knee. There was very little swelling.

"And how did this happen?" I asked.

"He was rolling in his paddock and caught his leg under the fence," Stephanie said indifferently.

"It's a common enough injury and it's healed well." I straightened up and got to my feet. "To be on the safe side, put him under light work for a few more days, gradually increasing his workout until he's up to full speed in about a week."

Stephanie snapped her gum. "So I can take him to Earlsdown, right?"

"I will decide that," I snapped.

She glared at me. "I've heard about you," she said between gritted teeth. "You old fart. Think you know more about horses than anybody else. I told Daddy not to put you on the committee. I told him! Nobody's stopping me from riding this year. Nobody!" She burst into loud and unattractive tears. "Everybody's against me."

"I can bar the horse from competition, and I will," I said. I pointed at the scabs on Beecher's neck. "That must stop. Immediately."

"We've got pigeons in the barn," she said sullenly.

"Lice would disqualify him, too." I picked up her hand and held it palm down. The quicks of the nail beds were as scabbed as her thumb. "But it's not lice. You have been picking at this horse."

She snatched her hand away.

"Your decision, young lady. Stop it at once."

"I don't understand," Marina said. "We need to get rid of the pigeons?"

Stephanie whirled and shrieked, "Shut up, Mom!" to which Marina had no response.

This put paid to any idea I had of appealing to the troubled child's parent.

"Can I ride, now?" Stephanie snarled. "I've only got ten days until the show. There's a ton of work to do."

I nodded. Stephanie hauled herself back onto the horse and urged him into a trot.

"If you want to leave the bill with me, I'll see to it," Marina said as she walked back to the tack room. "And we will see you tonight for dinner, won't we?"

I turned to follow her, and was just in time to see the horse stop, buck, and pitch the girl off into the sand.

Marina screamed. I swore. The horse trotted a short way down the fence and snorted. The girl groaned, sat up, and began to wail. Beecher snapped at his own hindquarters and began to race around the ring, kicking violently. He rounded the fence, reins trailing, and galloped toward Stephanie, who wailed all the louder. He swerved just before he reached her, his hooves flying past her forehead by a hairsbreadth.

Marina looked blank. She didn't move.

I hopped over the rails and dropped to the sand. The girl was my first concern. I helped her to her feet. She jerked her arm from my hand and stalked off to the gate. I waited for Beecher to round the far end of the arena one more time. He rolled his eye as he raced past me, and I said, "Whoa."

He slowed.

"Whoa."

He put his head down and walked on. I approached him at a diagonal, told him to stop, and grabbed the reins. I patted him absently, looking him over. He wasn't breathing hard, and he hadn't worked up much of a sweat. He snapped at his hindquarters again.

Puzzled, I examined his hindquarters more closely. A white-faced paper hornet crawled sluggishly over his croup. I took aim and smacked it.

"A bee?" Marina said at my elbow.

"Hornet. A vicious one. It's been unusually warm," I said. I picked the body of the hornet up between thumb and forefinger. "This fellow is out and about well before his time. It's been a warm spring. Just to be safe, I'd check the eaves of the barn for nests."

"Oh, I've got hornets, I know that already," Marina said. She stared over the fence. Her daughter stamped into the barn and slammed the door behind her. Marina, arms hugging her thin body, stared after her. "A whole pile of them."

Seven

～≋≈～

"GOOD grief," Madeline said over our very late lunch. "What a horrible morning you had."

She'd made French onion soup and a large green salad. That, and her own presence, went far toward mitigating my sour mood.

"And the horse is okay?"

"He seemed to be. Picking at his skin like that won't harm him. He's a horse. I doubt that he feels it. It's what the picking represents. The child is troubled. Animal abuse is a very bad sign, psychologically."

She sighed. "Well, I suppose we'll get through dinner tonight somehow. But he hit his wife, Austin." She shook her head, bewildered. "It's awful. Shouldn't we do something? I mean, if the poor woman's being beaten, don't we have an obligation to help? And what about calling child services about Stephanie?"

"Her parents provide a significant obstacle there. They're the legal guardians, of course. From what I can see, she's abusing her mother, not the other way round. And the police will only help the horse if there's evidence of abuse under the act, which there is not. We could," I added, in a mildly humorous tone, "call AA."

"The auto club?"

"Alcoholics Anonymous. I did observe two things about McClellan. There was a distinct smell of Scotch on his breath . . ."

"At eleven in the morning?"

"Which would argue for what I believe is called an intervention of some sort by the man's friends. If he has any. And when he hit his wife it was more of a bat than a slap." I pointed toward Odie, asleep, as usual, on her perch on the woodstove. "Much like the cat's attacks on Lincoln. Which would suggest that we leave the situation alone."

At the sound of his name, Lincoln thumped his tail on the floor.

"Well," Madeline said in a troubled way. "I suppose we have to leave it. At least for now. But I don't know how I am going to look any one of them in the face at dinner tonight. And you say they didn't call Grazley to come out to the farm?"

"If one of them did, it's been denied."

"Now what?"

"Now what?" I repeated.

"If none of the McClellans called Ben Grazley, and even if one *did*, they're denying it, which is just as good as guilty, in my book, we're looking at intentional murder. Just as you said. And if we aren't going to talk to the police about the family mess at the McClellans, are we at least going to let them know we're sure these shootings are deliberate murders?" Madeline finished this heated speech with her cheeks flushed and her considerable bosom heaving.

"Perhaps I should talk to Provost."

"Perhaps? What's with the perhaps? You bloody well have to, Austin. Or I'll do it for you."

I thought this a good idea. I have never known anyone to sneer at Madeline. More to the point, Provost would not decry *her* incisive insights into a certain shooting as amateurish.

"Except that you're the one who's made all these brilliant deductions, and you're the one who should get the credit." She reached over and clasped my hand proudly. "I'll bet the village council ends up giving you a citation, or something. When are you going to see Provost? This afternoon?"

"I have quite a bit of work to get through this afternoon," I said, a bit feebly.

"Nonsense. You might just as well stop in at the police station."

"I have a great deal of work to do here," I said firmly. "Not to mention the fact that I am on call, in case any of my patients need me."

"Stubborn old goat."

I set my jaw.

"Fine. But you'll get around to it? Talking to the police?"

I set my jaw even more firmly.

We finished the soup. Madeline disappeared into the laundry room. My work awaited. There was next week's column yet to do, and that review to write.

All desk work.

I looked out the window. The sun spilled all over the place. A light breeze rustled the tops of the maples. Time passed. I may have fallen into a light doze until Lincoln came and stood next to my chair, his gaze hopeful. Madeline swept back into the room, her arms filled with clean towels.

"Any farm calls?" I asked.

"No, dear."

Some days, I told myself, were bound to be slow, especially when a practice was just beginning to build.

"No messages?"

Madeline slung the towels to one hip, dug one hand into the pocket of her jeans and withdrew a disappointingly small stack of pink slips. "Not too many, sweetie. One for Allegra. One for Joe. You know what? I think we should run a little teeny ad in the paper. Let people know we're here."

Advertising. I shuddered. The dog shoved his head under my hand. I rubbed his ears, then rose, collected the coffee cups, and took them to the sink where I rinsed them with care.

"Oops," Madeline said. She unfolded a pink slip.

"What?"

"But there is this one from Rita."

The day became a little glummer.

"She wanted you to call her back. She said there's a problem with the column you turned in."

I sighed. "It's a pleasant day for a walk. I could go down there and discuss it."

". . . And she said it's *not* necessary to come down to the newspaper. She said not, not, *not,* as a matter of fact."

"Nonsense. Lincoln and I can use the walk."

"Did you write this week's column yet?"

"Actually," I admitted, "no genuine letters of inquiry have come in as yet this week. I'm afraid I must fall back upon the Socratic method. That is, I will pose and answer the question myself."

Madeline made a face. Madeline's face is highly expressive, and although she is a beautiful woman, at the moment she resembled the north end of a baboon. "Austin. I can't think of one pet owner in New York State who wants to know about bovine back fat."

"Bovine back fat should be of interest to anyone who . . ."

"As a matter of fact, I can't think of anyone in the entire United States who does. Or the Canadians. Or the French. Or the . . ."

Before she could get to the outer reaches of the Mongolian empire, I abandoned the dishes, retrieved my anorak, and left, accompanied by my dog. Madeline's shout trailed after me:

"Don't forget to talk to Lieutenant Provost!"

Outside my back door, spring unfolded. The temperature was benign, the sky was blue, and in their paddock, Pony and Andrew lifted their heads and whinnied a welcome as Lincoln and I stepped briskly onto the gravel drive. Either Joe or Ally had groomed both horses to trim perfection. It was with a sense of satisfaction that I set off on the mile-long walk into Summersville. I would compose both question and answer for this week's column as I walked.

Madeline did have a point about bovine back fat. Most pet owners are interested in the more practical applications of veterinary science. By the time I reached the portals of the *Summersville Sentinel*, I had a very satisfactory Q and A ready to dictate regarding the regular use of antihelmetics in dogs.

The *Sentinel* occupies a cut-stone building on the west side of Main Street in the center of the village. Even in the pale spring sunlight, the old stone glowed with a mellow geniality. The presses occupy the ground floor. The second floor holds the editorial offices. Lincoln and I jogged up the stairs to the second-floor landing just in time to meet Rita on her way out.

"You!" she said.

Rita is a small, trim widow in her mid-forties, with short brown hair, a great many freckles, and sharp gray eyes. Her late husband was, I believe, a journalist of some note, whose ethics remain a byword in the industry. Rita is as committed to truth, justice, and balanced reporting as he was. She is also peppery in personality. Generally, however, she is not excitable. But her excitement today was almost palpable.

"Austin, I don't have time to talk to you right now. Didn't Maddy tell you not to come down? Can't you just do the rewrite at home and e-mail me? I'm on a hot story! First murder in Tompkins County since that trouble last year up at the Inn at Hemlock Falls. I have to get to the press conference in half an hour."

"Rewrite?" I said, getting to the essential part of this stream of words. "There is absolutely nothing wrong with that column!"

"Sheesh!" Rita rolled her eyes, bit her lip with impatience, and glanced at her watch. "Okay. I've got ten minutes, tops." She wheeled around and pulled me through the door to the offices. The *Sentinel* offices occupy most of the second floor and are designed on what I believe is called the "open plan." This means that the only obstacle between the staff and the public is a chest-high counter that divides the desks from the entryway. Rita pushed through the swinging gate. I followed. She went straight to her desk and pushed papers around in a frenzy. "Here!" She thrust a sheaf of papers at me.

"It's the blueline." I said. (The *Sentinel*'s presses are antiquated, a consequence, Rita says, of the slender profit margin inherent in the publishing business.)

"Yep. And darn it, Austin. I was so busy this week I told Justine to edit it and I didn't see it until right this minute. And then of course we got the letter."

"What letter?" I demanded.

"You'll see tomorrow's paper!" She jogged up and down in agitation. "But it's *hot*, Austin."

I let this pass. My column always looks more impressive in typeface. I read it with a modest glow of pride:

ASK DR. MCKENZIE!

(The exclamation point is not mine. I prefer understatement, but apparently the advertising department felt it needed "punch.")

> Dear Dr. McKenzie:
> I found the dearest little possum in my backyard just before Christmas. I made a comfy nest for him in our garage. He went into hibernation just after we found him. I have tried waking him up now that the weather is getting warmer, but I guess he is still hibernating. What should I do now?
>
> Yours truly, M. W.

> Dear M. W.:
> Possums do not hibernate. Your pet is dead.
>
> Yours truly, Austin McKenzie, DVM, PhD

"M. W.'s diction could use some work," I admitted. "But I thought we had a policy not to interfere too much with reader letters. They are, after all, the voices of the people."

"Your *response* could use some work!" Rita said. She appeared to be in some dudgeon. "I mean—'your pet is dead'!? Couldn't you, like—I don't know—soften it up? It's like that old joke about the singing telegram. You know—da-da-da-da-dat! 'Your sister Rose is dead!' "

Rose? Soften it up? "This," I said with authority, "calls for Madeline. She will know precisely what to say."

"Good. Sit down at my desk and call her. Matter of fact, go home and ask her."

I pointed out it was nearly three o'clock and a Tuesday, to boot, and that three on Tuesdays had been the *Sentinel*'s deadline for twenty years.

"We're holding the presses until I get the whole story on the Grazley murder."

"This is most unusual, Rita."

"Yeah, well, I've got an unusual angle to this thing." She looked at her watch again, ignoring the imperative grasp of my hand on her sleeve. "The cops are holding a press conference at the courthouse, like, right now." She pivoted and resumed her march out the door. A press conference? About the shooting incidents, I presumed. An idea sprang fully formed into my brain. Lincoln and I followed Rita down the steps. I arrested her progress midway. "Is this press conference open to the public?"

"Nope. Press only." She hurtled forward, but swiveled her head and narrowed those sharp gray eyes at me. "Say. You know him? Grazley?"

I cleared my throat noncommittally as all three of us clattered down the steps. Rita stopped at the bottom, ran her hands through her hair, and then faced me. "Of course you know him," she answered herself. "All you guys know each other."

I said nothing, committing the sin of omission. If one were a Jesuit. Which I was not. I was also thinking rapidly, as is my wont. What if *I* spoke up at the press conference? A short, but succinct summary of the facts, delivered in my best classroom manner. Provost could hardly decry my efforts as "amateur" in teeth of a crowd I held in the palm of my hand!

"Austin?" Rita nudged me. Her elbow was sharp. "Look, Austin. You think you might be able to give me some background on this guy?"

"Possibly," I responded. It wasn't probable, since my one face-to-face encounter with Benny Grazley had been over the body of a dead horse fifteen years ago. But it was possible, depending on the nature of her question. I could certainly let her stand in line for an interview with me. Although I would have to consider the benefit attached with an exclusive to the larger papers. The *Times*, perhaps, if they were represented. "Grazley had called me in for consultation on occasion."

Well, once.

"All right. I'll risk it. I'll get you a press pass. You and the dog stay right here."

She raced up the stairs again and reappeared, moments

later, with a plastic card in her hand. "Here." She thrust a press pass at me. "You can come with me, Austin, but you keep your mouth shut, okay? What I want you to do is, if there's a question you think I should ask, you whisper it to me, okay? They find out you're a ringer, they can ban me from these like that." She snapped her fingers. "The last thing I want is to lose my press privileges on a big story like this." She skidded to a halt in front of her automobile. "What the hell are we going to do with that dog?"

"Lincoln is fully capable of finding his way home," I said, not without pride. "If you'll wait a moment, I'll just write a brief message to Madeline. Lincoln has carried messages to her before. If he arrives home without me, she'll worry."

"We can call her on my cell, Austin. As a matter of fact, why don't you carry a cell? Never mind, never *mind*, I don't want to hear another lecture on the general obnoxiousness of modern life."

"Very well," I said, with some dignity. "Be that way."

"Jeez-louise, Austin." She scowled. "Did I tell you how much I like you, you old goat? Stubborn old anachronism that you are."

"Rubbish." I held my palm up to summon my dog's attention. "Lincoln?"

He looked up at me, ears tuliped forward, eyes alert.

"Home. Madeline."

There was a brief—very brief—flash of disappointment in those brown eyes.

"Sorry, boy. But you must go home." I stressed the noun "home" very lightly. Lincoln's vocabulary is large, for a dog, but the words of apology meant nothing to him. He would forgive me the loss of upcoming journey in his own way. He heard the word "home" and obeyed. He pivoted and trotted back the way we had come, purpose in every magnificent line.

"Where is the press conference being held?" I asked as I folded myself into Rita's Geo.

"Ithaca courthouse. In fifteen minutes."

We made it in ten. Ithaca is only ten miles from Summersville and Rita's size-six shoe belies a heavy foot. She is an accomplished multitasker, too, and by the time we reached the courthouse, Madeline had been alerted to the fact of my absence for the remainder of the day, and she critiqued my oral transcription of my proposed column for the upcoming week.

"Worms are good," she said positively. "You can never get enough good advice about worms. But I swear to god, Austin, you try and run a picture of . . . what was it again?"

"Ascarids," I said. "Small, round parasites found in the stools of untreated dogs. They are visible to the naked eye, although by the time . . ."

"Excuse me. I know you find interrupting rude as all get out, Austin, but *no pictures*." She whipped the little Geo into a space that would have better accommodated a go-cart and turned off the ignition.

"You are quite an accomplished driver," I said with admiration.

"You'll find out I'm an accomplished pincher if you say one word aloud in here. Got it?"

I nodded and followed her up the courthouse steps.

I had passed by the Tompkins County Courthouse for many years without ever going inside. It was an imposing structure, made of cut stone as are so many of the older buildings in upstate New York. Inside, the ceilings were imposingly high. The floors were terrazzo, which always seems somewhat dirty, no matter how good the janitorial service, and the walls and stair railings of dark, battered mahogany.

The press conference was held in a small courtroom off to the left. We joined the pack of media people shoving and pushing their way in the confined space. With a few judicious applications of her right heel, Rita managed to drag me to the front of the room.

Before us stood a podium and lectern. An array of microphones splayed across the lectern's top.

"There appear to be no policemen present," I observed.

"Shh," Rita hissed. "And ten to one it's a policewoman, Austin. Just be quiet, okay?"

"I am using the term 'man' in its generic sense," I said, somewhat stiffly. "As a writer, you must be aware . . . ouch!" Rita's right heel dug into my shin.

A phalanx of policemen arrived all at once and distributed

themselves around the lectern, rather like a herd of sea lions beaching themselves on a favored shore. Rita pulled out her notepad and scribbled furiously. "They've got all the brass here, plus some extras," she muttered to me. "That's the chief of police here in Ithaca, and that's Simon Provost, the head of detectives for the Ithaca police force."

"I know him."

Rita let this admission pass. She pointed the end of her pencil at a tall, muscular man who had taken up a stand well to the rear. "And my gosh, that's Myles McHale. He's the biggest of the biggies. I heard he was off somewhere on terrorist duty. I wonder what he's doing here?" She snapped her head around and stared at me. "Wait a second. Provost. You know him, too?"

"I spoke with him earlier today," I said casually. "It was at the start of the investigation. And last night of course. You are aware that someone took a shot at me last evening?"

"No kidding," Rita breathed. "You catch me up on that later, okay? Maybe I ought to interview *you*."

Provost was short, stocky, with a heavy chin and a balding pate. His demeanor was far less cheerful than it had been the night before. He looked, in fact, careworn. I leaned down and whispered, "Would you care for a few pictures of me as well, Rita? To accompany the interview?"

"Shh. The chief's going to speak."

The chief of the Ithaca Police Department stepped forward and leaned into a microphone. He was familiar to anyone who had lived and worked in the area as long as I—a good man, the scuttlebutt had it, and an honest one. His manner was direct, uncompromising, and succinct:

Veterinarian Benjamin Grazley of the Canandaigua Equine Clinic was sixty-two years old. He had been traveling north on Route 96 and stopped at a gas station in the town of Covert. He was shot to death at approximately 7:15 A.M.

He left a widow and two children.

Rita shot up her hand and waved it frantically. The chief nodded, and she worked her way through the crowd to the podium. She grabbed the microphone, leaned forward, and said, "Ladies and gentlemen. Not thirty minutes ago, a message was delivered to the *Sentinel* offices. We don't know where it came from. We don't know who the author is. But I will read it to you now."

She withdrew a plastic-covered sheet of paper from her sweater pocket and held it up. "It says: ANYWHERE! ANYTIME! ANYBODY!"

A cacophony of shouts erupted from the mass of reporters, but Rita herself shouted the word that the entire room had feared to hear.

Sniper.

Eight

~~~~~~~

A sniper in Tompkins County?

It was hard to believe.

I returned home without speaking to Provost or anyone else about the evidence Madeline and I had pulled together. Any thought Rita had of doing an interview with me was squashed flat by the Summersville police department. Two patrolmen hauled Rita and her note off to talk to the investigators. I had to call Madeline to come and retrieve me from the courthouse.

The village was a hotbed of rumor and speculation, of course, and every radio and television channel was crammed full of spurious "specials" and "you are there" reports about the Summersville Sniper. Ersatz experts in psychology and sociology scuttled into the limelight and pontificated. The verb "pontificate" is a useful piece of language. I do not use it lightly. The only person who should pontificate is a pontiff. As far as the note was concerned? I was convinced it was a malicious prank.

I sat in front of the television and the Syracuse six o'clock news while Madeline squashed lamb patties into flat rounds. She was making dinner for Allegra and Joe before we left for dinner with the McClellans.

"There is one thing, Austin." She plopped the last lamb burger into the broiler pan and shoved it into the oven. "Austin? Are you listening to me?"

I scowled at the television. Some gasbag from CNN stood in front of the Grazley's front door, microphone clutched in one hand and fake compassion plastered all over her face. She'd just asked Mrs. Grazley how she felt. Mrs. Grazley shut the door in her face. She should have shoved the microphone up the reporter's nose.

"Austin!"

"You saw that, I take it?" I clicked the mute button and tugged at my mustache. "Bereaved by violence, and that reporter asks the poor woman how she feels? They should jail that flack. We need an amendment to the Constitution. I shall write to Senator Schumer."

"Good for you," Madeline said vigorously.

"Better yet, we should lobby for an addition to the Bill of Rights. This nation is in sore need of a Right to Civility. Come look at this, my dear. There is Simon Provost, at the courthouse steps."

Madeline thumped the cutting board with a package of frozen peas. This was to get my attention. I turned the television off altogether and walked into the kitchen proper. Lincoln got up with a sigh and followed me.

"Austin, have you thought about who is going to take poor Dr. Grazley's place on the Veterinary Commission?"

I sat at the table. Suddenly, I felt quite old. "Grazley will be quite a loss to the profession, you know. He has quite a reputation as a researcher. I used several of his papers on immunoassay testing in the senior seminars on equine infectious diseases. He will be difficult to replace." The cat Odie jumped to my shoulder and dug her claws affectionately into my shoulder.

"But what about Earlsdown?"

"My goodness. You're right. A second untimely death means the commission is short a veterinarian."

Madeline slapped the frozen peas into the microwave. "So, who we going to get on such short notice? Earlsdown's a rated show, right? We're going to need that fourth guy. And—you're not going to believe this—Marina's already called me back to make sure we're coming tonight." She shook her head. "She didn't say a word about what happened this morning, Austin. Not your visit. Not Grazley's murder. Not the so-called sniper. Not anything." She slammed a loaf of French bread onto the cutting board. "There's a lot of denial operating there."

There seemed to be a lot of denial operating here, too. Neither one of us wanted to discuss the shootings, or what we had surmised about them.

The microwave dinged and the broiler timer went off. Madeline smiled at me. "Dinner'll be ready as soon as I get the potatoes out of the oven. While you're thinking about poor Benny Grazley's replacement, go find the kids. It's time for them to eat."

I pulled Odie off my shoulder and set her down. She curled about my ankles in protest. She wanted her dinner, too.

By the time the kids and I trailed back into the kitchen, Madeline had fed Linc and Odie and tidied up the sink. Ally had the Lab puppy from the surgery cradled in one arm. Joe followed her in, looking fit to be tied. "The puppy shouldn't be here at all," he said to her back as he trailed her into the kitchen. "The cast won't be ready to come off for a week, at least. She'll heal better in the cage."

"You can put her over there, dear," Madeline said, pointing to the dog basket next to the woodstove.

Ally set the puppy into the basket as if she were a porcelain egg. Lincoln padded over and gave her a good sniff. Odie settled on the stovetop and glared down at her, her tail switching back and forth. (If Joe had had a tail, he would have been switching it, too.) I contemplated that peculiarly marked fur. Perhaps I was mistaken. Perhaps the bit of fur Provost found by the road at the scene of was from some other animal. Perhaps this whole series of events was a nightmare.

"She'll heal better with people around her," Ally said, a bit defiantly. She sat down next to me at the table.

"Miss Dog Expert." Joe sat at my other side.

"You've never heard of wellness psychology?"

They faced off over the dinner table.

It was precisely the same behavior exhibited when two new colts are introduced to a herd. I was interested in the activity, but I was ready to move and stop the fuss before somebody got kicked.

"What's for dinner?" Joe asked. "It smells terrific."

I exchanged a glance with my beloved. There was something quite poignant in that homely question, in the sight of the two faces at the dinner table. We had never had children of our own, a sorrow we had mourned and then put behind us.

"Oh joy," Madeline said suddenly. "Oh calloo, callay."

"You look startled, Allegra." I passed the peas to her. "Madeline misquotes Edward Lear when she is happy."

"What do you quote when you're not happy, Mrs. McKenzie?" Ally asked.

"She becomes very quiet," I said. "A rare occurrence for her." I chuckled. Nobody else did, including Madeline. Madeline looked at me. Oh, dear. I tugged at my mustache and cleared my throat.

"You're not eating, Dr. McKenzie?" Allegra asked. "Oh, that's right. You're due at the McClellans."

"That's still on?" Joe said. "I thought Grazley was a member of the Veterinary Commission, too."

"But the sniper got him," Allegra said soberly.

The sniper. I bit my mustache in disgust. I looked at the puppy in her basket. And I had an idea I should have had long before. "Excuse me a moment." I rose from the table and went into the living room. I called the ASPCA, an action I should have taken as soon as I'd picked up the puppy from the road. I returned to the table and sat down.

"There *is* no sniper," I said. "I'd bet my degree on it."

Allegra and Joe stared at me. "No sniper?" Joe asked. "I mean, there *is* a sniper, since two men have been shot at long distance. Do you mean it isn't a random killer?"

The boy was quick, I'll give him that. I didn't answer him. I needed time to turn this information over.

Madeline's brow creased with concern. "Austin?"

"My dear?"

"You look . . . unsettled."

"I am quite unsettled," I said testily. "And I don't wish to talk about it at the moment."

"I know who you can get to replace poor Dr. Grazley, Dr. McKenzie," Allegra said, after a second helping of green peas.

"Who would that be, my dear?"

"Dr. Bergland."

I paused.

"There's not much Dr. Bergland doesn't know about horses, from what I hear," Joe said.

"There is a great deal Victor doesn't know about horses," I said.

Madeline seized gratefully on this topic of conversation. "Now, sweetie. He's absolutely the last word on azo-whatever. You said so yourself."

"Azoturia myositis syndrome," I said. "Perhaps. Not as much of it about as there used to be, however."

"Compared to Dr. McKenzie, I'm sure Dr. Bergland doesn't know a thing," Ally said loyally.

Joe bit into a sourdough biscuit and stared at her while he chewed. "You've never met the man. How would you know how much he knows about horses?"

Ally tossed her head. "It's easy enough to tell about that sort of thing."

"You know what that was?" Joe said. He leaned over the table. "That was a suck-up comment. Just plain old suck-up."

Madeline stuck her oar in before we had a full-scale war over the lamb patties. "I can't think of anyone else we could get on such short notice, Austin."

"I'm certain he'll be too busy with university affairs to bother," I said.

"It's spring break," Madeline said. "And he only teaches the one seminar anyhow."

"There's a lot of vets around," Joe said. "Maybe some of the adjuncts at the school? I could ask. They'd probably jump at the chance to work with you, sir."

"Now who's a suck-up?" Ally muttered.

"Very few vets have the credentials required to attend a rated three-day event, that's true," I said. I mulled for a bit. There seemed to be no other candidate. "I suppose you're right, Madeline. I'll give Victor a call after dinner. With luck," I said hopefully, "Thelma will have break week all planned out for him and he'll have to decline. Last year, she hauled him on a ten-day cruise on the Bosporus with her mother." I grinned and exclaimed, " 'Cribbed, cabin'd and confined'!" to everybody's confusion, but Madeline's, since I quote Byron when I'm feeling nettled, and she'd heard it all before. "I'll give him a call. There may be time for him to meet us at the McClellans this evening."

But Brewster McClellan had anticipated me, and Victor and Thelma were to attend the dinner that evening.

Which is part of the reason why dinner at the McClellans' was such a bust.

But not all of it.

"WHAT in the world has gotten you so upset?" Madeline demanded, as soon as we were in the car headed to dinner.

"I called the ASPCA."

"You did? Why? Oh!" Madeline's comprehension was instant. "The puppy. You called to see if they had adopted out a part-Lab puppy." She turned to me, her eyes gleaming in the dark of the car. "And?"

"Four days ago."

"To whom?" Madeline's voice was filled with trepidation.

"Stephanie McClellan."

Madeline settled back without a word. After a bit, she said, "I don't believe it."

"We are speculating ahead of the facts," I admitted. "We don't know for certain, for example, that there is a match."

"Oh, come on, Austin. You're not facing up to this." She shifted in the seat. "So now what?"

"We will follow our noses. I wonder . . ." I fell into musing. "Do you suppose this all has something to do with Earlsdown? The one connecting factor here is that Grazley, Schumacher, and now I myself are on the committee in charge of qualifying horses. And if anything ever happened to prevent Beecher from competing . . ."

"She's killed two people because she thinks it'll keep her in a horse show?! I can't believe it! I won't believe it! She's just a child! And Austin, it's just an event!"

"McClellan seems to have put a great deal at stake, however."

All knew by now that Brewster McClellan bought his way onto the Earlsdown Committee with a generous cash donation, although to be fair, this is not as opportunistic as it might seem. Big horse shows cost a great deal of money. Without donations, the horse world would be a far smaller universe. But Brewster also bought his way into ribbon money with Faraway, who'd cost a huge amount of money, if Victor were to be believed, and all of that came to naught last year when the horse had died. This new horse, Beecher, had cost even more than Faraway, according to McClellan himself.

Fair play is characteristic of the horse world. It's one thing to win with a horse you've brought along with discipline and tears through the lower ranks of the circuit. It's another kettle of fish when you jump in right at the top with an animal somebody else has labored over. There would be a prejudice against Stephanie and her expensive horses from the beginning. "Everybody's against me!" she'd cried.

We drove on in silence, until we reached the edges of the property. I confess that I didn't know what to do.

The McClellans' place occupies one of the most beautiful spots in Tompkins County. There are acres of woods, meadows, and pasture. I had heard that one of Ithaca's wonderful gorges cuts right through the middle of the property. There's nothing happier than one of those gorges in the springtime. Water cuts through the limestone like a knife through butter, leaving layers of lichened rock. The water falls, cascades, spills, flows, dances, and weaves through these incredible caverns as if it's been loosed from a cage.

It's enough to make you believe in heaven.

"Do the McClellans live over the gorge?" Madeline asked as we drove into the evening.

"No."

She sighed. "Too bad."

"They live in the middle of five hundred acres of meadow. The gorge cuts through the back. He calls it the Manse."

"Well, *there's* a clue to his character," Madeline said.

I turned into the drive, which was lit along its length by electric standards made to look like gaslights. I pulled into the semicircular driveway. I braked and stared. I had never seen the front of the house before.

"Now, Austin."

"That's a full-sized replica of the fountain of Trevi," I muttered. "With those four stone horses rushing off into nowhere in particular."

"I'm sure they decided to copy the fountain because of the horses, sweetie."

"The place looks like a Florida restaurant."

"Well, maybe they'll serve us tropical rum punch and co-conut fried shrimp. Yum."

I parked the truck next to Victor's old Citroën and got out. I shook the dog hair out of my sports jacket and slung my coat over my arm. We slogged up the steps. The front door was as high as our barn door and split down the middle, like the doors of the cathedral in Rheims. I half expected a butler, but Marina herself opened the doors.

"It's Dr. McKenzie. How nice to see you again." She kissed the air on either side of my face. She seemed unnaturally cheerful. There was a foggy look to her eye. Had she been a horse, I would have suspected that she'd ingested a modicum of acepromazine. Just enough to make her woozy. "And Madeline?!" She spread her hands wide. "Who else could it be, but Madeline?"

She did the air-kiss maneuver with Madeline. "I love your caftan, Madeline. It's . . . it's . . . positively royal."

"My wife blooms in purple," I said. "And you look . . . er . . . well, Marina." I would be the last to criticize the poor woman if she were on drugs. Who had a better right?

Madeline smiled back at me. I had picked her caftan out myself, as a twenty-first wedding anniversary present. I like a lot of color.

"Aren't you two just the cutest things?" Marina asked the air. There was no possible answer to this, so I didn't make any.

"Well, we're all in here. Just follow me."

She tapped her way unsteadily down a long hall with black and white marble tile for a floor. She was wearing breeches, which made me wonder if we were going to eat dinner in the barn, and a white silk blouse and ruby necklace, which made we think we weren't. So we followed her wherever she was taking us and I finally asked where we were going.

She looked back over her shoulder. "Since this is an informal meeting, I put us in the library."

I brightened a bit at the word "library." But of course, it was no more a true library than I am the pope. Fake Stubbs on the walls. Hunter green walls and that shiny blond oak. And shelves and shelves of books, all bound in leather with gold titles, and not one of them looking like a real book looks, which is to say, as if somebody had actually read it.

"*South* Florida restaurant," I said.

Madeline nudged me. Hard.

"Madeline!" Victor said. "You look magnificent!" He hustled on over to give her a kiss. Thelma hustled on over faster than he, so he couldn't. She was wearing yellow-green, which was not a good idea. It made her look like an artichoke. I think Thelma came from the womb with a bad temper. Like the wolverine. Of course it could be bad digestion. One look at that yellowy skin and pursed-up mouth and it was obvious that her stomach bothered her on a regular basis.

Thelma gave Madeline a peck on the cheek and Victor an elbow in the gut. She passed her cheeks over mine in an air kiss. Her breath smelled like Maalox.

Madeline asked Thelma about her mother, and how she was settling in. (Ha!)Victor and I eyed one another. Then Marina grabbed Victor and the two of us and shepherded us to a little group gathered by the sideboard.

"Here's the rest of our little commission." Marina said with manic cheer. "I'd like to introduce Diana North. Here are the McKenzies and Victor Bergland."

"It's a privilege to meet you both." Diana North shook my hand, then Victor's. Diana North had a nice, healthy shape, a suntanned face, and a lot of thick brown hair cut short. She had a good smile, too. It was obvious that she'd calm any animal she met, just by her easy ways. You could also tell she was a little shy with humans since she shook hands with me twice. Then she said, "That's a wonderful caftan, Mrs. McKenzie."

"It was a present from Austin."

"This is Greg D'Andrea." Marina glanced up at him sideways, with a little private smile. Greg was one of those thirty-ish men that witnesses on *Law & Order* always describe as average, frustrating policeman like Lenny Briscoe. Medium height, medium weight, and as do a lot of people who don't smoke these days, he chewed toothpicks. But he had a good leg on him, and a straight back, which meant he was probably quite good on a jump course.

He didn't smile, but gave Victor a quick, loose handshake and nodded at me.

One of those little silences fell, the kind that happens when people who don't know each other can't think of a thing to say.

"May I get you a drink, Mrs. McKenzie?" Greg D'Andrea asked.

"Love one," she said.

He went over to the sideboard. There was a row of Waterford crystal decanters with the names of the liquor on brass tags around the necks. You should be able to tell bourbon from Scotch by the color and nobody with any palate at all drinks vodka, which meant that the clear bottle is always gin. And people who don't know what they're drinking shouldn't drink at all.

"I'll have a touch of the Laphroaig," I said. "And for you, my dear? I don't see any sherry—ah. Yes, I do. Over there, D'Andrea."

Madeline asked Greg if he was going to compete at Earlsdown, and Diana, too, and we talked about horses, which is a very relaxing thing to do, and then the commission duties, which Victor was rather pushy about, until Brewster McClellan came in from wherever he had been. He brought two more people with him. One of them was Lila Gernsback. I froze momentarily. Lila is a lushly built brunette of about Madeline's age. She is a widow, and I believe, a divorcée as well. She has, as Victor so bluntly states, the hots for veterinarians. For some reason, she has always fixated on me. She makes me highly nervous.

Lila caught sight of me despite my diplomatic retreat between the bookcases, shrieked, "Austin!" in a voice with the timbre of a steam whistle, and waved cheerily, which caused her generously exposed breasts to bounce. She stayed put, however. A riding accident some six months ago had slowed her down considerably. To my dismay, she was due to have the casts off and ditch the crutches in several weeks' time. She was quick with the cast on; she'd be even quicker with the cast off.

Lila was accompanied by a tall, heavily fleshed man with a bald head surrounded by red fringe. He wore bright red plaid pants and a blue sports coat. I glanced Madeline's way. She looked at Lila with an expression of comic dismay, then winked dramatically at me.

Marina skittered into the room and clapped her hands. "It's time, people!"

And we all marched into dinner.

The dining room had marble floors, Italian-style frescoes on the walls, and three chandeliers hanging over the table. It was not at all welcoming. But the far end of the room had French doors that had to front the pastures and meadows around the house. During the daytime, the view must have been spectacular.

Place cards at each setting were stuck into miniature pewter fox heads. Brewster sat at the head of the table with his back to the French doors; I was seated at his right. Marina sat at the foot, with Madeline on her right. That put the entire length of the table between us. The place to my right was empty. I took a look at the place card, which said "Stephanie" in elaborate calligraphy.

Marina caught the direction of my glance. "She's just finishing up in the stable." And sure enough, about three seconds later Stephanie came through the French doors and slouched into the seat next to me. She was dressed in breeches like her mother, but unlike Marina, she had made no concession to evening attire, with a silk shirt or otherwise. It was pretty clear from the sweat stains on her rear that she'd been riding. And even clearer from the smell that she'd been mucking out.

I rather like the scent of horse manure. It's a comfortable kind of smell, as long as the stalls are picked out every day (it's another thing all together if you don't and let it pile up). Besides, I'm so used to it, I don't care.

"Steph?" Marina said. "You didn't get a chance to wash up? I hate to say it, darling, but there's an . . . an odor."

Stephanie gave a snort of disgust, leaped up from the table, and stomped off through the entryway without a word.

Marina got up, too, and disappeared into what I suppose was the kitchen. She came back a few minutes later with a tray of soup. We ate the soup, which was a decent tomato cream, and then the salad, which was a Gorgonzola sort of thing that was too rich for my taste. By the time Marina came back with the main meal of beef filet, Stephanie was back, smelling like Ivory soap, but with a scowl that would have curdled hot milk on a cold day. Marina introduced Stephanie to the table. Whatever substance she had ingested prior to the party had begun to wear off. There were shadows under her eyes, and her skin looked pasty. She stumbled over the names. The fat man with the bald head and the red fringe accompanying Lila was named Phillip Sullivan, "Daddy's business partner from New York." She forgot Thelma's name entirely. And she called Diana "Susannah," which Diana accepted rather placidly, and ended up with Madeline, who was sitting next to her.

"Stephanie, this is Mrs. McKenzie."

Stephanie poked at her beef, dropped her fork, stared at me, and said, "Your wife?"

"Hey," Madeline said. "I've heard a lot about your horse. His name's Beecher, right?"

The kid kept staring at me.

"Stephanie," Marina said in a warning way.

She blinked like a lizard and turned to Madeline. "Yeah. That's right. Beecher." She ducked her head and poked at the beef again.

There was a strained silence.

"You're from New York, Phillip," Madeline said, turning to the fat man.

He leaned back in his chair and peered at her with slitted eyes. It was a most peculiar quirk. "Yep. The Big Apple."

"Phillip is interested in buying an event horse," Lila said in a rushed way. "He's up here for a few days, just to look around at all the . . . talent." She dimpled, implying perhaps that the talent was herself.

"Ha ha. That's right," Sullivan said.

"Sully's looking to get into bed with me and the vets," McClellan said from his end of the table.

"I beg your pardon?" Victor choked a little on his wine.

"Not *that* kind of bed, I hope." Lila twinkled merrily.

"Brew's got this good little business going, see," Sullivan said heavily. "FieldChek, innit, Brew?"

"At-point field testing for EIA," Diana said at my blank look, "or so Ben Grazley told me."

"A portable Coggins," Victor said alertly. "Ah. Quite a convenience for those who show."

It would be quite a convenience, indeed.

"We think it's got a nice little market niche," McClellan

said complacently. "Won't make us a ton of money, but you never know where something like that's gonna go." He belched.

"Ben Grazley was a partner in this group?" I asked.

"Was, yeah," McClellan said, "so we have room for another partner. You interested, doc? One veterinarian's just like another."

Nothing ventured, nothing gained. "Was Schumacher involved with this, as well?"

"Well, he was. Hard luck," Brewster said. "I see your point. No good investing in a nice little business where the partners drop off like flies, is there? Ha ha."

"Ha ha," Sullivan said. "We might want to talk to you, Mac, after dinner. I'm ready when you are. Anytime. Anyplace. Anywhere." He laughed, again. Loudly.

The table froze for a long moment. We had all gone to significant lengths to avoid any talk of the Summersville Sniper.

"This," Stephanie said loudly, "is, like, incredibly boring. Can I go now?"

"Sit right there, young lady," McClellan said. "You'll wait until we've finished."

"This party sucks," she muttered. She rose halfway from her chair. At the end of the table, McClellan raised his hand in a threatening way.

"Beecher's a Swedish Warmblood, I think," Madeline said loudly to Greg. "One of my favorite breeds for eventing. One of my favorite breeds ever, in fact."

Diana North jumped in, too, bless her. She smiled at Stephanie. "How do you find the breed, Stephanie?"

"And how is he over fences?" Madeline added.

"How is he over fences?" Stephanie repeated insolently. She sank back into her seat. She looked at her mother with a "get this" kind of expression. Marina fumbled into weary speech. "Forgive us, Madeline. You know how competitive the horse world can be."

"Well, sure," Madeline said, puzzled.

"It's just, we heard that Allegra Fulbright is staying with you. Is that right?"

"Yes," I said pleasantly.

Marina turned to me. "She's not competing, is she?"

"I don't believe so, no."

"She'd better not be," Stephanie said. It was the first time she'd spoken more than a few words at a time. The child had an unfortunate voice: whiney and high pitched and all of it through her nose. The whole table stopped talking out of sheer surprise. "I mean, like, you'd think she'd be ashamed to show her face anywhere near a horse show." That whine was replaced by a nasty giggle. "She's just a little bitch and everybody knows it. I mean, everybody knows she was screwing her brains out with all the top riders from Devon last year. She probably even screwed the judges. I mean, that horse of hers, where'd he come from, anyway?" She made a face. "Some auction, I think. I mean, like, who brings an auction horse to Devon and has it win unless there's something dirty going on?"

I looked at Marina. It's the mother's job, after all, to instill manners into the kits. She shrugged. "Well, from what we've all heard . . . I have to say that Stephanie isn't far off."

Which left the job to Madeline. Madeline looked gravely at Stephanie until the girl broke her gaze and looked down at her plate. Madeline's voice was soft, but there was no arguing with it. "That, young lady, is enough of that. Sit up. And remember your manners."

She sat up.

"And apologize to the dinner guests, please."

Stephanie muttered something that may have been an apology.

Marina sat with a face like a stone. Greg D'Andrea stared into his plate as if it were running the last twenty seconds of the Kentucky Derby. Diana North looked like she was somewhere else. Phillip Sullivan continued eating. And then Brewster McClellan broke the silence. The boozy son of a gun clapped his hands together one-two-three and shouted, "'Bout time somebody slapped that kid up the side of the head. Kids can get away with anything nowadays."

Now what could anyone around that table say to that?

Stephanie ate her steak with short, nasty stabs of her fork. I wanted to go home, sit down with Madeline, and swallow a large slug of Laphroaig. But McKenzies never back off. So I drank my water, ate the meringue Marina brought out from the kitchen, and made a polite mention of the food.

"Yes," she said dully. "Thank you."

"It's me you want to thank, doc. I'm the one that pays the bills from the Inn at Hemlock Falls." Brewster rose and shouted down the table. His half-full glass of Scotch tipped and spread the remainder of its contents over the white table-cloth. "You think she cooked this? Bullshit. It's fancy take-out." He tossed back his glass of wine. He was on his feet, so of course, all of us rose as well. "'Fore you all go, I wanna show you a *real* horse."

"Has someone been discussing fake horses?" I asked politely.

"Ha ha ha ha," Brewster said. "Come on, barn's out this way." He stumbled around in a half circle, found the French doors, and banged them open. Cold air rushed in. The rest of us exchanged looks of consternation. It'd been a mild March, but it was still pretty nippy out there. And I worry about Madeline.

"Barn's heated," Greg D'Andrea said to me. "And it's a short walk."

"I'm fine. But Madeline has no coat."

"I'll be fine, my dear." She laughed. "I'm pretty well up-holstered." This eased the atmosphere considerably. She put her hand on my arm. Stephanie had taken the chance to leave, and Madeline gazed at her empty chair in a considering way. "Quite a mannerless young lady."

Greg smiled for the first time that night. It looked good on him. "Quite an understatement. Are you sure you wouldn't like me to get your coat for you, ma'am?"

"Nonsense!" Madeline drew her arm through mine. "I've got my love to keep me warm."

Which was banal, but true. It did keep us warm all the way out to the barn.

The barn was spectacular. The barn was heated, and although this is a practice I find generally unhealthy for horses, it is quite comfortable for humans. And it was spotless. Most horse people care more about the barn than the house. I've even known a few places where the barn had hot water and the house didn't. One spends the money first on the horse, second on the horse, and third on oneself, if there's any left over after one and two.

This barn was built of pale stained oak inside and outside. And a barn is just where pale oak belongs. The stalls had double Dutch doors on the outside walls that led to the turnout paddocks. There was a hot water washroom, a grooming stall with hot blowers . . . and of course there was Beecher.

We stopped in front of his stall. He looked larger and more magnificent than ever against the wood.

"Pretty impressive, isn't he?" Brewster said. Someone had left a dressage baton hanging on the tack hook in front of Beecher's stall. Brewster picked it up and held it out as if it were an épée. Then he danced as if fencing with an invisible man. "Anyone want to take a bet on who's gonna win at Earlsdown this year?" He jumped forward as if to thrust home, a drunken simulacrum of Cyrano de Bergerac.

"He's wonderful," Diana North said. "Just wonderful."

"Take him out of the stall, Marina," Brewster said. "Let the folks here see him strut his stuff."

"Brewster, I don't think I should." Marina hugged herself and shivered. "He hasn't been himself lately." She twitched like a horse plagued by flies. "Where's Stephanie? Greg, go find Steph, would you? She can take him out of the stall."

I folded my arms and watched. This was a woman who was afraid of horses. Or of this horse, at least. You could practically smell it.

Brewster belched, with the pleased air of somebody who'd accomplished something. "Jesus Christ, do I have to *do* everything myself around here? Honest to god, I *pay* for everything myself." He fumbled at the latch and slid the stall door open with a clang. "Here, you sum-a-bitch. Get on out here." He gave us a sloppy grin. "Horse comes for me better than anyone else."

Now, most horses don't really care for the smell of liquor. As kind as he looked, Beecher didn't seem to, either. It was that, or the fact that Brewster was loud and pretty obviously blistered. So the horse jibbed and backed instead of coming forward. Brewster swore, swung the baton around like a baseball bat, and hit Beecher a hard one over the muzzle. The horse backed into the far corner of the stall, eyes rolling. Blood dripped scarlet onto the snip on his nose.

McClellan raised the baton again. I reached over, grabbed the back of his shirt collar, and dragged him out of the stall. I tore the baton out of McClellan's hand and threw it down the aisle. I took two steps forward and looked McClellan in the face.

If you'd hit the silence in that barn with a hammer, it would have shattered.

Diana North moved first. "We can fix that cut, Dr. McKenzie." She behaved as if she were on a routine barn call. She stepped past McClellan and into the stall as if McClellan didn't exist. "I'm pretty sure I saw a first-aid kit down by the tack room."

I stepped into the stall, too.

"I'll get the first-aid kit," Madeline said.

"I'll come with you, Maddy," Lila said.

Victor grunted, "Here you go, McClellan." And the old boy took Brewster by the shoulder and frog-marched him down the aisle. Greg D'Andrea sprang into action and went right along with them. Phillip Sullivan, on the other hand, blinked like a large somnolent lizard on a rock and said, "What's the big deal?"

Diana took Beecher by the halter and settled the big horse down. Greg and Victor began a falsely hearty conversation about where the horse had been and whom he'd competed against and what vet had done the prepurchase exam.

Madeline brought me the first-aid kit. She looked pale. I clasped her hand briefly. She pulled my head down and whispered in my ear: "Look!" She held the Red Cross kit in one hand; the other was clenched shut. She opened her fingers to reveal a pair of wadded-up gloves. She put her hand under my nose.

Gasoline.

I folded the gloves and put them in my pocket. I got the Betadine and cleaned out the cut. I ran my hands up and down Beecher's legs. All the while, Diana North held the horse by the bridle and spoke pleasantly to him. It took Beecher a while to settle down, but just as I'd thought when I'd met her, Diana had a pleasing way with animals. Fairly soon the old boy had dropped his head and relaxed.

Horses are amazing creatures.

I tucked the bloody swabs of cotton into my pocket, and felt to make certain that the gasoline-soaked gloves were still there. As I looked down to check, I noticed a glass vial in the bedding.

McClellan's raucous voice grated on my ear. ". . . I can tell you that. And then I had to fire the sum-a-bitch."

"McClellan." Nobody ignores that tone of voice from me. "Was I the last person to see this horse?"

McClellan didn't look up, but he stopped his gabbing to Victor and answered sullenly. "Who the hell knows?"

"You were the last one to see him," Marina said. "You said he was fine."

I frowned at the syringe. It was not dated, of course, but the record would be. "Did Schumacher leave you a bill that last time he was here?"

Any medication would be listed there.

"No. His office sends it on to us later. Why?"

"Did Schumacher say anything else about the horse?"

"Just that he was bruised from getting his leg caught," Marina said nervously. "And those, um, little lice bites on his neck." She looked into the rafters of the spotless barn, which was, of course, free of vermin of any type.

"That sum-a-bitch turns up lame for the show, he's gonna get a bullet through the skull," McClellan said.

"I wish you wouldn't talk like that, Brewster. He was a little off," Marina said. "That's all. He wasn't lame, as such."

"Anything wrong with that sum-a-bitch, I want my money back. A bullet in the head." He laughed. "Yep. That'll teach 'em."

That laugh was the straw that broke the camel's back.

Nine

MADELINE avers that my commitment to conduct a private inquiry into the veterinarian murders began when I lost my temper. Perhaps she was right. Paris's vow to avenge the death of Hector arose from just such a loss of temper: Trojan honor had been impugned with the desecration of the hero's body; veterinary honor had been assaulted by that crass boor McClellan. Not to mention the integrity of that wonderful horse.

Driven by righteous fury by the blow to the animal, fueled further by that sneering bellow, I escorted my wife from that overstyled pile of a barn and drove the both of us home.

As I hung up my anorak on the coat tree inside our back door, I realized I had come to a decision:

I wanted to nail McClellan.

"The man's a wart." I draped my muffler over my coat, removed my galoshes and went straight to the liquor cabinet. I needed a brandy, neat. "A smear on the windshield of life. A carbuncle."

Madeline hung her coat neatly next to mine. She'd swept her hair up on top of her head, and a few stray curls drifted around her ears. She looked beautiful, though tired. "I don't know, Austin. I feel kind of sorry for him. For all of them, as a matter of fact. Have you ever seen an unhappier family?" She slung her purse over the back of one of the kitchen chairs and sat down at the table.

"Sorry for him? Ha! With a trail of dead and discredited veterinarians in his wake! Hardly."

"Poor Marina. Can you imagine being married to him? And what about having him for a father! And, Austin . . ." She paused and took a deep breath. "What about the gloves?"

The gloves. I withdrew them from my coat pocket. The reek of gasoline permeated the kitchen. And the facts were strongly in favor of someone having drained a portion of gasoline from the dead Dr. Grazley's car.

"We'd better put them in a plastic bag," Madeline said. She pulled one out of a drawer and neatly sealed the gloves up. "Where? I know. The freezer." She tucked the package behind the ice cubes. "They'll keep just fine until you can get hold of that Provost character."

I frowned. "It doesn't seem too neat, to have found them like that? I take it they were in the first-aid kit?"

"Tucked underneath them. By themselves, they aren't evidence, Austin. I mean, there's a pair of gasoline-soaked gloves in *our* garage from the time you wrecked the lawn mower."

"I did not destroy the lawn mower."

"Did it work before you got your hands on it?"

I didn't dignify this with a response.

"And does it work now?"

I failed to respond to this, as well. "This is not getting us any further." I picked up the conversation where we had left off. "Am I sorry for his wife and daughter? Possibly. I'll have to think about it." I regarded Madeline with deep affection. "I must say, my dear, that I was enormously proud of you and the way you handled young Stephanie. The dispassionate, but eminently fair rebuke."

Madeline looked thoughtful. "Well, a little embarrassment is good for that kind of kid once in a while. But that was nothing to what you did, Austin." She raised her eyes to mine and said with heartrending simplicity, "You were a hero."

"Nonsense. As for McClellan? As I said—a wart." I poured two fingers of Five Star Hennessy into a glass, and then sank into my recliner. "I'm convinced he's behind all of this. Something's rotten here, Madeline. Very rotten, indeed. And I refuse to believe a sixteen-year-old is behind crimes of this nature."

"It's possible, however," Madeline said in a low voice. And she was right, my wife. There is a kind of ineradicable evil that may crop up anywhere. Even in those we think of as innocents.

"And there's something else. I found this in Beecher's stall."

I put my hand in my trousers pocket and withdrew the plastic vial I had discovered in the bedding.

Madeline looked at it and inhaled sharply. "A dose of that would kill him."

"It would, indeed." I held the deadly little vial up to the light. Acepromazine, in a lethal dose. "I doubt very much that Schumacher prescribed *this*. Besides, what kind of veterinarian would drop a glass vial in a horse stall?"

"You're right."

"Now, if McClellan is up to something and Schumacher discovered it . . ." I fell into a study. If Schumacher had indeed discovered some fakery and confronted McClellan with it, murder seemed a fairly drastic solution to McClellan's problem.

I leaned forward, "I would be *most* interested in determining whether or not Brewster McClellan owns a thirty-ought-six. And in determining the amount of the insurance policy on the horse."

Madeline's jaw didn't drop, exactly. But she was definitely alarmed. "That's the rifle the sniper used. You think Brewster McClellan's the murderer? That he's been doping and killing his own horses?"

"You remember Faraway."

"But . . ." Madeline bit her lip. "It doesn't explain all of it, Austin."

"In good time, my dear." I held the glass of Hennessy up and admired the amber color. "As you know, my dear, symptoms never occur in a vacuum. An elevated body temperature is an indication that some infection may be rampant in the system. A slow capillary refill time indicates a disturbance in the cardiovascular system. In short, where there is a vial of a horse-killing drug, there may be fire! Where there is the death of a horse named Faraway and a disgraced veterinarian—there may be corruption. Where there are two dead veterinarians, there may be murder."

Madeline merely stared. Then she walked over to my recliner and took away my Hennessy.

I rose to my feet and began to stride about the living room, an exercise that always promoted increased lucidity in my lectures at Cornell. "You don't find it a very low probability that not one, but three members of the Veterinary Commission have fallen afoul of McClellan? Are you forgetting Coughlin, who paid with his reputation? Grazley, who has paid with his life? And Schumacher, the same? You don't think I should follow in the footsteps of such investigating detectives as Sam Spade and Miles Archer?" Then, recollecting that Archer's death had established the premise for *The Maltese Falcon*, and that Archer hadn't investigated a thing, I amended. "Well, Sam Spade in all events. Ha!"

"Austin, ssshh! And, let me get this straight, you're going into the detective business because you think McClellan killed two veterinarians and shamed another one out of business?"

"The man struck his own horse. We were both there. We both saw it. He struck his wife."

Madeline closed her lips and nodded slowly. "I see your point."

"Capable of anything!"

"Oh, hush, Austin! You'll wake the house."

Which I had, of course. Lincoln galloped down the staircase—presumably from his spot at the foot of the bed in Allegra's room—followed moments later by Allegra herself. Perhaps I had been a trifle noisier than is my habit.

I greeted both girl and dog with a nod and continued, "Of course I am going to investigate this case. Three members of my profession have been removed from their proper sphere. Three! Coughlin, through disgrace, and now, Ben Grazley and Larky Schumacher through murder. I lay this all at that rat McClellan's door. In Spade's immortal words, 'When a man's colleague dies, he's gotta do something about it.' Well, I intend to do something about it."

"Sam Spade said 'partner,' I think. As for Coughlin . . . who? Oh!" Madeline's brow smoothed. "The poor guy from last year. The one who treated Faraway."

Allegra sat down at the table across from her and Madeline gave her a radiant smile. "How are you, sweetie?"

Before Allegra could reply, I swept on. "Coughlin hasn't had a moment's peace since that fatheaded boob saw him kicked off the Earlsdown grounds last year. His practice is virtually ruined."

"Now, Austin, who told you that Coughlin's practice has been practically ruined?"

"Victor, naturally. Who else? The man is in the know. I may just begin my investigation by interviewing Victor." I poured another dram of Hennessy and offered it to Madeline, who declined it with a graceful gesture. I sat down in my La-Z-Boy and regarded the amber drink with a darkling eye.

"Investigation? Of the McClellans?" Allegra asked. She looked both rumpled and defenseless.

"We were just kicking some ideas around. Did we wake you up?" Madeline looked charmingly apologetic. "Why don't I make us some cocoa?"

"I don't want any cocoa, thank you. And I wasn't really asleep, just sort of dozing off." She wore a baggy T-shirt and an even baggier pair of pajama bottoms. The ensemble emphasized her extreme youth. "Linc heard the car come into the drive and wanted to come down, so I got up and came downstairs with him." She settled onto the leather sectional, drew her knees up, and clasped her hands around them. "So, what's going on?"

"Not much," Madeline said in an absentminded way. "Except that Dr. McKenzie is thinking about going into the detective business."

Allegra tugged at her hair. "Something happened at the dinner party to make Dr. McKenzie want to go into the detective business?"

"The dinner party was a little skiffy."

Skiffy? Madeline, the most focused and forthright of women, was behaving in a strangely distracted way. I had fully expected that she deliver a tactfully phrased, but truthful, account of the evening, including the behavior of the despicable Stephanie. I agreed with the implied decision not to relate the story of Beecher's attack. It was an ugly incident, not fit to repeat. But as for the rest of the evening—I, myself, would certainly want to know if my name were being bandied about in a scurrilous fashion so I could paste the offender one in the snoot. On the other hand, I could understand why Madeline perhaps did not want to allude directly to the reasons behind my forthcoming investigation; such a task might be dangerous, and one did not want to involve the youngsters. Better then, to leave the suspected drugging under wraps.

"Ally?" The thoughtful furrow had not left Madeline's brow. "Have you thought about competing at Earlsdown again this year?"

"Me?"

"You have the points, right?" Madeline referred to Allegra's ranking in the eventing hierarchy. Anyone who had entered the show before as she had should have no problems with eligibility.

"Sure, I'd be eligible." She bit her lip. To my eye, she seemed to pale. "I don't have a horse, though. I mean I did, last year, but he's gone." Then she didn't say anything more. There seemed to be tears in her eyes. Most distressing.

"Well," I said. I cleared my throat. "Time to take Lincoln out for a walk, I see."

"Stay right where you are, Austin. Ally's not going to carry on, are you? Good. Who needs to cry when you can come out swinging? And I think that's what we all want to do. Come out of the corner and jump right smack-dab into the middle of the ring." Madeline put her elbows in the table and propped her chin in her hands. She seemed to have come to a decision. "Ally—if you had a horse, would you want to compete at Earlsdown?"

"Are you kidding? Of course I would! But, how? I don't have a horse."

Not much more needed to be said. Event horses do not grow on trees. Andrew had been a splendid competitor in his day, but the old fellow's heart condition meant those days were gone. And when Madeline's mare Duchess had died, we hadn't had the means to replace her.

"Well, let's think a little bit. What about . . . ummmm . . . let me think . . . Mrs. Gernsback?" Something in Madeline's tone of voice told me that she had not just pulled Lila's name out of her ear. My wife's thought processes can be amazingly quick. I am the first to admit she sometimes is ahead of me by a country mile. Despite this, I made a loud—if involuntary— grunt of protest.

"Oh, for heaven's sake, sweetie. I have never understood why a man who can castrate an unanesthetized twenty-five-hundred-pound bull is such a wimp around the likes of Lila Gernsback."

Lila Gernsback, you will recall, was a widow with, as Victor so bluntly put it, the hots for veterinarians. Or at least for me. She is loud. She is determined. And she is sneaky.

Madeline's eyes sparkled. "Oh, Ally. Mrs. Gernsback's got a horse. And what a horse. A retired eventer. He's a Trakehner cross. Twelve years old. He's perfect. She'd be over the moon to see Hugo work again."

"She's not competing herself?"

"Would if she could. Broke her leg in three places six months ago," Madeline said, with a regrettable lack of compassion. "Which just leaves her more time on her hands to make googly eyes at my husband."

"Wow," Ally said. "I mean . . . but the show's only a week and a half away. I couldn't possibly fit him up in time."

"There is that," Madeline agreed.

And for a moment, all three of us mulled this over. Eventing is arduous. Both horse and rider must be at the peak of athletic form. Allegra seemed healthy enough, but the back and leg muscles degrade quickly if not exercised regularly and she would be pushed hard. As for Hugo—well, Lila Gernsback was a good horsewoman. It was possible, although not probable, that the horse could be made ready in time.

"There's something else," Ally said. "I'd have to borrow the entry fees and expenses from you. It's never good to bet on winning enough to cover them—our farrier used to tell me that—so I'd have to work off the loan with my hours here."

Another obstacle to this quirky idea of Madeline's: show fees and expenses could add up to as much as three or four thousand dollars.

"Don't give that a thought," Madeline said. This from the woman who clipped coupons from the *Chronicle* every week and recycled tin foil until it disintegrated. Madeline *was* up to something, and I was beginning to fear I knew what. Madeline had worried about my physical well-being ever since my visit to our internist last year. She hadn't offered an opinion about my plans to become an investigating detective. And when Madeline is silent on a subject, she has a reason. Such as a fear of my demise among a hail of bullets on stakeout. Or broken limbs after being set upon by McClellan's goons. This plan to enter Allegra into competition was an obvious ploy to divert my attention.

"So, you think it could actually happen?" Allegra said hesitantly. "That I could compete next week?"

"The only way we'll find out if Hugo is available is to ask Lila," Madeline said merrily. "And the person to ask her is sitting right there."

Allegra turned a hope-filled gaze in my direction. I winced. Madeline laughed unfeelingly. "Phoo! You can wrap Lila Gernsback around your little finger, Austin."

"I don't care to be indebted to Lila Gernsback." I sounded feeble even to myself. "And I certainly don't want to be alone with her, even if she is on crutches. This is your plan, my dear. I think you and Allegra should talk to her."

"Nonsense, sweetie. All it's going to cost you is a little conversation. Besides, she'll end up owing us. She's got Hugo up for sale, you know."

I didn't know. On reflection, that made the whole suggestion more tolerable. One of the best places to buy an event horse is after you've seen it perform—so Lila would have a sound reason to lend Hugo out for the week. And if someone in attendance at Earlsdown were impressed enough with Hugo to buy him—Lila would owe us, or rather, Ally, who would receive a percentage of the sale price. Of course, if we were all involved in preparing horse and girl to ride, it would diminish the time available to me to investigate Grazley's death. How could Madeline think I hadn't noticed this attempt at diverting me from my purpose? I would be firm in denying my participation in this.

"Austin, it's just a terrific idea."

"Let me think about it, dear."

"Okay," she said cheerfully. "Think away. Now that you thought about it—why don't you give Lila a call right now? Just sort of explore the idea with her?"

"It's after eleven o'clock."

"She won't care," Madeline said cheerfully. "She's online every night on those Internet dating sites until two in the morning." She sprang to her feet. "You sit right there. I'll get the phone for you."

"Cooler heads will prevail in the morning, my dear."

Allegra rubbed her forehead. "Gosh, Mrs. McKenzie. This isn't right. It's too much time and money. I can't accept this from you. I barely know you. I'm supposed to be working for you."

"Of course you're working for us. You're undercover!"

Allegra shook her head as if she had water in her ears. Or ear mites. "Undercover?"

"If we're going to solve this case, we're going to need inside information."

"Inside?"

Madeline nodded. "No better place to get it than the show." Then she added wistfully, "I don't compete anymore or I'd do it myself. It'll give us an inside track on the case."

"Case?" Allegra said. "What case?"

"I wonder if we can get Joe to act as your groom," Madeline ignored Allegra's bewilderment and barreled ahead with enthusiasm. "He'd be a terrific help. He's a pretty shrewd guy and there's all that muscle if things get a little rough. I mean, what if McClellan decides to set his goons on Austin? What happens if we have to go on stakeout and we all get shot at?" She marched to the coat rack and grabbed her barn jacket. "I'm going out to the clinic to talk to him right now." She paused on her way out the door. Her tired look had vanished. "Call Lila, Austin. If she can't lend Hugo out to us, we're going to have to find some other way get Ally in the middle of things." She banged the door shut, only to reappear, "Jerry Coughlin's her vet, you know. He sees the horse twice a year, at least. I know that for a fact." She smiled brilliantly at Allegra and me. "So we kill two birds with one stone. You'll have to see Coughlin to discuss Hugo's fitness to ride. And you'll have the *perfect* opportunity to get the skinny on what happened to poor old Faraway last year." She twiddled her fingers at me. "Back in a few secs."

The door banged shut behind her before I could register another protest.

Allegra blinked at me. "I think maybe I'm not quite awake, yet. Mrs. McKenzie really wants me to ride at Earlsdown?"

I nodded. Allegra's expression didn't change, precisely, but as the information finally sank in, she looked lit from within. "On somebody else's horse? I can't believe this Mrs. Gernsback would loan her horse out to me. Would she?"

"There may be an element of danger, my dear."

Allegra dismissed that with a wave of her hand. "Everybody falls off once in a while."

"I didn't mean that." Allegra was right. Everybody *does* fall off once in a while. "We appear to be going into the detective business. Madeline has recruited you as an agent."

"Well, how cool is that?" Allegra asked.

I believed this is a rhetorical question among today's young, but I took her literally, just in case. "It may not be cool at all if there is a murderer on the loose," I said dryly.

"If there's a murderer on the loose, I want to catch him as much as you do," Allegra said with great force. "Especially if it means I can compete next week."

There was only one way to find out. I sighed. I looked at the phone. I thought of several excuses not to call Lila Gernsback, none that would wash with my wife. "Very well. I'll be happy to call and discover just what the situation is." A series of yips floated down the staircase, and Allegra glanced ceiling-ward, diverted from the task at hand. "Perhaps you should let the puppy outside while I do so."

She bit her lip a little guiltily. "I probably shouldn't have brought her upstairs with me, but she just hated being down here in her basket all by herself."

The yelps grew in pitch.

"You are in the middle of paper training?" I asked.

"Sure. You bet. They sure pee a lot, Dr. McKenzie. Puppies, I mean."

A succinct, albeit complete lecture on the development of the canine urinary tract was a highlight of my Small-Animal Practice seminar. Both Allegra and the puppy would benefit from such an overview. Perhaps something of my intent showed in my demeanor; Allegra sprang from her seat and said rather hastily, "I'll take him outside right now. And then you can be alone when you call Mrs. Gernsback, okay? In case she has a lot of questions you don't want me to hear." She paused on her way up the stairs and looked over her shoulder. "If she can't let me have Hugo for the week, that's okay. I know you just can't count on something like that. And Dr. McKenzie? She might have a lot to say about me if she turns you down. That is." She stopped, bit her lip, and then that chin went out at an angle. "I'd appreciate it if you'd tell me what she says. Exactly." She bounced upstairs without extracting a promise from me, for which I was thankful.

The kind of gossip young Stephanie had shoveled out at the dinner table was not only scurrilous, it was irrelevant to Allegra's ability to handle a horse. I was delighted that Madeline had ignored the substance of it. As I would, of course.

On the other hand, were I in Allegra's shoes, I, too, would demand an exact recounting. I pulled thoughtfully at my mustache. What kind of questions would Allegra not want to hear?

Lincoln pawed at my ankle, a little annoyed at my inattentiveness. "Not now, old fellow." I directed him to his basket. "I had better get the call to Lila over with. Madeline will only stop to make sure young Joe is reasonably dressed before charging back into the house with him."

Lila was in, Lila was awake, and in one of her more manic moods. As for unwelcome questions about Allegra: once Lila began her barrage, I was unwillingly enlightened.

"The Fulbright girl? Ride Hugo?"

"She's placed in the ribbons at Devon, or so I understand. You'll undoubtedly want to see her ride."

"You're right about that," Lila snapped. "And I'll want her sober, too."

I said nothing to this. But I confess to considerable surprise.

"It was out of line, no question about that." Lila swept on. "Even though the kid had a lot on her plate at the time. You heard about that father of hers, of course."

I made a sound of assent. Spurious, of course.

"But even so, I've got to have some kind of guarantee that the kid's not going to be boozed to the gills on my horse."

Lincoln sat up in his basket, his ears forward. Allegra came down the stairs, the puppy cradled carefully in her arms. She sent an anxious glance in my direction, and then let herself out the front door.

"Doc?" Lila's voice was insistent in my ear.

I'd taught for more than thirty years. There were no guarantees where students and liquor were concerned. Drugs were worse yet. But I was not convinced. Stephanie's gossipy tirade had made no mention of this particular problem. And the show world is rife with malice and innuendo, much of it downright false.

"I find it hard to think that would be a problem," I said.

"Huh. Well. If we can get that cleared up, and I see the kid ride, we might have a deal, doc." She lowered her voice. "Anyhow, I think we should get together to discuss it." She lowered her voice still further. "Just the two of us?"

Madeline swept in the back door, Joe at her heels. Allegra returned with the puppy. All three of them met in the middle of the kitchen. I dropped the phone in the cradle and rose to meet them.

"Well," Madeline said in a pleased way. "Here we all are."

The phone rang. I ignored it.

"Perhaps we should all sit at the table?" I suggested.

The phone rang again.

"Did you call Lila, Austin?" Madeline advanced on the phone.

"I did."

"And did you hang up on her, like you always do?" (A faint hint of exasperation there, I thought.)

"I don't think that's it," Allegra said, quietly, her eyes on mine.

"Well, whatever did she have to say?" Madeline picked up the phone as she spoke, and then said into the receiver, "Hello? Lila! We were just talkin' . . . ? No, I just came in. Did Austin talk to you about . . . ? He did?" She rolled her eyes at me. I'd been right. She was exasperated with me. "You just put him into a right old fluster, Lila. And he drops that old phone all the time. Now, about Hugo. Can you bring Hugo over here tomorrow? About nine? No? Why ever not . . . what?"

Lila would keep her for some time. And Madeline herself can keep a conversational ball in the air in a manner that defies conventional physics. I seated Joe, Allegra, and the puppy at the table. I put the teakettle on for the rich cocoa Madeline favors as a nightcap. I retrieved a lined yellow pad and sharp pencils from my desk and placed them on the table. By the time I had seated myself, Madeline had wound up the conversation with Lila. One look at her, and I knew that for the moment, at least, the Earlsdown case had been tabled. Madeline stood by Allegra's chair and looked down at her. It was hard to read her expression. Concern, dismay, and a modicum of anger were all there. "Allegra, honey, there's a few things we need to discuss."

"What did Mrs. Gernsback tell you?"

Madeline glanced at me, then Joe. "I think that's something the two of us should talk about, don't you?"

Allegra was pale. Her chin jutted out. "I don't have anything to hide. What'd she tell you about me?"

"I'd really rather we didn't discuss this in front of Joe and Austin, sweetie."

"Right," Allegra said grimly, "like the whole horse world hasn't heard something about me already. That jerk McClellan. He'd never seen me before. And the minute he heard my name, he got this look. If I do get to go to Earlsdown, you don't think it's going to be all over the barns in two seconds flat?"

Joe got to his feet. "Hey," he said, "Mrs. McKenzie's right. Maybe I should get on back to the clinic."

"You sit right there," Allegra snapped.

Joe sat.

The color rose in Allegra's face. She gripped the puppy so tightly that it protested with a yelp. She bit her lip and gently smoothed its ears. Then she took a breath. "She told you I destroyed my horse."

"Oh, honey," Madeline sat next to her, her hand on her arm. "She didn't say that. She said there was an accident. And the horse isn't dead."

"As good as." Allegra began to cry. I get quite uncomfortable when people cry. In my experience, which Madeline claims is limited, more women cry than men. It's one of the reasons I remained a bachelor until fifty.

Madeline sat back and folded her hands in her lap. Her gaze remained steady. "Lila may make googly eyes at every breathing male in three counties, but there's not a ounce of spite in her. She said you were drunk or high on something and you crammed your horse. Bowed a tendon. Said it only happened the one time she ever heard, that there'd been some brouhaha with your dad that could account for it. Just wanted to be sure that it wasn't going to happen with her Hugo. Can't blame her, sweetie."

"I wasn't drunk and I wasn't high," Allegra said tightly. "I'll swear on anything you like." She swiped her eyes with the back of her hand. "I think somebody slipped me a Mickey Finn."

"Chloral hydrate?" I said. "For heaven's sake, why?"

Allegra looked miserable. "There was this guy. He was with one of the event teams. I'd gone out with him a couple of times. Then he made some comment about my dad . . ."

I smoothed my mustache. " 'That' Sam Fulbright," I said rather quietly.

"Yes. Everybody knows about it." The tears poured down her face, unnoticed.

"I don't," Joe said frankly.

"Sam Fulbright was the CFO of Enblad," I said.

"Oh." Joe's face cleared. "The guy who messed up with the investments."

"That's the one," Madeline said. "Currently in the clink for ten years." She wriggled her eyebrows at me. I wriggled mine back.

Madeline reached over, took the puppy from Ally's lap and handed it to Joe. Then she pulled a fistful of tissue from her caftan pocket and dabbed at Allegra's cheeks. "What happened, sweetie?" she asked gently.

"I don't know!" Allegra pounded the table with both fists. "I swear somebody spiked my water bottle. Yes, there was some stuff going down at home. But there was always stuff going down at home. I never let that get to me before, and I can't . . ." She shook her head. "Anyway. I felt just fine, going up. Ready." She darted a shy glance at Madeline. "You know how it is? Excited? But all pulled together. Like your brain and your body have totally merged."

Madeline nodded, her eyes bright. "I remember."

"Harker was ready, too. When I mounted, it was like his brain and body were part of mine. We just—there was no way we could lose. I was really wound.

"It was a killer course. Thirteen jumps. But I'd walked it the day before, and of course, I'd watched all the guys who'd been up before me, and the one I was really worried about was the triple."

Joe raised his palm slightly. "You've lost me here."

"It's a series of three jumps, with a few strides between," Madeline said. "Some are in and out, that is, the horse lands off the first one and has to take off for the next without much more than a chance to get his feet under him."

"This combination was one and a half and two," Allegra said.

"The horse has a stride and a half before he takes off, then two strides," Madeline added.

Joe nodded. "Got it."

"The triple came off a water hazard." Allegra's eyes were distant with memory. "Harker loved water. So I was concentrating on keeping him straight—he liked to play in it—and then . . ." She thrust her fingers in her hair. "It was like, 'tilt!' "

"Tilt?" Joe said.

"Yeah. Like the world just went sideways. Then I got dizzy. I lost my center. So I must have leaned back. Harker pulled up, of course, and then I guess I just kept going. Anyhow. We lost it. I lost it. He took the fence sideways and all I can remember is that it was like being caught on one of those rides at Disney World, where you go around and around and you can't get off. And then . . ." She put both fists to her mouth. When she spoke again, her voice was husky. "Anyhow. We fell. The EMTs showed up, and the truck, and they hauled us both out of there."

"And then?" Madeline asked.

"And then the jump monitor told the judges I was reeling around in the saddle like I was drunk," Allegra said flatly. "So they made me pee in a cup and took a blood sample, and I came up clean, of course, but by that time everyone was talking about how I was drunk. And that's not all." She took a deep, shuddering breath. "Somebody turned my water bottle into the committee and it was loaded with vodka. And I *didn't put it there.*" She clenched her teeth and fell silent. "I think it was that guy I dumped. He took off after the accident, and I haven't seen him since."

"Hm," Madeline said. "But the blood and urine tests were negative?"

"Unless they were alerted to the contrary," I said, "They would have tested for liquor or amphetamines only."

"*I didn't drink anything!*" Allegra shouted. "You can call them and ask. Go on! Call them right now!"

"I believe you." Madeline tilted her head thoughtfully. "Why didn't everyone else?"

Allegra said fiercely, "My dad . . . people said . . ."

". . . That anything can be bought, these days. Even a negative drug test." Madeline looked at me. I raised an eyebrow, but forbore to comment.

"They said my dad was a crook and so was I."

"And what happened to the horse?" Joe asked.

Allegra wrapped her arms around herself, as if she were holding her ribs in place. She didn't answer for quite a long time. Then she said: "They took him."

"Who took him?" Joe persisted, a question that immediately occurred to me.

Allegra shut up completely.

Madeline frowned a little, and for a moment, I thought that Joe (and I, because I certainly wanted to know the answer) had gone too far in pressing the girl. Poor Allegra had certainly been through a grueling experience. But that stubborn chin had a great deal to say about the tenacity of her character. She mopped her face with her sleeve. "First off, I wanted to take him home, but they wouldn't let me."

I cleared my throat. "What was the precise nature of his injury?"

She took a deep breath, seeming to find relief, as I often do, in the recitation of facts. "He was limping hard, after the crash, I guess. I thought he'd broken his cannon bone. I didn't get to see him until the ER guys let me go back to the show. By that time, they'd taken X-rays. A stress fracture, they said, but they took care of that with a walking cast." A second deep breath seemed to steady her further. "But the tendon was bowed." She looked at me. "The scariest thing was whether or not they were going to put him down."

I mused about this. Without seeing the X-rays, at a guess the horse would be totally out of commission for a year, at least. And the chance of the leg regaining enough soundness to compete at Earlsdown levels was moot. The horse would be sound to hack, but nothing more, no matter how many years he had at rest. "Who performed the initial diagnosis, my dear?"

"The attending vet. Dr. Coughlin."

I would have known that, if I'd stopped to think about it. Of course it would have been Coughlin.

"And then Dr. Coughlin put his two cents in when my dad pressed him about it. He wanted to put Harker down."

Coughlin? I leaned forward with increased attentiveness.

"But he was your horse, sweetie," Madeline said. "Surely you could decide to take him home and retire him?"

"To where? We'd lost the house." A look of infinite bitterness crossed her face. "It was all about the money."

"I don't quite get it," Joe said. "You mean your dad wanted to put the horse down for the insurance money?"

"It seems to take you a while to get the picture, Turnbald. He needed every nickel he could get."

"So, did they?"

"Just shut up," Allegra said. "Just shut up."

Madeline and I exchanged glances. The connection between horse and rider was profound. Allegra was not exhibiting the extravagant grief one would expect from a youngster who had lost a horse under these circumstances. On the contrary, she looked a little smug.

"So where's the horse now?" Joe said.

"Never mind." She drew her knees up and rested her chin on them. "Safe. A whole year's got to go by before I can be sure that he's healed enough so that the policy won't pay out if he's put down. He's with some good friends of mine." She looked at us out of the corner of her eye. "The year'll be up in two weeks."

Madeline laughed suddenly. "I wondered why a voice major was so anxious to take a job with a veterinarian."

Joe and I looked at each other.

Madeline got up and smoothed Allegra's hair. "We've more than enough room. As you saw the day you showed up."

"I'll work the board off," Allegra said. She shot a bitter look at Joe. "If there's enough work to do."

"We'll see," Madeline said comfortably. "With Austin here getting these consulting jobs, and now that we're in the detective business, who knows what kinds of jobs'll need doing around here."

Allegra hiccoughed a little, in the way that one does after a bout of tears is over. "So. That's what happened at Earlsdown last year." She raised anxious eyes to Madeline. "Do you think Mrs. Gernsback will believe me?"

"Well, I believe you, in any event." Madeline rose and went to the stove. The electric teakettle had whistled and then turned itself off. She felt the sides with her hand, and then took three coffee mugs down from the shelf. She dropped healthy teaspoons of cocoa in each and then poured the steaming water.

"I can't tell her about Harker," Allegra said anxiously, "not until April sixteenth. That'll be a whole year after the accident. And then I can keep Harker alive. I talked," she added, with a rather quaint expression on her face, "to a lawyer."

"Lila's a lot of things, but she's a rock when it comes to giving folks a hand. And she'll make up her own mind, anyhow, partly on how you do with Hugo tomorrow. And partly on how Hugo does with you. She thinks the world of that horse. Besides," she added, with a smile to take away the sting, "she'll probably check the committee records from last year."

"She's coming over here, then?"

"So she can see you ride. Yes. She said ten tomorrow morning would be fine."

Allegra let out a long sigh. "I've got another chance, then. Thank god."

Madeline smiled and set the mugs of cocoa down. Joe grabbed one and knocked back a slug as if it had been beer. He burped, rather pointedly, I thought, and said, "Okay if I speak now, Miss Fulbright? I mean, do I have your permission?"

Allegra flushed a little. "A while ago? When I told you to shut up? I shouldn't have."

"No. You shouldn't have." He paused, both eyebrows raised.

"Sorry," Allegra said, through gritted teeth. Then, with a look even I recognized as one of spurious concern, she continued, "You can butt out of my business anytime, though. I haven't got a problem with that. Just in case you thought I wanted your stupid opinion."

"You know what you've got a problem with? When the conversation's not about you." He braced his feet against the table legs and tilted his chair backward. "You don't mind if we get off of the profoundly fascinating topic of you and get to what Mrs. McKenzie wants?"

Allegra closed her eyes and nodded to herself. "Suck *up*," she muttered, "just suck it on *up*."

Madeline pinched her lower lip, to keep, I judged, from laughing. Joe sat up with an indignant thump. "Ask yourself this, Fulbright. 'Do I really need to be here at this meeting?' " He fluttered his eyelashes, patted his hair, and said in a falsetto: " 'Shouldn't I be upstairs doing something useful like washing my hair?' "

"Like, get *over* yourself? Before it's too late?" Allegra said sweetly.

I rapped the table with my knuckles. This meeting was getting out of control. "Not only does Miss Fulbright need to be here, her contribution is essential."

"You're kidding." Joe scowled. "I mean, you're kidding, sir."

"It is?" Allegra asked with a pleased air.

"Yes. We will need someone undercover at Earlsdown. She is perfect. I am sorry to say this, my dear, but the mild—and unearned—disgrace you are burdened with at the moment is all to the good."

Allegra's expression was wry. She had very nice eyes, between green and brown, and with her hair sticking up and that mischievous smile, she looked quite elfin. "You mean because no one will believe I'm a good guy."

"Yes."

"And the crooks won't be as careful around me as they would around a virginal guy like Joe."

"Hey!" Joe said indignantly.

"I hope not," I said.

Allegra looked at me soberly. "So what is going on, do you think?"

I adjusted my spectacles. "Insurance fraud is my best guess. For the moment."

"You mean someone's killing horses and veterinarians for the money?" Joe was appalled. "I mean, I guess I can see if the horse is already down with a problem, the money might be a deciding factor, but you're talking about setting it up."

"My, my," Allegra mocked gently, "tough guy from the Bronx that you are. It's not like it hasn't happened before."

"Yeah, but that's racehorses. You're dealing with huge bucks, there. We're talking eventers. They don't make that kind of money, so they aren't worth that kind of money. And why would a vet like Coughlin risk his reputation for small bucks?"

"I'm afraid Allegra's story has changed my attitude about poor Jerry Coughlin," I said. "And 'small' is relative."

"Oh, dear," Madeline said. "That's the awful thing about crime. You find out stuff about people you'd just rather not know. Well. What a shame. Shall we keep case notes? I think we should keep case notes."

"You really think there's a case?" Joe asked skeptically. "You're basing this on the death of one horse and the suspected drugging of another? You think that's related to Dr. Grazley's shooting? And Schumacher's? How? What kind of real connections do we have here?"

"Of course there's a case," I said, somewhat testily. "We have symptoms."

This took Joe aback.

"I want to keep notes," Madeline said. She selected a yellow pad from the stack on the table. "First off, we need a file name, for the computer."

"The name," I said, tipping my chair backward and folding my hands behind my head, "should entirely cloak the nature of the case. A name that has meaning only to us four."

"It should?" Allegra asked in a puzzled way.

"To keep the operation suitably clandestine."

I believe Allegra giggled. Madeline certainly did.

"We shall call the file 'Roasted Onion.' "

I had anticipated disagreement. There was none. Confusion, yes. There appeared to be plenty of that. "Shall I elucidate?"

"Sounds like a rock group," Allegra said tentatively.

Joe scratched his head. "You're talking about the old colic remedy? The one where a roasted onion is put up . . . um . . ." He glanced a little uneasily at the women. His grandmother had taught him well.

"Butt?" Allegra said. "They stuck a roasted onion up a horse's butt? That was supposed to cure colic?"

Joe pointed out the basic chemistry of the cure. Decaying vegetation of any kind was bound to create enough carbon dioxide to result in an expulsion. Of the onion, if nothing else.

"Still sounds like a rock group," Allegra said.

"Good detective work is about matching cause to effect," I said. "Confusion to the enemy! I find the title suitably ironic."

Allegra got it instantly. She sat up. "Cool! And the roasted onion has *no* relationship to its effect on colic." She sent a kindly smile Joe's way. "Hence the reference to irony. In case you were wondering."

"I got it, thanks."

"With a little help from me."

"The day I need help in the brains department from you . . ."

". . . We're all going to need help from each other," Madeline interrupted. "Austin. We need to bring the kids up to speed on this."

So began the Case of the Roasted Onion.

Ten

❧❧

IT snowed the following morning, Friday. Eliot called April the cruelest month with reason. It is not at all dependable. The day before had been springlike. And now the snow fell at a rapid rate, clogging the roads, frustrating drivers impatient with its beauty, but above all, coating man's sins against nature with dumb beneficence. The snow made no difference in our plans for the day. A veterinarian must go where duty calls. A detective must go where the clues direct him.

Our first meeting on the case had gone well. There was a mystery to be solved, and like Athos, Porthos, Aramis, and D'Artangan, we were all for one and one for all in our commitment to uncover its nature. McClellan's careless reference at dinner to the business venture FieldChek had not gone unremarked by me. Both Grazley and Schumacher had been partners in this enterprise. Both were dead. Coughlin was also a member of this group. He was disgraced. What was the true nature of this business and why were three of the four principals victims? Our first step would be to interview Coughlin. I would shoulder this task.

We would need far more information on Stephanie than we had to date. Lila Gernsback would be a fount of information, as would the clients Joe and I were to see this morning, the Longworths.

Not unmindful of the basic rule of mysteries, which posits that the least-regarded person in the case is frequently the perpetrator, I volunteered Phillip Sullivan as a suspect. If only, I pointed out, because his John Wayne–like locutions were suspiciously similar to the language in the infamous Sniper Letter: Anywhere. Anytime. Anyone.

And there were the horses: Faraway and his death last year; Beecher, and the ominous presence of the lethal dose of anesthetic in his stall. The possibility of an insurance scam perpetrated by McClellan was all too real.

Finally, there was the possibility, as disappointing as it might be, that the police were correct. There *was* a Summersville Sniper, a vicious sociopath, roaming the countryside. There were two possible sources of information here, Rita and her crew at the *Sentinel* and Lieutenant Provost. As far as the latter was concerned, we obviously had a duty to lay the facts we had collected before the police, if not the evidence itself. The dog hair, the gasoline-soaked gloves, and the information garnered from Clarissa at the Grazley clinic would all be turned over to Provost. I assumed this responsibility. Ferreting information out of the *Sentinel* staff would be a lot more pleasurable; the paper's employees invariably gathered at the Monrovian Embassy for lunch. We would all meet there at noontime today.

Our objective, I suggested, was a methodical collection of data. Without data, we couldn't safely infer a conclusion. The current goal?

With that information assembled, we could begin a second, equally methodical investigation into the collection of sufficient forensic evidence to uncover the perpetrators.

Then followed a somewhat spirited discussion as to whom would accomplish what. Madeline and Allegra opted for a more aggressive approach than I felt was warranted; I could not see that breaking into McClellan's self-styled "Manse" and holding him at gunpoint while he spilled the beans about his horses could lead to anything other than jail time for burglars and an arrest for assault.

Eventually, we achieved agreement; I was holding out for total consensus, but Joe had been skeptical when Madeline had recruited him to the cause, and he remained skeptical throughout the discussion.

Duties were assigned and accepted. Madeline and I retired to bed, and slept well.

Only to wake to the snow.

We all four breakfasted early (more oatmeal, I fear) and set off on our various assignments.

The practice had three early farm calls scheduled for the morning, none of them emergencies. Joe and I would attend to these, since we could not abandon my responsibilities as a veterinary practitioner (nor the payment that would ensue). Lila had agreed to bring Hugo to the clinic this morning; this provided an opportunity to begin to collect information about the unfortunate Stephanie and the fate of her event horses. If all went well, Allegra would ride Hugo at Earlsdown and act as an undercover agent at the show.

I arranged to spend the afternoon with Coughlin, with the ostensible excuse of discussing Hugo's fitness to compete at Earlsdown. In actuality, I would discover all that *he* knew about the brouhaha at Earlsdown the previous year.

Our team, of course, intended to collect any stray bits of information relating to the case through adroit and clever interrogation techniques.

Despite this, I could not, of course, neglect my pedagogical duties. I summarized the nature of the farm calls ahead for Joe as we took the Bronco down the highway for our first appointment of the day. He listened without comment, then said, "You really think there's something funky about McClellan, doc?"

"We were discussing the principles behind immunization."

"I got a lot of that in Bergland's seminar last semester."

I negotiated a hillock of snow in the road by revving the motor sharply. Joe braced his foot on the dash, and reached back and hung onto Lincoln's collar to steady the dog. The plows had not yet been out on Route 15.

"The motive seems pretty weak. McClellan's loaded. 'Course," he added sarcastically, "we all could use an extra eighty thousand. That's what he claims Beecher's worth, right?"

"The horse is probably worth a little bit more," I said.

"And so Schumacher finds out McClellan's prepping the horse to die like Faraway did—in an accidental drug overdose and McClellan offs him. Now that Coughlin's been banned from the show grounds, McClellan brings Grazley in on the plan. Grazley freaks, and McClellan shoots him?" Joe shook his head. "I still don't buy it."

"As to the insurance fraud, I can't find another logical explanation for the vial of anesthetic in Beecher's stall. And although I'm not ruling out anomaly, I find it hard to arrive at any other explanation for Schumacher and Grazley's deaths." I downshifted yet again, with a fine degree of satisfaction. "I am convinced that McClellan shot him."

Joe released the dog, who stretched out in the back seat for a nap. "Not enough motive. The people angle's wrong."

"The people angle?" I queried.

"Yeah. I mean, Dr. Bergland is always telling us to look for 'why.' Grazley could blow the scam for them. So McClellan hauls out his thirty-ought-six and *bwoof!* Spang. There goes Dr. Grazley." He sat with his back slumped against the passenger door, his eyes somber. "Eighty thousand's not enough of a reason, doc." He didn't say anything for a moment, then added cockily, "Not even where I come from."

I downshifted, the better to negotiate another drift. "There are plenty of people for whom eighty thousand is sufficient motive."

"But a guy like that? He's rolling in it. Look at the cars, the house, the horses . . . I mean I don't get why we're investigating a case where the motive's not, like, right out there. What else would make McClellan kill but money, and lots of it? And if you agree with me, that the guy'd have to be crazier than an outhouse rat to go around knocking off people for eighty thousand bucks . . ." He slumped against the seat, frowning.

"Victor Bergland is a good man," I admitted (much against my inclination). "He's right. The answer to why frequently leads to the best diagnosis. My friend, something else must be going on here. Beyond the horse show. Beyond these particular horses."

"Like what?"

"I have no idea at the moment." I pulled into the driveway of the Longworth Farm and drew up to the aging barn. The lights were on in the farmhouse, but the barn was dark. "But we will find out. McKenzies don't back off. Now. To resume my summary of the lesson at hand. That is, the barn call. We have six horses here. All need vaccinations for equine encephalitis, rhinopneumonitis, rabies boosters, and West Nile virus. One of the geldings needs its teeth floated. One, who is headed to Earlsdown, will need a current Coggins. The Coggins is to verify that the animal in question is free of equine infectious anemia. You are aware that the test is required for any horse being transported off the home farm in New York State?"

"Sure."

"And do you know why?"

"Ah. Yes. Well. It's infectious, obviously." Joe drummed his fingers restlessly on his knees. He was the type of student that hates to be caught unawares. I like this type of student. They are well motivated. And they respond to the prod. "I'll check it out."

"See that you do, young man." I smiled to myself. There were several hours of hard study ahead for him in Cornell's excellent library. "It is an autoimmune disease of sufficient severity to be regulated by both the State of New York and the United States Department of Agriculture." I then delivered the prod. "Like the HIV virus in humans . . ."

Joe looked properly startled, as I had intended.

"It's sort of an equine AIDS?"

"Look it up."

"Equine infectious anemia," he muttered to himself. He reached down and rooted underneath the seat.

"There are several fine texts on the subject, as well as three or four monographs . . . is that your computer?"

"Yes, sir." He opened up and began striking at the keys. "I'm wireless," he offered, "and I'll get on NetVet and check it out right away."

I watched him out of the corner of my eye. He tapped away with concentration for some moments, then read off a complete description of the symptoms of EIA (depressed affect, slow capillary refill time, the prognosis—death, the recommended treatment—complete isolation from all other equines and complete protection from the insect that carried the virus, etc., etc.). I stopped him. With a great deal of annoyance. I'd had the same complaint the last five years of my tenure at Cornell: "Whatever happened to books?"

"Books are dinosaurs," Joe said with cheerful hereticism. "Or very nearly. If we can grab a half hour, doc, I'll teach you to use the Net."

"I am quite familiar with the Net, thank you."

"And you don't use it? You're a scientist, doc. How can you turn your back on one of the greatest technological advances in the world?"

"I am well aware of the advantages of the Net. I am merely lamenting the loss of the books." I pulled the handbrake up. "For the moment," I said decisively, "we have patients to attend to."

"Got it, doc. So, detecting's off till this farm call's over, too?"

"Not at all." I tapped the horn twice. "The horse world is a small one, and information can be found in some curious places." I smiled. "We will detect and vet at one and the same time."

The kitchen door of the farmhouse opened up, spilling light onto the tracked-up snow. Two bundled-up figures emerged and trudged toward us. "That will be Nora Longworth and her daughter Jennifer. Jennifer will be riding at Earlsdown. You will find," I said with a sigh, "that they talk a great deal. It is our goal to guide the talk to our purpose, delicately, with finesse. We are fly fisherman here, Joe, and the trout are wary." I looked over my shoulder at Linc, who opened his eyes, then went back to sleep. It had taken him no time at all to adjust to remaining in the vehicle while I went about my professional duties. Although he did have an unbreakable habit of taking over the driver's seat every chance he got.

The Longworths were good horsemen, making the best of an old and inconvenient barn. The stalls were clean, although small, and the animals well groomed and well fed.

Joe was deft with the vaccinations, as I had noted before, but unfamiliar with the process of floating teeth, that is, forcing a large rasp over the horse's molars to even out the sharp edges. It was while he was hauling the dental harness over the beams that the first small bit of information emerged. Jennifer's mother rose to my cast, as I had hoped she would.

"No, Gunny doesn't have a bit of Swedish Warmblood in him, Dr. McKenzie. He reminds you of Stephy's Beecher?" Jenny said, after I made a (calculated) remark about the generous bone in Gunny's legs.

"A bit, perhaps." I assessed Gunny's amiability by forcing his jaws open with the dental vise. It resembles nothing so much as a medieval rack, which was used by the Knights Templar to extract confessions from those they believed to be recalcitrant heathens. Gunny took immediate exception to the intrusion, like the poor serfs before him, and backed up the entire length of the aisle, shaking his head violently the while.

"I'm afraid we'll have to tranquilize him, Jenny. Prepare an injection of acepromazine, if you would, Joseph."

"Poor old Gunny," Nora said, patting his neck. Joe injected the tranquilizer, and within minutes, Gunny fell into a light doze. I reinserted the vise, forced Gunny's jaws open, attached the pulley, and directed Joe to pull the horse's head high enough so that I could apply the rasp. Then I braced both feet and set to work.

"Gunny can outjump Beecher any day of the week," Jenny said. She was still stewing over my reference to Beecher. She stood next to the somnolent Gunny, one hand on his neck, and peered worriedly into the distance.

I concentrated on Gunny's oral cavity and didn't respond. The rasp is long, heavy, and it can be a bit tricky to keep the pressure sufficient to round off the sharp point of the teeth. I had intended to pass this information along to Joe. However, I didn't seem to have breath enough to offer instruction. It had been some time since I had floated a horse's teeth. I had used Andrew and Pony as test subjects for my students in the past. "It's the dressage I'm worried about," Jenny added. "I don't know, Mom. I heard Beecher's qualified for fourth level."

"You'll do fine, honey," Nora said. Nora hadn't been attending to her daughter at all. She was watching me. With a slight note of alarm in her voice, she put her hand on my back and said, "Dr. McKenzie, are you sure you don't want to take a break?"

"I'm fine." I increased the angle and the pressure of the rasp, to get to the pesky molars in the rear. And the damned rasp slipped. The saw-toothed edge ran along the gum line, bright red blood spouting in its wake. Even in his tranquillized state, Gunny jerked his head back.

"I wouldn't trade Gunny for twenty Beechers," Jenny brought her attention back to her horse, Then, with a shriek, "Dr. McKenzie! He's bleeding!"

Nora cast a sharp, perceptive gaze at me. But all she said was, "You bleed at the dentist's, too, Jenny. It's no big deal. Gunny is fine. Give it a rest." She moved her hand on my shoulder. "Are you okay, Dr. McKenzie?"

"You said I could take over the back teeth now, sir," Joe said.

Rasping a horse's teeth is tiring work, I admit. But there was no need for this display of concern from either my client or my assistant. "I'm fine," I said shortly. "I will, however, take a breather."

"I'd really like the chance to handle this, sir." Joe took the rasp from my hand, which, I admit, was aching in the cold, as were my shoulders and chest. "Thank you for the opportunity." He smiled at Jenny. "You don't mind, do you? I'm very good at it."

Jenny blushed and muttered, "Sure." Then she turned to her mother and giggled.

Joe rasped away, and I observed that he was just fine at it, although he, as I had, worked up a fine sweat in about two seconds flat. I stepped aside and joined Nora Longworth from her observation post by the feed bin. "Gunny should do quite well at Earlsdown," I said after a moment. "You've gotten him in fine shape."

"Yeah, well. We'll do our best." She sighed. "Money can buy so much, Dr. McKenzie. Sometimes I get so tired, struggling the way we do."

Any response would be either condescending or untruthful. So I maintained an encouraging silence.

"She doesn't actually own that horse, you know," Nora said over the noise of teeth being grated to a smooth round edge. "Stephanie, I mean. I heard they paid half a million dollars for it."

I stared at her. "Half a million? For an event horse? I find that hard to believe. Now, if he were headed to the Olympics, perhaps that wouldn't be an outrageous sum."

"Well, he's syndicated, isn't he?" Nora said stubbornly. "Just like Faraway was."

"Were they both syndicated, indeed?" I said slowly. "Would you happen to know who other than McClellan is a member?"

"Dr. Grazley is what I heard. And some lawyer, I think."

Now, who else could that be, but Sullivan!

She brightened. "I don't suppose you'd want a share of Gunny, here."

"If Madeline and I could afford it, we would indeed," I said, as gallantly as I could. "Perhaps Beecher's other share-holders would be interested in Gunny."

"If I knew who they were, I'd ask 'em," she said with the air of one who is hard put to find grain money every month. "As it is, I've got to be realistic. Steph and Beecher will walk all over poor Gunny. Some people think they can buy their way into the ribbons. The hell of it is that they can."

"Talent, hard work, the love of the animal . . . all those count, too, Nora."

Nora gave this bromide the dismissive snort it deserved; as good as he was, Gunny's basic conformation meant he didn't have much of a shot at the blue. "I'll tell you what, though. It doesn't matter where Gunny places next week—at least he's going to come home as healthy as when he left."

Again, a politic silence seemed to be called for.

"It never crossed your mind that poor old Faraway was losing his classes when that vet killed him?"

I hadn't known that. The value of a syndicated stallion lay in the mares that were brought to breed with him. There was little value in a loser. "Officially, the injection was an accident, Nora."

"Everybody says so," she said stubbornly. "And of course, you vets stick up for your own." Her look softened. "But everybody knows you can't be bought. So what does everybody know, anyway?"

Joe and I completed the barn call without any further revelations about Beecher, McClellan, or Faraway. We were back on the road by eight o'clock.

I mulled over my conversation with Nora; feeling about

Faraway's death and the McClellans was evidently running high a year later. Joe swilled down half a bottle of spring water and wiped his forehead with the back of his hand.

"Okay," he said. "I heard that about half a million. Now I'm willing to buy the motive. I don't know anyone who couldn't use that amount of cash in the old bank account."

"McClellan told me eighty thousand."

"And you think he's an honest murderer?"

I smiled at that. "Data," I said. "We will never convict him without data. If nothing else, we need it to reconcile the anomalies. But we now know there's a syndicate. We shall have to discover who else belongs. You heard that Grazley was a member. I wonder if Schumacher was, as well."

"We'll have to find out." Joe rolled his shoulders. "We have more dental work this morning? That's some workout. Don't they have motorized rasps?"

"They do," I said. "Perhaps next year, after the practice picks up, we will purchase one."

"Expensive, huh?"

"Quite."

"And we're going to float more teeth again today, aren't we? I appreciate the chance to do some real hands-on work, Dr. McKenzie. Thanks for letting me take over in there."

The boy was tactful, I'll give him that. My hand had slipped, my shoulder muscles had given out, and Gunny's gums had suffered as a result. "I'm afraid my arm isn't yet up to the rigors of that particular job. I've been thinking of joining a gym."

Joe nodded.

I cleared my throat. "It's not necessary to mention this to Mrs. McKenzie. That I wasn't up to . . . that is, that my hand slipped."

Joe nodded again.

"She would only worry."

A silence elapsed. I didn't care for the quality of the silence at all.

"Young man," I said, finally, "I am getting too old for this business." The Bronco slid a little in the greasy road. I corrected the skid. "I apologize to you. I should apologize to Nora Longworth, who is no fool. There is nothing more important than the well-being of the patient. That has been compromised. By vanity."

"You're past some of the physical stuff, sure," Joe said, with the devastating candor of the young, "but I'll tell you something, doc. It's good to see that you've got one weak point, at least. I was beginning to think that this whole job was some kind of charity gig, courtesy of Dr. Bergland, and that you didn't need me at all."

"Oh?"

"Yeah." He stared out the window at the snow-covered fields. "I was on full scholarship last year, until the school lost some grant funding. If I'd been into research, Bergland could have come up with something for me, but I don't want to stare into molecular microscopes eight hours a day. I want to be outside. In the air. Not . . . locked up." He was quiet for a long time. Then he said, angrily, "I can't stand to be locked up. So my tuition's paid for, but I'm on my own as far as room and board. And, god, but everything's expensive. I wasn't getting real far with minimum wage. But I was handling it." He grinned, dispelling the hostility. "I was eating, at least. And buying my books."

Madeline and I had surmised that Joe had appeared to be carrying the sum of his worldly goods in his car; it appeared we were right.

"Then we have an excellent chance at accommodation, you and I. You are now in charge of dental work. And I am in charge of you."

He rubbed his forearm thoughtfully. "We have a lot more floating on the ticket today?"

"Just two," I said. "And we're drawing one wolf tooth. You'll enjoy that." I smiled. "And, with luck, we'll also draw our little bit more about Beecher and the repellant McClellan."

"You really think this stuff's connected?"

"You're dubious?"

"Well, it all could be, sure. But how's picking up gossip from people like Mrs. Longworth going to get us anywhere?

Shouldn't we be getting hold of police reports? Tracking down eyewitnesses? You know." He socked one fist into the other palm. "A little action."

"I am reserving that sort of action for lunch," I said. "In the meantime, please pull the records for the next barn call. The client is named Pulcini. The patients are a pair of Belgian draft horses, Pat and Mike."

The next two farm calls gave us nothing more than an interesting anecdote involving a well-known dressage trainer, an electric horse clipper, and a newly bald Palm Beach socialite, and a diatribe against the fees charged by the late Benny Grazley. By the time we'd finished the last call, it was close to ten, and time to return to the farm and watch Allegra school Hugo. Lila Gernsback was a nexus of gossip in the horse world. With luck, we would gather more solid information. My first day as an investigator was proceeding in a most satisfactory way.

Eleven

WE pulled into our drive just before ten o'clock. Allegra and Madeline were waiting outside in anticipation of Lila's arrival. I parked the Bronco well to the side of the drive, giving Lila and her rig plenty of room to maneuver. Joe disappeared into the barn to see to chores. I walked over to our small outdoor arena. Madeline and I hadn't used it much, of late, but I keep the sand surface level and free of debris. The sun was well up and the snow already melting.

Allegra had braided her hair this morning, and the chocolate-colored pigtail hung down her back like a shiny exclamation point. Her breeches were well worn, but clean. She looked like a rider, and there is nothing neater, tidier, or more pulled together on this green earth. I stood next to the two of them at the fence and nodded at her with proud approval. "You look well, my dear."

"Like a pro," Madeline said with a smile.

Allegra shifted nervously on her feet. "What's Mrs. Gernsback like, Maddy?"

Several emotions chased themselves across Madeline's expressive face. "Well," she said, "to tell you the truth, if I had my pick of who to get stuck in an elevator with, it wouldn't be Lila Gernsback. The train that used to whip by my old house in Memphis every night at two o'clock in the morning had a whistle that shrieked a little louder than Lila does when she gets excited. But not by much. And she's one of the bossiest people you'll ever meet, excepting maybe my great-aunt Liddy. Not to mention the fact that she makes googly eyes at Austin every chance she gets . . . but I've already mentioned that, I think. So I wouldn't want Austin stuck in an elevator

with her, either. But I'll tell you something about Lila Gernsback. She's a real horsewoman. Lila has the eye and the brains
and she's honest as they come."

"Well, that's good." Allegra picked at her thumbnail. Then
she grabbed the end of her pigtail and chewed it.

"She's loud, when she gets on a roll, and she's always on a
roll. I know that's not going to bother you. In fact, I don't
think much anything about Lila or the horse is going to bother
you. You'll be just fine, Ally. And Hugo's a peach."

Allegra's shoulders relaxed a little. "You've seen Hugo
show?"

Madeline shook her head in admiration. "Have I! He's not
a lot to look at, at first, is he, Austin?"

"His looks are quite deceptive," I admitted.

"He's just under eighteen hands, built like a Hummer, and
kind of cloddy, the way that sort of horse can be."

Allegra grinned. "I think I know what you mean. They sort
of mog along until there's a reason to get going. And then . . ."

"Ka-chang! Katie bar the door," Madeline agreed. "You understand. So a luggy rider or a nervous one isn't going to get
much out of him. He's just going to stand there and go 'duh' if
you let him get away with it. Hasn't got much of a mouth on
him, either."

Ally looked at her hands, which were long, strong, and
slender. The nails were unpolished, but neatly trimmed.

"From what I've seen of him, he's fairly strong on the bit,"
Madeline offered. "Lila doesn't like to use anything but a Pel-
ham on him, though, with a straight snaffle."

"Too many horses are bitted up," Allegra said firmly, for all
the world as if she were a forty-five-year-old veteran on the
circuit. "Does she have a large place?"

"About twenty acres, several miles from here," Madeline
said, "and here she is."

Lila's red pickup bumped up the gravel drive, her stock
trailer clattering along behind. A high, loud whinny came from
the depths of the trailer; Hugo, saying hello as he scented Andrew and Pony. Both our horses galloped excitedly to the
fence of their paddock, then whirled away again, kicking

snow and mud high in the air. Lincoln dashed to the rig, plumey tail waving.

Lila backed the rig expertly to our arena fence and disembarked.

Her dark curly head was bare to the skies, and, as I had noticed at last night's party, she was no longer on crutches, but used a cane. Her expression, however, reminded me of a scowly poodle.

"Hey, Lila." Madeline splashed through the melting snow to give Lila a hug. "I didn't get much of a chance to talk with you last night. How's the leg?"

Lila swung the cane around in a peppy circle. "Pretty good. I won't be needing this sucker in another month. Maybe less." She eyed Allegra. "You're the Fulbright girl?"

"You're looking just great." Madeline took her arm, and linked it companionably with her own. "I swear you've lost five pounds since I saw you at Christmas."

Lila had a figure, I must admit. A large bosom, small waist, and curving hips. It was not at all difficult to surmise what men saw in her.

Lila looked down at herself, startled out of her sharpish glare at poor Allegra. She was wearing a puffy barn jacket, a bright red sweater, and jeans. She was also made up like the runner-up in the Miss Caloosa County contest, but then she always was. Madeline thinks Lila sleeps in the stuff. "You think so?" she said. "I don't know how you can tell with these jeans on."

"Waistband's loose," Madeline pointed out.

"I've been working at it," she admitted. But, like an ICBM, she was not to be diverted from the job at hand. She looked at Allegra and her voice got testy. "So here you are."

"Yes, ma'am," Allegra said, firmly. "Here I am." She stood with her saddle canted over one hip, her field boots dangling from one hand. "I'd like to thank you for the chance to meet Hugo." Lila opened her mouth, but Allegra forged bravely ahead. "And I'd like to get your questions about the accident at Earlsdown last year out of the way right up front."

Then Allegra did a very wise thing. She stopped talking altogether.

"I'm glad to hear that, young lady," Lila said sternly. "I care a lot about this horse."

"Yes, ma'am."

"From what I've heard about you, if Dr. McKenzie himself hadn't called on your behalf, I wouldn't even consider it."

Ally blinked.

"He knows his horses. None better." Lila cast a dimpled smile at me. "If Maddy and I weren't such good friends, I'd have him vet mine."

Madeline drew in her breath with a "hah!"

"Ma'am?" Ally asked in a bewildered way.

Lila gave me a knowing smirk. "Let's just say that Dr. McKenzie and I have more than respect for each other." Madeline calls Lila's style sneak and shoot, and at this juncture, I began to see her point. Lila abandoned her flirtatious mien before Madeline could intervene and got down to the business at hand. "I called Les Whyte this morning. You know who he is, Allegra?"

"Um. The chair of the Earlsdown committee?"

Lila nodded once. "Right. He swore on his grandmother's grave that the blood and urine tests they did after the train wreck you had were negative for alcohol."

"I don't drink," Ally said. I watched her, waiting for her chin to go up, the way it did when she lost her temper. But she held it together.

"Not at all?" Lila's glance was skeptical. "I don't know any college kids that don't drink at all."

Ally admitted that she didn't mind a beer with her friends once in a while. "But never around horses," she said. "It's, like, just too stupid."

Lila nodded again. "Okay. So tell me how the train wreck happened."

Ally shifted the saddle on her hip. Then she looked down at her feet. Last night, we'd all discussed the possibility that a competitor had slipped something into her water bottle. The date-rape drug, or perhaps chloral hydrate, the notorious Mickey Finn. But this was supposition. Ally merely said, "I hadn't eaten for a couple of days, Mrs. Gernsback. There was some family stuff going down, and I just kind of forgot about it."

Lila looked envious. "Forgot about eating? God. Don't I wish I could." She ran her eyes over Madeline's size-sixteen jeans. "I bet you do too, Maddy."

"Never once," she said in mild surprise. "Eating's an essential part of a happy life."

Lila's eyes narrowed. "So, what happened? You were riding on an empty stomach . . ."

"Dr. McKenzie thinks I had a precipitate drop in blood pressure," Allegra said, with just the smallest air of reciting a memorized script. "He thinks it's an anomaly that shouldn't occur again if I just keep a granola bar handy."

"That's correct," I offered.

Lila's razor glance turned to me. "So you're treating people now, Austin?"

I shrugged.

"Anyhow," Allegra continued, with a practical air, "I got dizzy. I think I blacked out for a second. Plus," she added, with a strike of inspiration, "I had my period. I get pretty bad periods."

I am afraid I blushed. I also quelled a cowardly desire to remove to the clinic. Allegra's embarrassing remark, however, proved to be a brilliant tactic. Lila's face softened in sympathy.

"Oh, you poor kid. Mine are just awful. Awful. My gyn says he's never seen periods as bad as mine."

I decided I didn't want to hear anything more about Lila Gernsback's physical condition, even though she was behaving less like a prosecuting attorney every second, which was all to Allegra's advantage. So I changed the subject to the only thing she'd pay more attention to than sex. "How is Hugo doing these days, Lila? Those students Victor sent over to help out while you were laid up keep him pretty fit?"

Lila swung the cane in another peppy circle. "Worked out so well I'm thinking about breaking the other leg, now that this one's on the mend." She turned around and stumped to the barn. "I'll bring him out and you can see for yourself."

We followed Lila across the way to the trailer. "Hey," Lila said as we approached, and the horse rumbled back at her. She let the back gate down with a crash and backed Hugo out onto the drive.

Trucking affects horses in many different ways. Some are tense and anxious, others take it in stride. Hugo was of the latter type. He stood half asleep on his big feet. He flicked one ear forward, then nosed Lila's vest, with a "hey, you have food for me?" look.

Hugo was squarely built, with a big chest, hindquarters like a semi tractor trailer, and thick bone. His neck sloped at the correct angle into his withers. When he craned his head around to rub at an itchy spot on his barrel, you could see how supple he was.

"He looks good, Lila," Madeline said. "He looks *really* good."

"Um-hm. Kids Victor sent over to help while I was laid up kept him going pretty well." She dug a currycomb and brush out of her vest pocket and handed them to Allegra. She shook her head at Allegra's saddle. "That's not going to be wide enough for him. I've got a wide body in the truck. Get him brushed out and we'll saddle him up."

"Okay." Allegra bit her lip. "And thanks."

"Don't thank me yet, kiddo. We have to see how he goes for you."

Conversation stalled for a bit while the women fussed about getting Hugo tacked up. When he was saddled, bridled, and gleaming enough to suit the three of them, Lila led him back to our arena. I opened the gate. Our arena is 180 feet long, standard for dressage, and we have two jump standards in the middle. Allegra pivoted the toe of her boot into the deep sand and smiled tentatively at Lila. "Great footing, at least."

Lila didn't smile back. "Okay. Mount up." She gave Allegra a leg up. Hugo stood there a second, his ears flicking backward and forward. Ally settled neatly into the saddle and gathered the reins.

Hugo yawned. His head drooped. If he'd been a person, he would have scratched his belly in boredom. Allegra gave him a nudge. He took a couple of steps forward, then stopped and swung his head sideways like the pendulum on a clock. *Work? Forget it.*

Lila was smiling now. More of a smirk, really. Then Allegra straightened up, drove her butt into the saddle, dug her spurs lightly into his flank, and shortened the reins, all at once. The horse rolled his eye in pleased surprise. Then he shaped up, moved out, and settled into work. It was a marvelous thing to see. It always is.

"Hmph," Lila said, pleased.

Allegra went around half the arena at a collected walk, moved into a trot, a collected trot, and by the time she'd worked him up to a collected canter, Lila had relaxed and so had the rest of us.

"*You* look happy about this, Madeline," Lila said.

"Well, I am. Both of them look terrific. I have to say, Lila, I'm amazed at how set up he is. He's fit enough to go the whole three days at Earlsdown and then some. Someone's been giving him a lot more than just exercise. He's been working."

Lila had her attention on the pair in the ring. Hugo was taking the jumps in easy, efficient strides. "Yeah, well. I was planning on selling him this year, so I made a point of getting him fit for show. He's twelve. Got a lot of good years in him, yet, but you know what'll happen if I wait too long to put him. out there."

We did. People have uninformed ideas about a horse's age—especially a performer like Hugo. He'd be worth a great deal less if Lila waited until he was thirteen.

"Already had an offer."

"Do tell," Madeline said, interested. "Anybody we know?"

"That guy I was with last night. Phillip Sullivan." She interrupted herself and shrieked like a steam whistle at Ally. It was a mercy the horse didn't bolt. "I'd like to see a couple of dressage moves, please. Settle him down and take him through some second-level work."

Allegra kept her eyes focused just between Hugo's ears. She nodded without turning her head and slowed Hugo to a trot. She brought him to a complete standstill and asked if she should change saddles.

"Won't make all that much difference to him," Lila shrugged. "He's about as sensitive as a slab of granite."

Allegra lengthened her stirrups to get more leg, sat back so that the cantle almost pressed into her backside, and shortened the reins. Hugo tucked his chin in and got to work. He was in the middle of a truly well-executed half pass across the arena when Madeline said, "I didn't get much of a chance to talk to him last night. Is he from around here?"

Lila frowned. "New York City. Lawyer. With an interest. You know."

All horse professionals are aware of these types. Often the first thing new millionaires do is buy themselves expensive horses. It seems to be a rite of passage.

"He saw Hugo on my website. Gave me a call and I checked him out. Gave me his bank references, the whole bit. We talked back and forth on the phone. Stephy McClellan had ridden him for me at Devon and a couple of other places, so he checked Hugo's performance out. He said he'd pay for a prepurchase exam, so I got that done. Then he came down to take a look." She flashed her dimples. "Said he wanted to take a look at me in the flesh as much as Hugo."

"You say that Stephanie has ridden Hugo for you?" I interjected.

Lila's eyes darkened, momentarily diverted. "That kid. What a mess. On top of all her other troubles, she lost her dog. Showed up at my place the other day in a huge temper. Claimed somebody stole it. Insisted on searching through my barns. I would have felt sorrier for her if I liked her better."

"Someone stole her dog?" Madeline said.

Lila shrugged, "Guess so. She was in a state, that's for sure."

Madeline, Allegra, and I exchanged glances. Perhaps we could strike the girl from our suspect list. Perhaps not. It would have to be verified.

"But you didn't take to Sullivan?" Madeline asked. "You seemed pretty friendly last night."

"You know that I have a pretty good eye for men, Maddy." She looked woeful. I saw Madeline bite her lip. "But I guess I was wrong, again. I thought I really liked this guy, Maddy. We'd had such a great time chatting each other up on the phone. And he'd gone to a lot of trouble to make sure that seeing Hugo work was worth the trip down. Of course," she added, "he was coming to see me as much as the horse. Anyway. He came down late on a Friday. He booked a suite over at the Inn at Hemlock Falls. We had a terrific meal there, and things were going along just fine. You know." She rolled her eyes a bit. "Anyhow. Saturday I got Stephy to come over to ride Hugo for him. The kid's a real snot, no question, but she's a good little rider. Anyhow, Hugo did great. Just great. And then Phillip offered me a quarter million for Hugo."

Madeline clapped her hand over her mouth. I was not as amazed, of course, since Nora Longworth's information had already prepared me for such a sum. "Dollars?" Madeline said, faintly.

Lila shifted uncomfortably. "Uh-huh. Said he was in the market for a winner. That he'd lost a few horses over the years and was ready to try again."

I felt my face would betray me if I looked at Madeline, so I did not. Lost a few, eh? There were far too many ways to kill a horse undetected. I bit my mustache in disgust.

Lila went on, oblivious to the undercurrents. "Now, I was thinking asking maybe seventy, eighty thousand for him. If that girl of yours does justice to him at Earlsdown . . ."

So she would let Allegra ride Hugo at Earlsdown. I breathed a silent "thank you!" to whatever horse gods were looking out for the two of them.

". . . We might even get a bit more than that. But two-fifty?" She looked at me and shook her head. "Something really funny there, Austin."

Madeline dragged Lila's attention back. "So you said no?"

Lila hitched her shoulders and said irritably. "Are you crazy? Guy wants to drop that kind of cash, you bet I'm going to catch it. I said I was thinking more about three hundred, but I'd consider two-fifty. So we dickered a bit and settled on two-seventy-five. That's one of the reasons I was in such a good mood at that party last night."

We waited for the denouement.

"And then he got a phone call this morning and he up and left, just like that. And I haven't heard from him since."

"Without buying Hugo," Madeline said.

"That's right. Like I said," she added with an airy wave of her hand, "there's something funny there."

I exchanged meaningful glances with Madeline. My first thought had been that poor Lila had been talked into bed for the price of an elaborate dinner at the Inn at Hemlock Falls and then dumped, as had happened all too frequently in the past. Perhaps Sullivan was merely a cad, and not a crook. But why go to all the trouble of vetting the horse out? Why call and ask about Hugo's show career? Madeline's mind is always congruent with my own, for she said, after a moment, "Now, Lila. Do you think maybe he left for some reason other than not wanting to buy Hugo? I mean, sweetie, you know how . . . umm . . . enthusiastic you can be over a new man in your life."

Lila was not one to pull her punches. She said, with that devastating honesty that endeared her to one and all, "You mean, you think he took off 'cause I talked about marriage?"

Lila was the veteran of perhaps three marriages; no one was precisely certain.

"Well, Lila, dear . . ." Madeline said.

"I know, I know. I'm a total idiot about men. I always have been. Maybe." She brightened. "So maybe he'll be back if he really wants Hugo? Do you think? I could really use that money."

Now, like a lot of people who'd been through a failed deal, Lila wasn't above skimping a bit in relating the whole picture. But I'd never known her to lie outright. So it appeared that Sullivan had indeed offered Lila Gernsback $275,000 for an $80,000 horse. And if she had been truthful about that, she surely had been truthful about his comment that he had "lost a few" horses along the way.

I had a great deal to mull over as Ally finished her ride and began to cool Hugo out.

"Well, she'll do, I suppose," Lila said.

"Allegra?" I put my mind back to the job at hand. "Of course she'll do. I had no doubts at all."

Then we had a short discussion about the finances. Lila was unusually practical about money, so it became a trifle spirited. But in sum, she agreed to pay the entry fees, and to give Allegra 5 percent of the purchase price if anybody made a reasonable offer to buy Hugo. By the time Allegra had brushed Hugo down and turned him out with Pony and Andrew in the paddock, Lila had pulled a copy of an agreement to ride from a file in her pickup and handed it over to her to sign. Allegra read it, signed it, shook hands with Lila, and threw her arms around Madeline. I then invited Lila to lunch with us at the Monrovian Embassy.

"Lunch sounds great," Lila said. "But I've got a pile of work to get through at home." She shook Allegra's hand. "You'll give me a call pretty often, let me know how he's going on?"

"I will," Allegra said. She wrung Lila's hand fervently. "And thank you, Mrs. Gernsback. Thank you."

I recalled Joe from his duties in the clinic. We decided to take two vehicles to lunch. Madeline and Allegra wanted to change out of riding gear. I had made an appointment to see Jerry Coughlin at two that afternoon, and I didn't want to rush through the hamburgers. "We've done extremely well," I said as we prepared to depart. "Phillip Sullivan made a ludicrously high offer for the horse. And did you catch what Lila said? He'd 'lost a few.' A few indeed. I wonder how much blood money the man has collected over the years."

"It's awful," Allegra agreed.

"Yeah, but I don't get it," Joe said stubbornly. "If he was going to buy Hugo, why did he beat it out of town this morning?"

"My guess is, he'll be back. But it will be at a safe distance from Lila," Madeline said a little ruefully. "That poor woman just falls into the dumbest traps when a man's involved. If Sullivan is behind an insurance scam, she's going to feel terrible." But she smiled at me. "All the same, this detecting business is fascinating, Austin. I don't know why we didn't think of it before."

"It's proving quite a challenge," I admitted.

"Well the next challenge is going to be your lunch at the Embassy, Austin. You are not, I repeat, *not* to have that artery-clogging hamburger special. You stick to the tuna salad plate."

"Of course, my dear."

Twelve

❧❧❧

"THERE are two items of information I wish to take away from this fact-finding mission," I said to Joe as we approached Summersville's finest diner. "As well as the finest hamburger plate in central New York. The first concerns the sniper letter. I believe it to be bogus. A red herring. The second concerns McClellan himself. We need to know more about the man. Our source for this information is the *Sentinel* reporter, Nigel Fish."

"You think McClellan's behind all of this?" Joe asked.

"I do indeed. And if Nigel is unaware of McClellan's significance to the sniper story, we shall soon make him aware of the fact."

I like eating lunch at the Monrovian Embassy. It is a large square space with high ceilings. Battered wooden booths line one side, and an equally battered mahogany bar lines the other. Rickety tables with a job lot assortment of metal, wooden, and plastic chairs march down the middle. Three beaten-up doors are set into the back wall: the center leads to the kitchen, the left and the right to the facilities. Admittedly, it is shabby. Madeline generally refuses to accompany me there, primarily, I think, because of the cholesterol-laden menu. She also says it smells like horse pee, which doesn't augur well for the cleanliness of the kitchen. It certainly smells. But a combination of beer fumes, the scent of old French fries, and the odor of unwashed student is not at all bad once you get used to it.

"There is a great deal to be said in favor of a good local bar in a town like Summersville," I remarked to Joe as we settled into a corner booth. "It is a place where the denizens feel at ease, where lips may be loosened by both the familiarity of the surroundings and inexpensive alcoholic beverages. It is also the place for the best hamburger in three counties. The Monrovian Embassy Special. Ah! My quarry is in view. Quick! Hide yourself behind the menu."

"Do what?" Joe seemed at little slow on the uptake. Perhaps it was the difference between the cold air outside and the warm air inside that gave him that somnolent expression. I saw that my instructions required clarification. "I do not," I said, in lowered tones, "wish Nigel Fish to see us just yet." I had raised my plastic menu in front of my face; behind its concealing shape, I nodded toward the front door.

"That guy?" Joe said, pointing.

Nigel Fish headed toward a table in the center of the room and dropped into a chair. I doubted that he was more than thirty, but he was already bald on top, with a fringe of baby-fine brown hair around the area of the medulla oblongata. He had a pudgy face and an equally pudgy little belly. He raised a finger in the direction of Colleen the waitress. She nodded and headed toward the bar.

"Nigel is Rita's star reporter," I elucidated, "with ambitions to move to the upper reaches of journalism and a byline with the *New York Times*. The only story big enough to do that for him is the Grazley shooting and the Summersville sniper story. However, the two of us do not get along well. He has on occasion resented any support I've offered to clean up his prose style. As a result, he is prone to quick exits when he sees me, unless approached at the right moment. You see? He has ordered his beer and burger. He's committed to staying now." I lowered the menu and drew breath, in order to be heard over the babble of diners. "Nigel!"

He jumped and looked around in wild surmise. Then he saw me. It may have been my imagination, but I believe he blanched.

"Join us for lunch, Fish," I said. I smiled widely. "It's on me."

That did it, of course. Rita does not throw money around on employee salaries. Nigel gave me a reluctant nod.

I thumped my menu on the table, thus drawing Colleen's attention. "Two burgers and two beers over here, my dear.

And Nigel is going to join us. Put his lunch on my tab." I waved the reporter over. He stared at the door for a long moment, perhaps contemplating escape, but cupidity overcame caution. He shoved his chair back and slouched over to our booth. "Hey, Dr. McKenzie."

"Hey, yourself," I replied genially. "May I introduce my assistant, Joseph Turnblad? Joe, this is Nigel Fish. A reporter of some aptitude." Nigel looked surprised, as well he might. Among Nigel's many literary sins was inattentiveness to his participles. I had castigated Nigel for sloppy grammar on more than one occasion. The two young men nodded to one another. I rose and pushed Nigel firmly onto the bench. "I'm delighted to see you, Nigel."

He looked even more surprised. "You are?"

"Although I do have a small bone to pick with you regarding last week's feature on the mayor."

"Uhn." Nigel grabbed the beer Colleen placed in front of him and drained half of it.

"Diction, Nigel, diction. 'In between' is a tautology. 'Except for' is another. But by and large"—I sipped my own beer, which was quite cold and refreshing—"the piece was well done."

"It was?"

"I thought so. I can see why Rita assigned the sniper story too you."

"Who told you I was on the sniper story?"

"An assumption, merely," I said, casually. "You're the most tenacious reporter Rita has. I can't think of a man better suited to take on the killings. And Brewster McClellan's a significant part of the story on the sniper shooting, isn't he?"

"Ah, yeah," Nigel said uncertainly.

"I know you know he should be." I took another swig of beer. "Or perhaps she is saving that part of the feature for herself. It's bound to be hot."

Colleen set three plates in front of us. The burgers were large, juicy, and smothered with Gorgonzola cheese and bacon. The French fries were thin, crisp, and seasoned with a concoction of spices known only to Manfred Schmitt, the chef. The look and smell of the meal was almost irresistible.

Nigel resisted it. The man was a perfect bloodhound when it came to news, and bloodhounds will drop from hunger before they abandon a scent.

"You know something you want to tell me, doc?"

"Perhaps. But we want to eat our lunch before it gets cold."

"Now, look, doc. You got a hot lead, I'd sure like to hear about it."

I held up my hand. "All in good time, Nigel."

The consumption of the meal occupied the three of us for some moments. Eventually, Joe sat back and said, "So, Nigel, McClellan a big noise around here?"

Nigel snorted through a mouthful of bacon. "Likes to think he is. You ever met him?"

"I've been to his home," I interjected. "And yes, Joe has met him, too. If we're speaking of the same McClellan. He's on the committee at Earlsdown this year. His daughter will be eventing this year."

"We're speaking of the same McClellan, all right. And that daughter of his? Crazy as an outhouse rat. Kid's got a rap sheet a mile long for petty theft."

"Is that so?" I said.

"Obnoxious kid. Lost her pet dog a couple days ago, came into the paper and wanted to take out a full-page ad. Couldn't pay for it, so no go. Nobody felt sorry for her, either, which tells you something."

"It does indeed," I said. I mulled over this verification that Stephanie had searched for her pet. I then brought matters back to the point. "You may know that I am head of the Veterinary Commission at Earlsdown this year."

Nigel shrugged.

"So we'll be working closely together, Brewster and I."

"So? What's all this got to do with the sniper killing?" He frowned. "There's some horse angle here? That what you're telling me?"

"Did you know that Ben Grazley had been out on a barn call at McClellan's home prior to the shooting?"

"What are you talking about?" Nigel didn't go so far as to affect a fedora, the way reporters in old Ben Hecht screenplays did, but he did wear a ratty tweed sport coat with leather patches on the elbows. He dug in his breast pocket and withdrew not a well-worn steno pad, but an electronic dingus.

"Nice BlackBerry," Joe said.

"Yeah. Can't beat it for notes." He tapped at the keys with a stylus. "Huh. All that's part of the police report is that Grazley was coming back from a call on Route Fifteen." He looked up at me. "Route Fifteen is where McClellan lives, isn't it? In that huge new mansion he built. So you think something happened out there? Maybe he pissed McClellan off? Maybe McClellan shot him?" He poised his stylus over the keyboard.

"Whoa," Joe said. "You're going a little fast there, pal."

"There's been no indication at all that McClellan was the author of the sniper letter," I said. "Or has there?"

"Police figure the letter's a prank," Nigel admitted. "Or that's the official story line, anyhow."

I smoothed my mustache. "I thought so."

"Yeah? How come you thought so? It's got a lot of people going, that letter has." Nigel's beady little eyes were alight with reportorial passion. "Hey, you guys want to stay off the record, I got no problem with that. I'll quote you as reliable sources. Use that term all the time."

"I think," I added, "that we would need to know a lot more about McClellan himself before we could be any kind of source at all."

"What is this, a trade-off of some kind? You scratch my back, I'll scratch yours?"

To be truthful, I had not anticipated the full ramifications of a foray into the detecting business. It was clear my inclination to have all aboveboard might prove impediments to a successful investigation.

"Don't like the idea of a quid pro quo?" Nigel slouched against the booth and grinned unpleasantly. "You look like you're sucking lemons, doc. Hey. You lie down with dogs . . ." He shrugged and put his BlackBerry away. "Suit yourself. Let's back track a bit. Why you so interested in McClellan, anyhow?"

"Dr. McKenzie already mentioned he's going to be doing some business with him," Joe said. "They're working together on the Earlsdown event."

Joe was getting quicker on the uptake. Perhaps I'd worried unnecessarily about the quality of our teamwork. I picked up the baton and ran with it. "And I needn't tell you, Nigel, about my concerns for the show's success."

I needn't, indeed. For all of me, they could cancel the damn thing. It'd been the site of one equine death already.

"Huh. Well. R-i-i-ght," Nigel said, with an irritating drawl. "So, this vet Grazley goes out to McClellan's for what did you call it? A barn call. What'd he do at the barn call? Moo?" Nigel's laugh is particularly annoying. He drew his nose up like a Duroc sow in heat and snickered, "Heh-heh-heh."

"He was to examine one of the horses stabled there," I said repressively.

"And then what? Was there an argument?"

"You'll have to ask McClellan about that. The evidence indicates he never got to the farm."

Nigel took out the BlackBerry, made a few notes with the stylus, and packed it away again. "Okay. Thanks. I guess."

I took a deep breath. "What I wish to know is who McClellan is."

"Who he is?"

"Where did he come from? What does he do? What is the context of the man?"

"Heck. That's easy enough. He's a venture capitalist."

"A what?" Joe asked.

"You know, he goes around raising money for new businesses. He's from New York City, originally. All of those guys are." He sighed and looked wistful, perhaps thinking of the offices of the *New York Times* and the newly gentrified Times Square. "Anyhow, he either takes a cut of the business itself, through equity participation, or a commission on the money he raises. Seems to be doing pretty well, if you look at the cash he's spread around here."

"Does he specialize?" I inquired.

"You mean, like high tech, low tech, no tech? I don't know for sure. But I can find out. I do know that he's one of the movers behind that estate development plan."

"What plan is that?"

Nigel shook his head. "Tsk. Tsk. Tsk. You know, doc, I think

the only part of the *Sentinel* you read is your own column.
Rita'd be pissed about that. The Gorges Group has been mak-
ing headlines for the past couple of months. All the liberals at
Cornell are as steamed as hell about it."

"McClellan's a force behind that?" I stroked my mustache,
a habit when I'm amazed.

"What is it, some kind of housing thing?" Joe asked.

"Some kind," Nigel snorted. "McClellan's got that three
hundred acres of prime meadowland. Wants to turn it into a
combination housing development/office park sort of thing.
He's got the state guys here to do permits, the whole shebang.
Word is he's got the mayor in for a piece of the action . . ."
Nigel's eyes grew dreamy. "Now, *there's* a story for you. If I
could tie McClellan into Grazley's murder all hell would
break loose about that development for sure."

None of this had anything to do with dead horses or disgraced veterinarians. I was not unable to see a red herring
when it was staring me in the face. And Colleen had deposited
the bill for lunch in front of me in her usually impetuous fashion. "That's all very well and good, but it doesn't appear to be
germane to the horse business."

"What about Mrs. McClellan," Joe said. "Do we know anything about her background?"

"Marina? She's a software developer, or was."

"Really?" I said.

"Yeah. To look at her now, you'd think she couldn't develop
a cold. But yeah, she's no dummy. You wouldn't believe it, the
way she comes across now. Not to mention the fact she's got the
roundest heels in Tompkins County." His gaze drifted beyond
my shoulder to the dining room proper. His eyes widened.

I was startled. "Round heels? You mean she's what my
grandfather would call a loose woman?" This was extremely
hard to believe. I began to doubt the veracity of all Nigel's
statements.

"Having an affair with some young vet, they say. D'Andrea? Was that his name?"

Hm. If it were true, more power to the poor woman. But
Nigel paid no further attention to me. He sat up. A slight red
flush suffused his cheeks. I turned around. Nigel's gaze was

riveted on Allegra. She was looking particularly fetching. Her complexion was rosily flushed with the chill of the outside air. Little tendrils of chocolate-colored curls floated about her forehead. Her eyes were brilliant and she was smiling happily.

She was accompanied by my beloved. Madeline was looking lovely, too, if one overlooked the expression of extreme disapprobation on her face.

I was keenly aware of the remains of the Monrovian Embassy Special on the plate in front of me. My thoughts moved as lightning. This was a booth for four, wasn't it? And there were only three at table. Rising to greet the arrivals, I shoved plate, cutlery, and beer stein to the unoccupied place to my right. I could make careless reference to Rita's arrival and precipitate departure, perhaps. Rita was notoriously fond of the hamburger special.

"Austin." Madeline's mellow contralto momentarily silenced the din. "You haven't been eating greasy junk again, have you?

My lunch companions snickered. Madeline sighed, then crossed the room, a sloop in full sail, Allegra trailing her like a bright little dinghy. "Well, Nigel," Madeline said sunnily, "we haven't seen you for a while. How've you been?"

Nigel, staring at Allegra as if she were a Monrovian Embassy special, made a vague noise of welcome.

Madeline considered him for a long moment, then said, "Shove over, Joe, so we can sit down."

"Sit here!" Nigel shouted. "I mean, you can sit right across from me, Mrs. McKenzie. Joe, if you slide over a bit, she, I mean, you can sit next to me." He waved his paw in Allegra's face. "Nigel Fish," he said. "Journalist."

"Allegra Fulbright," she said. Then, with a mischievous glance at me, she added, "Eventer."

"I knew you would knock Lila's eye out," I said with no little satisfaction. "You and Hugo are well suited."

"Hugo who?" Nigel demanded.

"Ally's going to be competing at Earlsdown next week," Madeline said. She, too, was beaming. She gave me a kiss on the cheek. "I wish you'd seen the two of them working out, Joe. She got that big rock of a gelding moving right along."

"Hugo's a horse, then," Nigel said, with a degree of intelligence I hadn't credited him with, heretofore.

"Hugo's a horse," Allegra agreed. "A really nice horse."

"And Ally's going to take a ribbon or two on him, if I'm any judge," Madeline said happily.

"No ribbons. It's way too late for that. I might finish, if my legs don't fall off first." Allegra bent and rubbed her calves. "The horse is in great shape. I'm not so sure about me."

"We'll have to feed you up," Madeline said. "I don't know about you, sweetie, but I'm about starving to death." Madeline waved at Colleen, pointed to the plate by my side and called, "We'll have two of what Austin had." She relaxed against my side. "So, did you two have a successful morning at the Longworths'? We didn't have a chance to talk about that earlier." She kept her eyes on Nigel for a moment, then turned and looked at me. One eyebrow quirked up in an unspoken question. There are many advantages to a long and happy marriage, chief of which is the ability of two compatible partners to read each other's mind.

"Nigel was just leaving," I said.

"Oh, I can stick around a while," Nigel said eagerly. "Are you new in town, Allegra? I don't think I've seen you at the Embassy before."

"I'm a senior at Cornell."

"And far too young for you, Nigel," I said briskly. "And I said I would buy you lunch. I wasn't anticipating the pleasure of your company for the rest of the afternoon. Nor do I want it."

Madeline intervened with some celerity, "What Dr. McKenzie means, Nigel, is that he has several more calls to make this afternoon, and we'll all be leaving shortly. But it was very nice to see you again."

I don't know how Madeline accomplishes these things. Nigel left the table with reasonable grace, for a journalist, and we were left alone.

"So, did you learn anything from Nigel?" Allegra asked eagerly.

Joe drained his beer and set the schooner on the table with a thump. "McClellan's on thin ice financially and Stephanie's got a rap sheet a mile long."

"Interesting," Allegra said, her brows raised.

"What did he mean, rap sheet?" Madeline asked with a frown. "Anything serious?"

"Shoplifting, a small amount of drugs, petty stuff," Joe said.

"We think Stephanie's pretty much out of the picture as a suspect," Allegra said, and then explained why.

"It's McClellan's financial worries that are of great interest here," I said. "With a modicum of luck, Coughlin will be able to shed a little more light onto the situation." I glanced at my watch. "I should be getting along to the interview I've set up with him soon."

Madeline nodded, "And, I'm going to get groceries if we're to count on any supper, and I want to drop Ally off for her afternoon class. But I didn't want the whole day to go by without discussing what we've discovered so far." Colleen set two platters of the Monrovian Embassy Special down on the table. Instead of beer, she'd brought hot tea. I instantly deduced that Madeline frequented a place she had forbidden me. I seem to be a natural at this detective business.

"Don't chew your mustache, Austin."

"McClellan is in the middle of this up to his crooked neck," I said. "We suspect Sullivan of insurance fraud. Sullivan wants to buy into McClellan's Coggins business—what was it? FieldChek, whose other shareholders are mainly dead. That is, Grazley and Schumacher. Beecher is owned by a syndicate, whose partners are the late Benny Grazley, the highly suspect Sullivan, and the nearly bankrupt McClellan. Things could hardly be more suspicious."

"It looks like it," Joe said. "Interesting."

"You were dubious that McClellan could to be linked to the crimes this morning," I observed.

"Not dubious, exactly. But the links seemed pretty weak to me, doc. Not now. There's something off, that's for sure."

"I have no doubt of it. You search for the cause of a disease process system by system. If a horse exhibits symptoms of colic, you begin by an examination of the gastrointestinal system. If nothing is unearthed, you move on to the endocrine. What you do not ignore, as a diagnostician, is the fact that something is wrong. And if something is wrong, there is a proximate cause. One may search for the cause of crime in the same systematic manner."

There was a lengthy pause at the table. I tapped my fingers impatiently. "The crimes against Faraway, Grazley, and Coughlin are all connected to McClellan in one way or another. One of the man's 'systems' if you will, is what he does for a living."

"Well, what is McClellan's business?" Madeline asked.

"He appears to be a real estate developer, primarily. With a hand in some small business start-ups."

"A real estate developer?" Allegra echoed.

"Not on his own behalf. He raises money to develop developments." I took a moment to examine this locution. I didn't like it.

Allegra looked perplexed. "What in the world does that have to do with horses?"

I said nothing. Madeline gave me a nudge. "Austin?"

"I don't know," I admitted. "We aren't in possession of sufficient data. We need to know more about this Sullivan, for one. We need to know his exact relationship to McClellan. And it'd be well to discover the extent of McClellan's debts and to whom he owes money. We are quite a way from establishing a motive for these murders." I sighed. I knew that the path to bringing the murderer to justice might be a twisty one, but this was getting to be positively tortuous. The amount of data that needed to be gathered was mountainous.

"You said Sullivan's a lawyer with offices in New York, Madeline?" Joe asked.

Madeline nodded. "A divorce lawyer, according to Lila."

"I could hop on down there and make like a client," Joe suggested.

"You and your string of ex-wives?" Allegra asked politely. "Funny."

"Or we could break into McClellan's offices," Allegra said, with a blithe disregard for the man's civil rights.

"We have a specific objective," I pointed out. "Which requires a much more focused approach."

"I've got it," Madeline said, "Why don't we just ask him? It's my experience that men like McClellan love to talk about their business."

I may have mentioned that my wife is frequently three

steps ahead of me. I love her dearly for it. "Excellent," I said. "And why stop there? I will call on McClellan after I've finished with Coughlin. I shall demand to know all about Phillip Sullivan, the syndication of Beecher, and his relationship with Grazley and Schumacher."

Joe coughed. Allegra twiddled with her hair. Madeline put her arms around me and said, "I think you should reconsider, dear!"

"You think my approach, in general, is too direct?"

"I think your approach could get you killed, if McClellan is the murderer," Madeline said.

"This is how I see it, Dr. McKenzie," Allegra said. "You're the brains of the operation. Madeline's the interrogator. I'm in charge of covert operations—I'm the one going undercover at Earlsdown, right?"

Joe cleared his throat.

"And of course," Allegra said with an airy wave of her hand, "We need muscle, occasionally."

Joe smiled calmly. "You know," he said casually, "You might take a few minutes to examine your retro-sexist, gender-biased attitudes. They're bound to get you in a lot of trouble in the veterinary business."

"Is that so? Who says I'm gender-biased? I know a lot of dumb, muscle-bound women, too."

"You know what? I was wrong. I admit it. It doesn't seem to be an attitude at all. More like a character trait." The two of them leaned over the table, almost nose to nose.

Madeline sighed. It was so deep, so heartfelt, that Joe and Allegra broke off their squabble. Allegra and Joe looked at her in concern. I, of course, knew better. A heartfelt sigh was one of Madeline's favorite tactics. It works to advantage in all kinds of unusual places.

"Are you all right, Mrs. McKenzie?" Allegra asked anxiously.

"I'm fine!" she said, briskly. "Just breathing. So, we've agreed that I'll be the one to pry information out of Brewster, preferably without his realizing I'm prying at all. We should come up with some excuse to meet up with Brewster. A natural one. Not fakey."

I mulled a bit. "I wonder if Beecher's Coggins is current," I said, finally. "You and Joe can drop by tomorrow morning to check. A nice neighborly call. And if it isn't current, Joe, draw a blood sample to send off the to the lab."

"Perfect," Madeline said. She dropped a kiss on my head and gathered her purse and coat about her. "Allegra's off to class. I'm off to Wegman's." She glanced at her watch. "If you've got a two o'clock with Coughlin, sweetie, you'd better get going. Poor guy'll pitch a fit if you're late."

I was twenty minutes late, as luck would have it. But it didn't matter to Coughlin.

He was already dead when I got there.

Thirteen

❦❧

JERRY Coughlin had sold his large house and successful clinic two years before, a consequence of an unusually unpleasant divorce. The practice was now located near a stretch of abandoned railroad tracks outside the village of Covert. I pulled into the graveled driveway and looked at the premises in some dismay. The house badly needed a paint job. Not to mention a new roof. The barn was sound, at least; the roof had been newly shingled and the north wall had been totally replaced with T1-11 siding. The outside paddocks were clean and well kept.

I knew something was wrong the moment I pulled the Bronco to a halt. For one thing, Lincoln was uneasy. He shifted restlessly in the front seat, ears up. He pawed at my knee and whined. I rolled the driver's window down. I could hear lowing cattle. I got out of my vehicle. At the sound of my feet on the drive, a dog began to bark—short, high-pitched yelps that indicated a high degree of canine anxiety. Lincoln pushed his head out the window and barked back. The yelps increased to a crescendo. Jerry's dog was an Akita, a beautiful breed that can be temperamental when under stress. Her name, I recalled, was Juno.

It would be prudent to avoid a dogfight. "Leash, please," I said to Lincoln.

He stopped barking, gave me a brief, reproachful look, then retrieved his leash from its place under the front seat. I attached it to his collar and let him out of the car.

Juno appeared at the south corner of the house. She barked, spun around, and dashed back out of sight. Linc and I followed at a jog.

I had an intimation of disaster when I heard the sound of a truck motor. Jerry garaged it in a somewhat ramshackle shed at the back of his house. The intimation strengthened to surety when I saw the rolls of pink insulation jammed under the closed overhead door. Juno stood in front of the door, all four feet braced, the yapping nonstop.

I unsnapped Linc's lead, told him to stay, and whistled for Juno. She danced frantically up to me. Age has sapped a bit of my strength, but not, thank god, my response time. I grabbed her collar, leashed her, tied her to the nearest shrub, and raced to the overhead door. I pulled at the handle, which was not locked, and flung the door upward.

Clouds of carbon dioxide–laden exhaust rolled from the space within. I took a breath and jumped over the insulation to the inside. Jerry had backed the truck in; I saw him slumped over the wheel. The driver's window had been rolled down an inch or two. Plastic tubing ran from the exhaust pipe to the clearance. I tore the tubing away and pulled at the door handle.

The driver's door was locked.

Lincoln raced back and forth between me and the frantic Juno, ignoring my command to stay down. I backed out of the choking air, took another breath, and returned inside. I had to get Jerry out of that vehicle.

There was nothing at hand to break the window. What I could see of Jerry's face—his forehead, his right cheek, his chin—was a bright cherry red. His right eye was open. It was too dim in the garage to see if the sclera was suffused.

He didn't blink when I pounded at the glass.

I ran back to the Bronco, retrieved the tire iron from the rear, then went back a third time. This effort at smashing the glass was successful; the window broke into shards mostly contained by the safety glass coating. I swept at it, reached in, unlocked the door, and pulled Jerry from the truck into the open air.

I sat down next to him, unable to get enough air of my own. Lincoln behaved in a most annoying fashion, leaping at me and licking my face. I think it was more irritation with my dog than anything else that roused me from my stupor.

I straddled the poor man and began cardiopulmonary re-
suscitation. I stopped, put my thumbnail to that ghastly opened
eye, and pressed down. No reaction. No pulse, either at throat
or wrist. I resumed CPR for some minutes, then stopped, at
last, for good. Jerry Coughlin was beyond what assistance I
could give him. I went back to the Bronco and radioed
for help. I then walked through the barn and checked on the
animals.

Simon Provost and the Summersville emergency crew arrived simultaneously, some twenty minutes later. I sat on an
upturned crate next to the body, both dogs at my feet. The
EMTs spoke little; one went to the corpse and removed the
horse blanket I had placed over him, the other two removed a
gurney from the back of the ambulance. I rose at Simon
Provost's approach and extended my hand.

"How do you do, Lieutenant?"

He nodded, unsmiling. The last time I'd seen him had been
at the press conference at the Tompkins County Courthouse;
he had looked tired then, and he looked even more tired now.

"Well, well, well. If it isn't my amateur Columbo. You call
this in?"

"I did."

He walked over and gazed down at Jerry's face for a long
moment. The young man who had been taking Jerry's vital
signs shook his head. Then he walked back. "You have a reason for being here, doc?"

"I do. We had an appointment for two o'clock."

His eyes narrowed. "I saw you at the press conference with
Rita Santelli. What are you doing out here? How do you know
Coughlin?"

"I am a veterinarian. He is a veterinarian. Of course we
know each other. And I'm impressed that you recall my presence at that event, Lieutenant. You were fairly well occupied
at the time."

"You stuck out a little," he said. "The crowd was a bit
younger, on average. Now, you want to tell me what happened
here?"

I gave Provost a succinct, unembellished account of events.
He made notes in a much-battered steno pad. Then he walked

to the shed and peered inside. I followed. The dogs followed me. He turned abruptly and seemed taken aback when confronted with the three of us. "I don't want any civilians back here," he said. "Would you mind?"

"There were some anomalies about the scene that you may not have noticed, Provost. I was going to point them out to you."

"Anomalies, huh? Great. Why don't you tell me about them back over there?"

Being a law-abiding citizen, I acquiesced. As we returned to the upturned box, I noted that the EMTs had not only loaded Jerry onto the gurney, and into the van, but that they were preparing to drive away.

"You're not waiting for the pathologist?" I said, in dismay. "What about the forensics people? What about evidence collected in situ?"

"You moved the body, Dr. McKenzie. And the forensics team isn't going to be real happy to be called out on a suicide."

"It wasn't a suicide," I said flatly.

"You know something I don't?" Provost's entire *mien* was stern. He turned and walked back toward me. If I hadn't known better, I would have thought that he suspected *me* of untoward activities.

"Perhaps," I said, somewhat testily. It had been, after all, a trying hour and a half. "Yes, I moved the body, but you'll agree I had no other choice, and yes, I do know something you don't because vital evidence—of necessity—has been disturbed. Please refer to your notebook."

He blinked at little. He opened his mouth—perhaps to consider registering a protest—but closed it again. Instead, he took out his notebook.

"Refer to the statement I made about the condition of the insulation around the garage door and the driver's window."

He licked his thumb, turned to the relevant page, and said, " 'Insulation tucked in from outside.' "

"That is not verbatim, but it is essentially correct." I waited for him to expand upon this, somewhat impatiently, I admit. It didn't take long.

"You mean you think someone stuffed the insulation in after the doc was in the truck?"

I raised my eyebrows. "Bravo."

"He could have gotten in the passenger-side door."

"Unlikely. That side, too, was stuffed from the outside. I checked. As a matter of fact, you may see that for yourself. There was no need to remove it."

Provost scratched his ear with his pencil. Then he went into the garage, examined the truck from all sides, and came back.

"Now refer to the statement I made about the animals."

He paged through the notebook. " 'Stock not fed.' "

"Again, that is not precisely what I said. But it is significant."

Provost's gaze was politely disbelieving.

"No veterinarian would leave his stock untended. I don't care how depressed the man was. Rather than leave the cow unmilked, the calves unfed, and the surgery patients without water, he would have shot them all."

This took Provost aback, as I had intended it should.

"Or at least seen to their welfare," I amended.

"But he knew you were coming to meet him, didn't he? You're a vet, too. He knew you would have taken care of the critters."

This hadn't occurred to me. "Hm," I said. "You have a point."

I heard the familiar chug-chug-chug of an ill-maintained motor. Provost stiffened, much in the way that Lincoln does when he senses an intruder. "Now, who the hell is this?"

I turned to see Joe's Escort pull into the drive. "My assistant, Joe Turnblad."

"You gave him a call?"

"I did."

"To give you a hand with the stock, here?"

"Yes."

"There's some sort of veterinarian's oath? Like the Hippocratic oath for people doctors?" He didn't wait for an answer, but held his hand up so that Joe wouldn't park too close to the garage. "You notice anything else while you were prowling around the joint, Dr. McKenzie?"

I reflected a moment. "There were one or two things. They can wait, however." Joe unfolded himself out of the Ford. It is a very small car for someone of his height.

"Mrs. McKenzie got me on my cell after you called her,"

he said as he came up to us. I introduced the lieutenant. Joe greeted him soberly, then stooped to ruffle Lincoln's ears. He gave Juno a considering glance. She had responded to the death of her master like Greyfriars Bobby was reputed to have done; she lay where his body had lain, muzzle sunk onto her paws. "Sorry to hear about Dr. Coughlin."

"And I'm sorry to drag you out of class, Joe. But we need to transfer these patients to Sunny Skies. I'll need your help to load them up. Take the Bronco, return home, and hitch up the stock trailer. We'll need it here."

Provost raised his hand in protest. "Hang on a minute. You can't take anything from the property."

"You can't have it both ways, Lieutenant. Either Jerry Coughlin killed himself, knowing that I would arrive to take care of his responsibilities, or he was murdered." I paused, for the effect of my next point. "In that case, of course, you stay and take over the clinical duties. I will be happy to leave you instructions."

Provost didn't look happy. Worse yet, he didn't look convinced. "Can't you send someone over once a day? My wife goes over once a day to feed the neighbor's cat when they go on vacation."

I held up one finger at a time as I enumerated. "There is a gravid mare, who looks to be due within days."

Provost rolled his eyes at Joe.

"She's pregnant," Joe clarified.

"There is a very fine, show-quality heifer with mastitis. She has to be milked carefully twice a day."

"Infected teats," Joe said. "Probably pretty messy, Lieutenant."

"And there are the chickens."

"Oh god," Provost said. "Chickens. I hate chickens."

"The hens can be extremely quarrelsome," I agreed. "But we will have to leave them here anyway." I turned to Joe. "According to Victor Bergland, Coughlin was involved in some research for the CDC. We'll have to carry out SPF procedures in caring for them until we review Coughlin's records."

"Specific pathogen free, Lieutenant," Joe said, rather merrily. "He's talking biohazard gear, here."

"Are you talking contagious?"

"The concern is more for the contamination of the chickens," I said irritably. "Although I believe Coughlin's research had to do with various strains of avian flu, yes."

Provost swore rather colorfully. Then he said, "Are these all Coughlin's, these animals? He had a practice, didn't he? You can't just haul off somebody's property."

I shrugged. "I have no way of knowing unless I go through the records. But the heifer should be under medical care. I'm not certain about the mare. She may be Jerry's own event horse. Madeline will be able to identify her if that's so. But, ownership notwithstanding, we have to deal with the pregnancy. The statistics for healthy delivery in the equine are surprisingly low."

"Stop," Provost said. "I get the picture. You charge by the word, doc?"

I didn't dignify this with an answer.

Provost sighed again. I was beginning to think the man had an oxygen deficiency. "Okay. This is what I'm going to do. Hold your right hand up, Dr. McKenzie."

I demurred. "I'm not adept at the ritual known as the high five."

"I'm going to deputize you, dammit. You, Turnblad, you're a witness. Got that."

"Got that," Joe said.

"And wipe that shit-eating grin off your face, Turnblad."

Deputize me? I raised my right hand. I believe I had a shit-eating grin on my face, too.

Provost scrubbed his face hard with both hands. "Jesus Christ. I can't believe I'm doing this. Okay. Hang on a sec. You have a record, doc?"

"Do you mean a sheet?" I said jovially.

Provost muttered something, then said, "Yeah. A sheet."

I thought a moment. "Yes," I admitted, rather proudly.

Provost's face fell, perhaps at the thought of caring for the sick chickens. "What the hell for?"

"Felony parking."

"Felony *parking*? What's that when it's at home?"

I explained about the $300 parking violation at Earlsdown

the prior year. "And as I understand it, misdemeanors are separated from felonies in part by the value attached to the
penalty. Three hundred dollars certainly falls into the felony
category."

"Bullshit," Provost said. "Bullshit, bullshit, bullshit. Raise
your hand, McKenzie."

And so I was deputized. Provost did not have a badge
handy, but promised that one would be sent in the mail. Then,
with further profane fulminations, he retired to his cruiser, returned with a digital camera, and proceeded to take photos of
the crime scene. Not that I could get him to admit that it was a
crime scene. He did, however, warn me off taking anything
from Coughlin's files.

I sent Joe home to retrieve the stock trailer, then went to the
house in search of information about the patients. Halfway
into the kitchen, I stopped at Provost's behest, which took the
form of "What a minute, godammit." He ran up the steps and
shouldered his way past me. "You can't just trample all over
the place, McKenzie. This may be a crime scene."

"It *is* a crime scene," I said agreeably. "I do, however, need
the records on Coughlin's animals. Particularly the chickens."

Provost ran one hand over his chin. "You said something
about research? I've read about avian flu. It's pretty dangerous
stuff."

"I doubt that Jerry was involved in any research involving
pandemic diseases that affected humans. This location is not
secure. Besides," I added, somewhat absently, as I looked
about the kitchen, "the research wouldn't have been original.
He would have been carrying out experiments under a senior
scientist somewhere." I sighed. "Provost," I said. "I find this
kitchen very sad."

The area was clean, that was all that could be said for it.
The window that looked out on the desolate backyard was cur-
tainless. The linoleum on the bare floor was cracked and peel-
ing. Yellowed newspaper had been spread under Juno's water
bowl and food dish. An old tin pot sat in the sink next to a soli-
tary bowl and soupspoon. A stack of empty, rinsed-out Camp-
bell's soup cans lined the worn counter. An old, humpbacked
refrigerator clanked away in the corner. I opened the door.

The sole contents were three loaves of Wonder Bread, a jumbo jar of peanut butter, and a six-pack of Budweiser beer. Provost opened and closed a scarred wood cabinet. "Cans of tuna fish. And some cereal."

"An arid existence," I observed. "He was a bachelor, you know."

"Poor guy had a limited diet," Provost agreed. He shook his head, "Thank god my wife's Italian."

"Lasagna," I agreed. "Pasta puttanesca. You're a fortunate man. But it's more than a lack of the feminine, Provost. There is a poverty of the senses, here. The man was depressed."

Provost looked smug.

"It was not a suicide," I said.

"There'll be a note."

"There will be no note."

"Probably in his office."

"He didn't keep records in the barn. That's what will be in the office, and that's what we're looking for, here."

"A small percentage of suicides leave a note."

"There will be no note." What there would be, I was convinced, was something that would link McClellan to this crime.

The rest of the small house was as unlived in as the kitchen. No color. No life. And in the small second bedroom that Coughlin used as an office, what few personal mementos he owned were shoved carelessly aside on his desk. A picture of his ex-wife, whom I vaguely recalled, now that I saw her face; a high school graduation photo of a young man who bore a close resemblance to Jerry; and a large, expensively framed picture of the young man grown up, with wife and toddler.

"A son," I observed.

"We'll have to track him down." Provost opened the desk drawers one by one. The center drawer was filled with the usual assortment of office supplies: pens, boxes of staples, paper clips. And two glucose testers of the type used by diabetics, still in the pharmaceutical packaging.

"What're those?" Provost asked. "They look familiar."

"You've probably seen these advertised on television," I said. "Or perhaps someone you know is a diabetic?"

"Not that I know of." Provost picked up one of the packages and turned it over. "So Coughlin was a diabetic. Might be another reason why the poor guy was depressed."

"Possibly." I turned to the filing cabinet, which held files in alphabetical order, by patient name. I immediately went to the Ms. And there it was, McClellan, Faraway. "Ha!" I said. "We are partially in luck, at least."

Provost peered over my shoulder. "You find a note?"

"There will be no note," I said firmly. "No. This, I hope, will give me some insight into what transpired at Earlsdown last year."

"Have anything to do with Coughlin's death?"

"I don't know. Possibly."

"Then give me that. It's evidence."

I held the file out of Provost's reach. "This is a patient file. It concerns the health of a horse. You are prepared to wade through thickets of veterinary terminology in the hope of discovering a clue?"

"No."

"Then I will wade through it for you. If there's anything relevant to the case, I will let you know immediately. I am, after all, a duly deputized member of this team, am I not? Although I do not yet have a shield."

"Yeah, yeah, yeah."

"Which brings me to a small matter of the honorarium," I said. "We haven't yet had an opportunity to discuss it."

"You mean you want to get paid to stick your nose into county business?" Provost seemed somewhat exercised.

"You do pay consultants, do you not?"

"Jeez!" Provost rubbed his scalp, which, I was pleased to see, was almost as bare as my own. "All right, yeah, why not. I'll talk to the mayor."

"And you'll be sure to send the appropriate ID through the . . ." I broke off. Provost's complexion was becoming choleric.

"Don't push it, McKenzie. And give me that file."

"The chickens," I said, "may well need daily doses of antibiotic. Would you care to learn how to dose a chicken?"

"No." He glared at me. "We had chickens when I was a kid. I hate chickens."

"It's all in the handling," I observed. "A professional rarely gets pecked."

He smiled to himself. "Oh yeah? Keep the damn file. Keep all of the damn files. Just let me know when you're handling those chickens. I'd like to see it."

I didn't tell him that the CDC was more than likely to send someone to pick up the chickens. Either that, or order them dispatched to chicken heaven.

"Very well, then." I laid the Faraway file on the top of the filing cabinet.

We worked at our respective tasks in silence for some minutes. "Well," I said, frustrated, "I see nothing to do with the chickens. Not even a contact number. At home, you know, we are in the process of computerizing our patient files. Are you finding anything in the way of a computer?"

"Nope. But there's evidence he had one. There's a printer cable, an extra battery for a laptop, a peripheral for a disk drive . . ." Provost looked under the desk, pulled all the drawers out again, then slammed them shut. "Nope. No computer."

"I find that highly significant," I said.

Provost shot me a look. "You do, do you?"

"Don't you?"

"Maybe. Maybe not. Unless it turns up in the truck, or something. You about through here? I want to finish taking those pictures."

"I'll take a moment to see if I can find any information on the mare and the cow."

Provost clattered downstairs. I thumbed rapidly through the manila file folders. Coughlin had had quite a few clients, I was glad to see. There was a file for Gernsback, Hugo, and I pulled it. It contained the usual: X-rays, records of vaccinations, a current Coggins. A casual scan revealed nothing more unusual than a note on the Coggins form: in red ink, a downward pointing arrow, which seemed relevant to nothing.

Except that a quick scan of similar patient records revealed that same arrow on almost all of the Coggins exams. Curious.

I found the pregnant mare's records listed under Coughlin, Sunny. There was an arrow on her Coggins, too. But she was Coughlin's event horse, evidently. The heifer appeared to belong to Liversedge, Britney. Liversedge Longhorns was famous, locally, for show cattle. That was one issue that could be resolved expeditiously. I would call them about the heifer as soon as I returned home.

I tucked the Hugo, Sunny, and Faraway files under my arm and went back outside. Joe had arrived with the trailer as reinforcements for me. Reinforcements for Provost had arrived in the form of two uniformed patrolmen. Provost leaned against his cruiser, writing furiously in his steno pad. The patrolmen stood at semi-attention, evidently waiting for him to finish. He looked up as I approached. "We're going to do a search before you haul all the stock out." He closed the book, crossed his arms, and looked at me. "You said earlier that you noticed a couple of things when you walked through the barns. What things?"

I beckoned. "Come with me."

They did. All of them, including Lincoln and a much-subdued Juno. I led them through the barn, which was small and tidy enough, but in need of fresh lumber and a bulldozer to grade the floor even. The barn itself was about thirty-six by thirty-six, with an overhead door facing the drive, and two man doors on either side at the rear. A dirt aisle ran down the middle, with two open pens on either side. The cow and the horse occupied two of the four pens. The heifer shifted quietly as we passed by. The mare, Sunny, stood with her head down, dozing peacefully. The hay I had given earlier hadn't been eaten, although she had drunk half of her water. I paused for a moment, noting the shape of her swollen belly.

"The odd thing is the horse?" one of the young patrolman asked.

"No," I replied. "But if she isn't eating, she may be close to delivering the foal." I slid the door open and stepped into the pen. There was something very good about the thought that a new life might come out of this tragedy. I checked her teats, which were swollen, but not milky. "Another day or two, perhaps. But it would be as well to move her quickly as possible."

"*We're* ready to move," Provost said pointedly. "Now what did you want to show me, doc?"

I gave Sunny a pat on the neck and came out of the stall. "The chickens are in an isolation building to the rear of the barn. You see that fire door?" A steel door was set in the middle of the back wall. A Level One Biohazard sign warned intruders off. "The door leads to an antechamber." I walked to the door and opened it. "And the necessary gear to enter is right here." I looked over my shoulder. Joe was behind me, but the assorted constabulary was not. "There's no danger," I said impatiently. "This is for the chickens' sake, not ours."

Provost hesitated, then motioned his confederates ahead. He peered over my shoulder. "How do you know?"

I nodded at the gear hanging from a peg on the wall. "Because this is just a clean coverall and a gauze mask. There are paper booties to slip over your shoes. It's so you don't bring contaminants in, not to keep containments from escaping out. There are three tiers of wire cages inside. Probably twenty-four chickens—I didn't count." I closed the door behind me and stepped back into the barn. "It's what is behind the isolation shed that piqued my interest."

Provost shifted uneasily. "There's something behind it?"

"A larger shed." I went through the man door on the east side and turned right. "The isolation shed butts flat up against the barn and runs its entire width, as you see." I began to pace off the length of the isolation shed. The others followed me like imprinted ducklings. "But the interior depth is about twenty feet. The exterior width . . ." I paused at the end. The rear of the shed faced a welter of rusted automobile parts, an exhausted washer, and a lumpy pile of smooth wire.

". . . Is more than forty feet," Provost said, who had been pacing along behind me.

"Exactly."

We all turned and surveyed the shed. It was a steel building, about twenty feet high with a metal roof. Ventilation soffits were placed at regular intervals under the eaves. There was one door, a fire door that faced the pile of junk in the brush. "What do you notice about the soffits?" I asked instructively.

"They're made of a fine mesh," Joe said. "Soffits are usually made of aluminum slats. And there's a lot of them for a building that size." He shrugged modestly at my approving look. "I work construction in the summers."

"Precisely. And what may that mean?"

"Well, you'd want that much ventilation if you had a problem with condensation," Joe said. Enlightenment dawned. "Jeez, doc. He has animals in there?"

"Excellent deductive reasoning, Joe. And yes, I believe there's an animal in there."

"Hang on a minute," Provost said. "What kind of animals? Why would he lock them up?"

"How should I know?" I asked irritably. "We have to go in to discover that." I stepped carefully around the snow mat in front of the fire door and rattled the handle. "There is a door from the inside, but it's locked as well." I stepped back and gestured at the patrolmen. "Open it."

"Open it?" Provost repeated.

"If there is an animal in there, it undoubtedly needs to be fed."

Provost hesitated. "But if it's locked up like that . . ."

"For heaven's sake, man! What can you possibly be afraid of?"

"Be reasonable, doc. This guy was into all kinds of weird experiments . . ."

"Research in avian flu is hardly weird."

". . . and god knows what's in there." He eyed the lock. "And this is a bugger of a lock. We'd have to break the door down. What if whatever's in there escapes?"

I pointed to the path beneath our feet. "It snowed this morning. Note the footprints. Somebody has already been in and out this door this morning."

"Those are your footprints."

"They are not," I said indignantly. "Those footprints are quite small. I stepped to the side, the first time I was here, and ⸳ in a few moments ago. They are not my footprints. For all ⸳ ⸳ y, they may be the footprints of the murderer."

"⸳ ⸳ y with size-seven feet," Joe said, peering over my ⸳ ⸳ Or a woman."

Provost rubbed his chin. "Take a picture, Frank."

The older patrolman had been carrying the digital camera. He took a picture. Then he measured the footprints and wrote the results down in the ubiquitous steno pad.

"Now get the door open," I said.

Provost's scowl was impressive. "Are you sure about this? We get a lot of memos from the Feds about terrorist crap and that."

"Quite sure." I looked up at the eaves. The mesh in the soffits alone was enough to convince me that nothing wildly contagious lurked there. Coughlin may have been depressed, but he was not a fool. "You must have a battering ram of some sort, Provost."

"Not so's you notice," Provost admitted.

"We could ram it with the cruiser," Frank the camera cop suggested.

"I'd sooner ram you with the cruiser," Provost said with a look of disgust. "Jesus. Ram the door with the cruiser."

"What about the keys?" Joe said.

"The keys?" I said.

"In Dr. Coughlin's pickup truck? Wouldn't he have a key to this on his key ring?"

He did.

There was an animal inside. And she was dying.

Provost was first inside. "Oh, hell," he said. "I hate these cases. I hate them."

"And what kind of case would that be?" I snapped.

The mare was in a wire-enclosed pen. She was in the last stages of starvation. Every rib was visible. The bones of hip and stifle protruded like doorknobs. Her belly and legs were swollen through ventral edema. She lifted her head a trifle as we came in, and dropped it down again, indifferent to all but her own internal voices.

"Abuse cases, that's what," Provost snapped back. "Where you going, Frank?"

"Outside," the unfortunate man muttered. His face was green. "Just give me a minute, okay?"

"This isn't an abuse case," I said as I approached the stall. "Or rather, not a typical abuse case." I glanced around. Both patrolmen had gone. "Tell Frank to close the door behind him."

"What is it, then?" Provost demanded.

I went into the stall. "Curious," I said.

"What the hell are you on about? Curious!" Both Provost and Joe were at my side. Madeline says that often the first human response to tragedy is to walk away. I believe that one may take the measure of a man this way.

"Coughlin had spent money here, and nowhere else." I indicated the automatic waterer, the rubber mats on the concrete floor. I squatted down. The bedding wasn't fresh, but there was little manure and less urine. Her digestive system was close to shutting down.

Joe squatted next to me. "Is there anything I can do, sir?"

"My bag, please. It's in the rear of the Bronco."

"Right." He left without further comment.

Provost stroked the poor beast's neck. "You say it isn't abuse."

"She's a test subject," I said shortly. "You see the IV apparatus there?" A rack with saline bags was fixed to the stall wall. "And the hypodermic needles and collection vials on the shelf near the door?"

"God," Provost said. "It's enough to make you join those folks that picket the animal labs."

"She's on a morphine solution, at least. Or was until this morning. She's been disconnected, and now, I'm afraid, she is suffering. Ah. There you are my boy. Thank you." Joe returned as silently as he had left. He carried my aluminum case into the stall and set it down. "We'll take her vital signs first," I said. "And draw at least forty ccs of blood. I'll handle it after that. Make it quick as you can, my boy."

"You think you can save her?" Provost asked. "McKenzie, something funny's going on here."

I didn't feel like responding to this, so I didn't. Joe was very quick. He took her temperature, her respiration, and noted the capillary refill time. He peered into her eyes and her mouth, checked the rectum, and drew the necessary blood samples. Then he sighed, quietly. "Shall we get her out of the stall first, sir?"

I shook my head. "Let them tear the damn place down if they have to get her out."

"Okay by me."

"What's going on?" Provost demanded.

"We're doing what we can to ease her," I said shortly. I turned to Joe. "I need twenty ccs of morphine sulfate." He prepared the syringe. I took it.

"They put me on morphine once," Provost said. "Busted a couple of ribs. Don't remember much about it, but I can tell you, I didn't feel a thing. She'll feel a little better after the shot, won't she?"

"You might want to stand outside," I said.

"Oh. Sure." He took up a post by the open door. "Let me know if I can give you a hand."

It's never easy, even when the need is as clear as a chime at twilight. I always put my hand over their eyes. I'm not sure why. Joe stood at her near side, his hand on her halter.

I injected her in the left carotid. She sagged to her knees, sighed deeply, and fell. The newer drugs are fast. And she was so weak.

"Hey," Provost said.

Joe smoothed her eyes closed. I placed the blood samples in my case and picked it up.

"You put her down!" Madeline would have been able to sort out the emotions in his voice. I was not.

"We put her down," Joe agreed. The two of us walked to the door.

"Goddammit." Provost trudged after us. "She was evidence."

"Possibly," I admitted. I turned to face him. "Provost? You're going to have to find Coughlin's laptop. And while you're at it, you might notify the FBI."

Fourteen

❧❧

THE episode with the mare upset me, I admit. I wanted to see my wife. At four o'clock, I found her standing in the middle of the vegetable aisle at Wegman's in front of the peppers.

She greeted me with sigh of relief. "Austin, I've been so worried about you!"

Neither of us is prone to public displays of affection, so I merely said, "Are you planning on purchasing the peppers?"

She picked up a scarlet pepper and held it in her hand. "They're just beautiful, aren't they? I was just thinking how those greens and yellows and reds would look piled up in the blue bowl in the kitchen." She put the pepper back in its place and gazed at me searchingly. "So, poor old Jerry Coughlin's dead?"

"Yes. Provost believes it to be a suicide. It is not. It is murder."

"Oh, Austin. You're certain?"

"I am. This person has to be stopped, Madeline."

"You're right. What are you going to . . . ouch!"

The "ouch" was due to Lila Gernsback, who had snuck up on the two of us and given Madeline a friendly pinch on the arm. At least, I surmised the intent was friendly; Madeline looked momentarily as if she wanted to hit Lila over the head with a milk bottle.

"How're you, Lila?" she said, rubbing her arm.

"You remember Phillip Sullivan?" she said abruptly. Lila wasted little time on social niceties. And she was excited. Her cheeks were pinker than usual, and her eyes were sparkling.

"Of course we do," Madeline said a little impatiently. "What about him?"

"He's back."

"He's back?" Madeline cast me a look of dismay. "He doesn't want to buy Hugo, does he?"

Lila nodded vigorously. "He sure does. I told him Ally was going to ride Hugo at Earlsdown, and he was fine with that, but Madeline, he's going to buy him for three hundred thousand dollars!"

And insure him for five hundred, I thought cynically.

"Well, my goodness," Madeline said feebly.

"And I knew it had to be something serious to make him take off so fast. I mean, I know men, Maddy. And he was definitely falling for me. And sure enough, his grandmother died."

I've had a couple of students with multiple grandmothers that keeled over at the drop of a term paper deadline. But I said I was sorry to hear it, and so did Madeline.

"He was very close to her," Lila said, earnestly. "It upset him terribly."

"I can imagine," Madeline said. "But his grandmother died this morning and he's back already?"

"Yes." Lila sighed happily. "The funeral was this morning. In Syracuse."

This was all quite strange. I filed it for further reflection.

Madeline took it all in stride. "I see you have a nice rolled roast of pork in your basket, Lila," she commented. "You do that with a marmalade glaze, don't you? It's delicious. And I see two nice yams. He's coming over? And you're giving him your Jamaican dinner?"

"Yes. He's coming over tonight, as a matter of fact."

"That's a terrific meal," Madeline said sincerely.

"Do you think he'll like it?" she asked worriedly. "Should I try something different?"

"When you made it for Austin and me, we both loved it. I think it's the perfect choice. As a matter of fact, we'd love to have it again, any old time."

My sagacious wife! Sullivan could provide vital clues to our investigation—and here she was, providing a natural, unsuspicious way of accomplishing just that.

"Oh." Lila looked blank. She doesn't pick up social cues at

all well. A dinner invitation was not forthcoming. But Madeline persevered.

"And have you thought about dessert?"

Lila looked in her basket, as if expecting the dessert to show up unannounced, like in-laws on a Sunday afternoon. "Mrs. Smith's Pecan Pie?" she asked. "There's a special on it here."

"Oh, you don't want to give him a store-bought pie. I would love to make you a pecan pie for this evening," said my shameless wife. Admirable woman!

It took Lila a long second. "You want to come to dinner with Phillip and me?"

"Aren't you the nicest thing!" The sheer nerve it had taken Madeline to demand to be invited to a private dinner party made her sound a little too enthusiastic; Lila cocked her head with a puzzled look. Then she smiled, darted a highly salacious look at me, and said, "You're *sure*," with a wheelbarrowload of meaning. "I mean, you don't mind about Austin? I don't want you upset at dinner when he flirts with me."

"I don't worry at all about Austin," Madeline said, which was the perfect truth, since she well knew that Lila scared me to death. "What time would you like us to be there? And can I bring anything else besides the pie?"

So we settled on eight o'clock, which would give Madeline enough time to bake the pie and pull something together for Allegra's dinner, as well, since Lila became reckless and invited Joe as well.

We returned to the farm, and after I had helped Madeline unload the groceries, I sat at the dining table with the full weight of the day suddenly on my shoulders.

Madeline took one look, made me a cup of hot tea, and then went on with preparing Allegra's dinner. She was mixing meatloaf when Joe came in, carrying the foal monitor. Juno was with him. Lincoln padded in after them, and came and bumped his head under my hand.

Madeline patted Lincoln, hugged Joe, put a bowl of water down for Juno, and put the meatloaf in the oven to bake. Juno curled up on the floor and put her nose on her paws.

"This is Juno," Joe said.

"Hello, Juno." Madeline set a bowl of kibble down for her. She ignored that, too.

I got up and attached the foal monitor to the barn intercom. I looked a question at Joe.

"The mare's fine. But she sure looks like she's ready to foal any minute. You might want to come and take a look at her, sir."

"Is she fairly comfortable? No stress from the ride here?"

"She seems to be okay."

The rustle of the mare's hooves in the straw of her stall came over the intercom. She coughed once, then sighed.

"We'll be able to hear her when labor begins," I said.

"Can I get you something, Joe?" Madeline asked. "The two of you had quite an afternoon."

"Just coffee for me, Mrs. McKenzie. But only if it's made." Joe turned to me and asked, "Can I get you a Scotch, doc?"

Well, here was a small victory amid the gloom of the day. So he'd finally dropped "doctor" and "sir." "Thank you," I said, "I'd appreciate it."

Joe went into the living room to the liquor cabinet. I heard the thump of Miss Odie's paws coming down the stairs and Joe's voice greeting her. Juno raised her head, looked briefly in the cat's direction, and went right back down again. This was one depressed dog. Miss Odie sauntered into the kitchen, stopped dead at the sight of the intruder, snarled, and jumped up to settle on top of the woodstove.

Joe handed me the Scotch and sat down at the table. Madeline had made oatmeal raisin cookies, and he began to eat them absentmindedly.

"It is now," I said, "a matter of some urgency. We need to get at the bottom of this affair, and soon. Phillip Sullivan has returned and has made a ridiculously high offer for Hugo."

Joe ran his fingers through his hair, which was short, as is the fashion these days. "I don't quite understand how this scam works, doc. If Sullivan pays Mrs. Gernsback for the horse, how can he make any money when he kills it? Oh, wait. He must insure it for more than the purchase price."

"Precisely," I said. "One would up the value of the horse by say, a third. It's easy to make a case to the insurer that the

horse has increased in value, particularly if there is an inter-
vening show or two before the animal's demise. Hence Sullivan's willingness to let Allegra take Hugo to Earlsdown."

Joe hunched forward, his face thoughtful. "So let's say
Grazley, McClellan, and Sullivan all agree to buy horses for
an inflated price, insure them for an even more inflated price,
and then the vet knocks them off so that it seems to be either
an accident or of natural causes."

"And Coughlin," I said wearily. "I'm certain that he was involved as well."

"But no one's onto them. Except us, I mean. And we
haven't told anyone. What does this have to do with the
shootings?"

"And today's debacle. Let's not forget that. I don't know
yet. That, young man, remains to be seen."

We remained in silence for some time.

A good slug of Scotch is quite a reviver. The horror of the
day's events receded and my curiosity revived along with my
spirit. I settled my spectacles on my nose and reached down to
open my carryall. I pulled out the rack of sample tubes I had
taken from Coughlin's lab.

"You collected those this afternoon, sweetie?" Madeline
asked. She came and rested her hands on my shoulders.

"Yes. These"—I tapped four of the tubes with my
forefinger—"are equine. I need to get them to Victor. And
those"—I tapped the two remaining—"are avian. I'm not certain what to do with those."

"They're from Coughlin's place?"

"Yes, I suppose Victor might have an idea about those, as
well. I have no idea for whom Coughlin was doing his research."

"There wasn't anything in his patient files?"

"His computer's gone," Joe said. "Our best guess is that the
records were on it."

"Oh, my." Madeline went back into the kitchen proper and
called over her shoulder, "Did that Simon Provost have any
idea where it'd got to?"

I snorted. "Ha! I had to lead the man around by the nose
before he began to accept that this was murder. He hasn't a
clue about the laptop. I had some doubts about his capability

as an investigator before the debacle this afternoon. I have significant doubts, now."

"He did get a forensic team in the mare's room, Mrs. McKenzie," Joe said.

"Call me Madeline, Joe, if you would. And you say there's a forensics team there now? Getting fingerprints and whatever?"

Joe grinned. "Actually, the doc here convinced Provost to call in the Feds."

"The FBI?" Madeline almost dropped the salad bowl. "Why, for heaven's sake?"

I picked up one of the tubes. It was labeled with the date and nothing else. "The mare had equine infectious anemia. I'd stake my reputation on it."

"Although we won't know for sure until we get the Coggins done," Joe added.

"The ESL test is faster," I said, "Victor can give me a definitive answer in a few hours. That's why I'd like to get this sample to him as quickly as possible. Coughlin kept this mare alive as a reservoir for the virus, I'm sure of it."

Which was insane. McClellan had said FieldChek had a product that allowed at point testing for EIA. But the development of such a product could have just as easily been done through the use of a stored virus. There was no need at all to involve a live animal. And, unless the man was involved in some kind of goofball government research, which, I admit, was possible, what he did was a violation of at least two federal laws, not to mention the cruelty of it. Every veterinary practice knows that EIA's regulated by the Department of Agriculture. Which, of course, was why the FBI had to be in the middle of things, now. I was about to suggest that I run the test tube over to Victor at Cornell when a rush of cool air came through the kitchen and Allegra walked in. She was carrying the Lab puppy. "There's a pregnant mare in the barn!" Ally said excitedly. "And a little horned heifer. Are they new patients?"

"Dr. Coughlin was murdered today," Joe said bluntly. "The animals belong to him."

"Murdered! You're kidding." Allegra stared at us for a minute. Then she set the puppy in its box by the stove.

"Watch out for Juno," Joe said sharply. He lunged forward and grabbed Juno's collar. "She's an Akita, in case you hadn't noticed. Don't you know anything about Akitas?"

Akitas have a black mask, and a coat the color of fresh, pale butter. They can also be a little bitey. But Juno was too depressed to eat, much less defend her territory from another dog.

Ally snapped back. "She looks pretty quiet to me."

"She was Coughlin's dog. She's not quiet, she's depressed." Ally rolled her eyes.

Then Juno noticed the puppy. She wiggled under Joe's restraint. Then she growled. "Told you," Joe said. "Get the puppy out of here and let me handle it."

The puppy sat up in her box, her little cast stretched out at an awkward angle. She gazed up at Allegra with an anxious smile and a lot of panting. Juno pulled forward against Joe's hand on her collar, sniffing like mad in the puppy's direction, her tail wagging hard. Lincoln watched the two of them, his tail set mid-low, his ears at attention.

"You can let Juno go, I think," I said, after a moment of observation. "Linc will handle it." I got up, came over, and put my arm around my wife.

Linc handled it. Joe let Juno loose. Juno leaped to the puppy's box in one bound. Linc was faster. He straddled the puppy like some doggy Colossus and barked once. Juno barked back. Linc curled his lips over his eyeteeth, to show he really meant it. Juno flattened herself. Then she jumped up, licked Linc's muzzle to show she was going to be beta dog, and there was a confusion of sniffing and tail wagging and a few yips in the bargain. After it was all over, Juno curled in the box with the puppy looking as contented as a dog should look. Linc came and nudged my knee, then went back to where Juno and the puppy lay cuddled together. He lay a few feet away from them, paws, out, head high, looking like the king of the universe.

While Jorrocks says there's nothing for the inside of a man like the outside of a horse, I would have to say that that applies to dogs, as well. Even the kitchen seemed warmer.

* * *

ALLEGRA volunteered to take the vials of sera to Victor, so the last hope I had of begging off Lila's dinner party was gone. "You're coming," Madeline said, "and that's flat. It's bad enough that I strong-armed her into an invitation. It'd be even worse if you didn't show up at the last minute."

"Very well, my dear. But you are far better than I at interrogation techniques. We established that this afternoon."

"Then you just sit there and keep quiet."

And so the three of us set off for Lila's pork roast and Jamaican yams. Not to mention Madeline's pecan pie, which Joe held on his lap in the backseat. Lila's twenty acres are not far from us. She has an old, if pleasant barn, and she's meticulous about care of the grounds. The house was set well back from the road, and we bumped over the gravel drive for some moments before we arrived at the house.

Joe leaned forward and peered out the windshield. "You suppose that's Sullivan's?"

A big, fire-engine red Escalade obstructed the path in front of Lila's front door. "It sure isn't hers," Madeline said. "Good lord. What that man must pay for gas."

"What that guy must *earn* to make enough to pay for the gas." Joe hitched himself out of the passenger seat, then came over to Madeline's side of the Prius to help her out.

Lila opened the door before Madeline pushed the bell. Joe stepped back a bit. He hadn't seen Lila in full evening garb before. She was dressed Lila-style, which meant a bright red T-shirt that scooped down to Australia and extremely snug jeans.

"Come in, come in," she caroled and we followed her through the hall to her living room.

Some horse people make sure to leave every single bit of horse-related gear in the barn. Others stow it in every possible space in the house. Lila was the stow-it-anywhere kind. She had her ribbons and trophies in a large trophy case in the living room. A pile of halters lay in a basket by the fireplace. Copies of *Equus, The Chronicle of the Horse,* and *Eventing* sat in a heap on the coffee table. The place smelled like good used leather and pork roast.

Sullivan sat on the sofa, as big and red as his Escalade.

Same red hair, red face, and red plaid pants. And he wore white patent leather loafers on his feet, which were oddly small for a man his size. Lila introduced Joe, and reminded Sullivan that we had met two nights ago.

"Call me Phil," Sullivan said. "Take a pew." So we sat down. He lumbered on over to the breakfront where Lila keeps her liquor. "What's your poison, folks?"

Madeline requested a glass of chardonnay, Joe a beer, and I a Scotch, which meant that Lila had to run into the kitchen to retrieve the wine and beer from the refrigerator. Sullivan poured himself a rum and Coke and stirred it with his finger.

"You're from New York City?" Madeline asked. "Are you here in Summersville for long?"

Phil had very small blue eyes. He squeezed them shut as if thinking hard. Then he opened them suddenly. "Long as it takes."

"I know you and Lila met over horses. Is it something you just got into?"

He blinked. "Pardon?"

"Is your interest in horses recent?" Joe asked.

"Good tax shelter." His eyes flickered over Joe. "But you people should know about that."

Uh-oh. My scalp prickled. I glanced over at Madeline. But all she said, "Well, it's a fine sport. And Lila's one of the best people I know to introduce you to it."

Lila hurried back in with the wine and the beer. She also brought a bowl of mixed nuts and set it on the table. Sullivan leaned over and picked out all of the hazelnuts. He chewed them with his mouth agape. Then he picked out all of the cashews. Then the Brazil nuts. Then he offered the remaining peanuts around to us.

"Dinner's ready in two minutes," Lila said. She headed back on to the kitchen.

"We didn't get much of a chance to say 'hello' to you last night," Madeline said chattily. "I know you were out of town today. You haven't had much of a chance to see Summersville. Do you prefer Syracuse?"

Excellent woman, my wife! What a clever way to lead into queries about his activities!

"Hah? Never been in Syracuse in my life."

"Really," Madeline purred. "Lila said you were in Syracuse this morning."

"Oh, that. Huh. I spent the morning looking at another horse. Didn't care to mention it to Lila. Thinks I'm going to buy Hugo. But I thought I'd better check around a bit."

"Oh?"

"Yeah. In a way, one horse is as good as another, in my book. But you never know. Went to Greenacres stables for a couple of hours. You know it, doc?"

"Yes," I said, rather glumly, since all this was verifiable.

"Then I stopped by some pile of garbage. Longworth's, that's it. Guy at Greenacres said they had a likely prospect, but the horse looked like a pile of junk to me."

"Did it," I said coldly. "I know the horse. It's quite a good eventer."

"And then I had the best burger I've ever had in my life. Place called the Mongrovian Embassy. You ought to try it."

"It's Monrovian, not Mongrovian," I said testily. "And we were there ourselves. I'm surprised we didn't see you. The place isn't that big."

"Yeah?" He opened his piggy eyes wide. "I was there at eleven. I would of seen you, place was half empty. With these popular places, see, it's good to get there early. You don't have to wait that way."

I was morose. It looked as if we had spent the morning just missing Sullivan. And Colleen would undoubtedly remember a person this objectionable. It looked as if Sullivan was in the clear for Coughlin's murder.

"Are you thinking about moving to Summersville?" Madeline asked. She was as downcast as I.

He said he might be. He had a million or two that he thought he might spend on a country place. The way things were going in the city, it was time to have an escape plan.

"I'd have a hard time living with all that concrete," Madeline admitted. "My husband and I like to visit there, though."

"Concrete's okay," he said, dead serious. "It's the towel heads and the jigaboos that're taking over the streets that I can't stand." He shook his head. "Only one real solution to that." He brought his arms up as if he were firing a rifle. *"Blam!"*

We went into dinner.

It got worse.

Problems with Iraq? Nuke 'em. Arabs and Jews can't get along? Nuke 'em. Not to mention teacher unions, welfare mothers, abortionists—if you couldn't slap them up the side of the head to see reason, well, just . . . *blam!*

As for Jerry Coughlin, never heard of him, but Lila'd told him the guy'd been through a divorce, and you could bet the broadie had taken the poor slob to the cleaners. Women were behind half the male suicides in this great country of ours.

I left the brunt of the conversation to Madeline. Aside from getting a little red around the ears with Phillip's disparaging ethnic references, Joe spent most of the dinner staring at Sullivan's feet. His grandmother did a good job of raising that boy. I tuned out, since I have learned long since, there's not much to be done about people like Phillip Sullivan.

Just after the salad and before the pork roast, I rose from the table to give Lila and Madeline a hand in the kitchen. It was either that, or wrap a lamp cord around Sullivan's throat.

Lila hadn't said a word all through the first course, although she drank more wine than I'd ever seen her drink before. She hasn't the head for it. I collected the salad bowls. Madeline took the plates. We carried them straight to the sink.

"I like what you put in this salad, Lila." Madeline smiled, rinsed the salad plates under the tap, and started putting them in the dishwasher. I leaned against the refrigerator and wondered how the pregnant mare was doing. "And I keep forgetting how much I like fresh peas in greens. That was a nice touch!" Madeline was positively chirping.

"Oh, don't be so gosh-darned social, Maddy." Lila folded her arms, leaned back against the kitchen counter, and scowled. "I can't stand it when you get that polite thing going. I know you want to smack him as silly as I do."

Madeline kept on rinsing.

"He wasn't like that before," she burst out.

There's a time for the "social thing" and a time for truth. Madeline knows the difference. "You mean such a creep?"

Lila ran her hands through her hair. "He's awful."

"It's the kind of awful that's hard to mistake for anything else, that's for sure," Madeline said frankly, "When he was here before, what'd you two talk about, anyway?"

"Well, we talked about horses, and he talked about some of his cases—I guess he's really good at what he does, Maddy. He's here to handle the McClellan divorce, as a matter of fact."

"Is that so?" I said.

"I have to say I can't blame the poor woman," Madeline said.

"Oh, it's not her divorcing him, it's him divorcing her." Lila veered back to the more important topic, which was, of course, Lila. "Anyhow, with Sullivan, what with talking about one thing and another, things got kind of well, you know." She made a whirly gesture with one hand, which accounted, I supposed, for the time they weren't talking, (and what they *were* up to, I sincerely did not wish to know) "but I never had him around other people before. God. I'm really sorry about this."

"What kind of lawyering *does* he do?"

"He says he's with a big firm that does everything from patents to wills. He's the divorce partner. His clients are very famous. I mean, I told him tonight was just a nice, social evening with some good friends, and he was so happy about that, Maddy. He was really looking forward to meeting my friends. He says he doesn't have much of a social life at all."

"That's hard to believe."

They looked at each other. And they both got the giggles. Lila laughed until the mascara ran down her face, and then she shrieked, "and I went out and bought this new top!" and Madeline laughed so hard she couldn't stand up straight.

Women.

Finally, Lila wiped her eyes with a paper napkin. "Oh, god. What am I going to do? He left his keys and his wallet and his suitcase right in my front hall, Mad. He's planning on spending the night."

"Throw up," I said.

"Huh?"

Madeline nodded vigorously. "Austin's right. Works a treat.

About halfway through this nice pork roast, put your napkin over your mouth, roll your eyes a little bit, and excuse yourself from the table. I'll go after you and then I'll come back and say that it must have been something you ate and that I've made you go lie down."

"What if he wants to stick around and make sure I'm okay?"

"Honey, that kind of guy's out the door at the first sign of inconvenience to himself."

"Really?" She looked sad. "I'm a lousy judge of men, Maddy."

"That is *so* true, darlin'."

"And what about his offer for Hugo?" She shook her head. "What am I thinking of? I don't want that bozo anywhere near my horse."

As I said, Lila's a true horse person. No amount of money would tempt her to sell Hugo to a man like Sullivan.

Lila put the pork roast on a platter, with the marmalade around the sides. The outside was crisp and it sat on a bed of green beans. It made me quite hungry to look at it. I picked the platter up to take it into the dining room. Madeline carried the Jamaican yams. Lila clutched at her.

"You're sure barfing will get him out of here?"

"Count on it."

"He'll think I'm a terrible cook!"

"You're a wonderful cook"—which was true—"but it'll get him out of your hair without a big hassle. Just wait until I've had seconds though, okay? I've been dyin' for that meal all afternoon."

When we came back to the table, Joe had disappeared somewhere. He'd undoubtedly decided to walk home rather than eat the rest of the meal with Phillip Sullivan. But he returned just as we'd finished the pork roast—and just as Lila threw her napkin over her face and began to heave like a bellows.

"You all right, sweetie?" Madeline said, right on cue.

"I feel *sick!*" Lila shrieked. Sullivan was at Lila's right, of course. She swayed dramatically toward him. Apparently, he couldn't decide whether to keep his beady little eyes fixed on her heaving bosom or help her out of the chair. As it was, he edged away from her toppling figure.

Madeline took a last bite of pork roast before she came halfway out of *her* chair. "You think you're going to throw up, sweetie?" (It would have come out a lot more clearly if she'd swallowed that mouthful first.) Lila screamed, *"Yes! Yes! Yes!"* in a very convincing way.

That was the determining factor for Sullivan. He jumped out of his chair and backed up against the wall. Joe, on the other hand, went straight to Lila and put his arm around her shoulders in concern.

Madeline thrust him firmly aside. "Thank you, Joe. If I get Lila right up to bed, I'm sure she'll be right as a cricket in the morning." She pulled Lila's arm over her shoulder.

"You sure you're feeling nauseated, Mrs. Gernsback?" He looked into Lila's face, eyes narrowed. "Honestly, your color looks okay. Do you have any other symptoms?"

Madeline gave Joe a meaningful nudge. He drew back a little. Then she flicked her eyes to Sullivan and back to Lila. The penny finally dropped, the young idiot. He bit his lip (to keep from laughing, I presume) and grabbed Lila's other shoulder. "I think you're right about getting her to lie down, Maddy. Your room's upstairs, Mrs. Gernsback? I'll give you a hand."

They dragged Lila to the entryway, where Madeline paused and said, "We'll be back in just a minute, Phil. You go right ahead and finish that pork."

He looked at his plate uneasily. "Could *be* the pork, couldn't it? Yeah, I guess I'd better go." He paused. "You think maybe I should stop by the emergency room. Maybe get my stomach looked at?"

"Oh, no. Why, Joe and I and Austin are just fine and we ate just what Lila ate. No, no, this is the flu. There's a nasty bug going around."

"Yeah? I doubt it." His tone was disgusted. "I want a plastic baggie. I'm going to take some of the pork with me, get it tested. Just in case."

"In case of what?" Joe asked.

"Well, y'know. The meat could be bad." His beady little eyes swept around Lila's dining room. She'd used her Limoges china and her Baccarat crystal for the meal, and her second husband had left her a genuine Stubbs (a small one) that hung over the sideboard. It was clear what Sullivan was think-ing. "If the rest of us get sick, too, we need evidence. For the doctors," he added ponderously. "Not that I'd think about su-ing. But you can't be too careful these days."

Lila growled like a dog. Madeline grabbed her head and forced it back onto her shoulder. Then she patted her back. Hard. "You feeling a little worse, honey?"

Sullivan's mean little eyes drifted over the triple crown moldings. "The homeowners policy would cover it, though. How much coverage you got, Lila?"

The next growl was more of a snarl, I suppose. It was a good thing her head was buried in Madeline's neck.

"Next election," Joe said to the ceiling, "I'm voting for tort reform."

"Pinko," Sullivan said without surprise. "You New York types are all pinkos."

"I'm taking her upstairs now, Phil," Madeline caroled. "You just sit there and have another piece of that roast."

"No, thank you," he said, quite rudely.

"Well, you'll stay for a little bit of Lila's pecan pie, won't you? I'll be right back down for a bowl for Lila to spit up into, and I can cut you a nice, big piece."

By the time the three of them gained the upstairs, old Smilin' Phil had thrown his gear in the back of his Escalade. By the time they crept back downstairs, he was roaring down the drive in a spit of gravel. He took the pork roast with him.

Lila sat down in the middle of the ruins of her dinner party and held her head in her hands. Madeline sat down next to her. Joe shifted from one foot to the other. I sipped at another Scotch.

Madeline coaxed Lila's head up. "Shall I fix you some of that pie, sweetie? Dessert always makes *me* feel better."

She shook her head.

"You want some help with those dishes?"

"No."

"You," I interjected, "would like us to go home."

She looked at me in relief. "Yes, I do, Austin. Do you mind?"

"Not at all."

"Take the pie with you."

"Are you sure?" Madeline's pecan pie recipe comes from her mother's side of the family. It is stupendous.

"*Yes!* And good-bye, Maddy."

"Good night, sweetie."

So we were back in the Prius headed home a little earlier than I'd anticipated.

"Well, that was a dead loss," Madeline said, "except for the pie. And for crossing that deadbeat off the suspect list."

I stopped at the end of Perry City Road and waited for the traffic to clear so I could turn back onto Route 96.

"Not quite a dead loss." Joe was in the backseat. He reached down and hauled up the kind of briefcase that holds a laptop computer. He held it under the dashboard so I could see the initials embossed on the top:

GAC, DVM

"What we have here," Joe said in a very satisfied way, "is Gerald Arthur Coughlin's computer."

Fifteen

❧❧❧

MADELINE set a piece of pecan pie in front of me. A very small piece.

"It was Sullivan's feet," Joe explained with becoming modesty. "Size seven. Same size as the footprints in front of the shed."

My wife set quite a large piece in front of him.

"You can tell people's shoe size by just looking at them?" Allegra demanded. She refused the pie with a regretful look.

"I worked one summer as a shoe salesman."

All four of us were seated at the dining-room table. The purloined laptop sat in the middle. Madeline had moved a vase of daffodils to accommodate it.

Madeline eyed the laptop with a certain amount of trepidation. "Do you think we should call the police, Austin?"

"My dear, we *are* the police. Or rather, I am."

For the first time in twenty years, I had truly astonished my wife. Victor had not received the news of my deputization half so well. In point of fact, he had been quite rude about it.

Madeline closed her mouth and demanded to know what I was talking about.

"It's true, Maddy," Joe said. For some reason, the whole idea seemed to tickle him. He was grinning like a chimpanzee. "Lieutenant Provost deputized him this afternoon."

"My badge is in the mail," I affirmed.

"Your badge! Oh, my goodness." Madeline blinked. "Austin, you're not going to get a gun, too."

"I hadn't thought of that," I said, much struck.

"You can stop thinking about it right this minute." Madeline has a full-lipped, beautifully shaped mouth. At the moment, it was set like a steel trap. "If anybody has a gun," she went on after a moment, "it should be me."

"That's very true," I said to the children. "She's a far better shot than I."

"Are we going to need to shoot anybody?" Allegra said doubtfully.

"Certainly not," Madeline said. "Well, Austin. I'm dyin' to know what's in that computer of poor Jerry Coughlin's."

So I opened it up and logged on.

I had been fearful that the files would be password encoded; they were not. I opened the first that came to hand: ENZYMES.

I began to read, only to be interrupted by Madeline's warm hand on my cheek. I gave it a kiss, rather reflexively, I must admit. "In a moment, my dear."

"It's been more than a moment, sweetie. More like an hour and a half."

"Eh?" I looked up, considerably startled. I checked the clock in the kitchen. It was almost midnight. Joe and Allegra were gone. "Goodness." I looked down at the file that had absorbed me. "You know, my dear, Coughlin was engaged in some extremely useful work. It's quite amazing, really."

"Does it have anything to do with his murder?"

I frowned. "I don't know at this juncture. It's a damn shame, his murder."

"Well, yes. Of course it was."

"In a general way of course, all murders are dreadful. That's not quite what I meant. I hope someone else can pick up this research, that's all. It's quite interesting. It will be a genuine boon to the scientific community if it works."

Joe clattered in the kitchen door, startling us both. I was surprised to see that he was not only fully dressed, he was wearing Carhartt coveralls over the white shirt and tie he'd donned to go to dinner. "She's still leaking colostrum," he said. He took a breath. "And she's dilated a little more. I think you'd better come out to the barn, doc."

"The mare's foaling," Madeline said. "That's why I came to get you."

Now fully disengaged from Coughlin's fascinating foray into enzyme-linked immunoabsorbant assays, I saw that

Madeline's cheeks were pink with excitement. A rhythmic grunting came over the foal monitor. Joe glanced at it and chewed his upper lip. "Is Allegra with her?"

"Yes, sir."

"Then go on back to the barn. Make sure the infrared lamp is on. The foal will need the warmth. And then get my tackle from the Bronco."

"Tackle, sir?"

"I'll get it," Madeline said. "It's in case he has to pull the foal out, Joe."

Joe made a face. "I don't think I wanted to know that."

"Madeline knows what to do. Go, both of you. I'll be out directly."

The two of them rushed out the back door. The puppy stirred in her box and whimpered. Juno jumped up and circled the kitchen, head low, tail wagging anxiously. She stopped beneath the foal monitor and listened, her head cocked to one side. Then she went back to the box and grabbed the puppy by the back of the neck.

That wouldn't do. The pup's leg was healing well, but I didn't want Juno dragging her all over the floor in an effort to find sanctuary. Linc, by contrast, was an old hand at this, as was I. He stood in the middle of the kitchen, interested in the goings on, but not alarmed.

I shut Juno in the pantry, over her shrill protests, and pulled my own Carhartt coveralls off the peg by the back door. Then the screen saver on the laptop winked and went dark as it went into sleep mode. I debated but an instant. The habits of a lifetime came into play. The files were of too significant an import to leave unattended. I shut the computer down. Lacking the time to think of any more secure place, I put it in the refrigerator. I then scrubbed my hands and forearms at the sink, followed by a good dousing with Betadine.

The grunting from the foal monitor came at faster intervals now. The sound of a mare in labor is like no other: deep, guttural, pain-filled, and oddly patient. I whistled to Linc and went out to the barn at a jog.

The three of them stood outside the mare's stall, hugging themselves against the evening chill. Andrew and Pony had their ears up. Both looked interested. More interesting to me was how quiet they were. I have observed this equine behavior at many foalings. The most irritable horse will settle until a foaling is over. I believe this is an atavistic response. Horses have no defense against predators except their speed and the ability to kick. A quiet herd decreases the chance of being discovered by a hungry creature.

Human behavior at a foaling is equally ubiquitous, except it is tension, not quiet, that characterizes the responses.

"She's sweating really hard," Allegra whispered as Linc and I went into the stall.

"That sweating is usual, my dear."

Joe had turned the infrared lights on, and they spread a decent warmth. Someone, my guess would be either Allegra, Madeline, or both, had added a good foot of straw to the stall floor. A completely feminine touch, this. The surface of the stall would make no difference to the mare.

The mare was up, her flanks dark with sweat. She rolled an eye at me, but seemed to welcome the dog. I took her pulse and her respiration. Rapid, but that was to be expected.

"This is her first, according to Jerry's file," Joe said behind me.

"Gosh," Allegra said. "She looks scared."

I noted the panicked roll of the eye. "She is." I went to her rear and eyed her cervix. "May I have my gloves, please?" Joe brought them in. I put them on and thrust my right hand into the birth canal. "Good."

"Good?" Joe said. "What d'ya mean, 'good.' Oh! The foal's presenting the right way."

"Correct. Hind end to." I withdrew my hand and stepped back.

"Austin?" Madeline said. "We don't know her name."

"Sunny." I laid my hand on her neck. She sighed.

The contractions stopped.

"Oh, my god," Allegra said.

"That's not unusual." I smoothed my mustache. "Mares are among the very few mammals that can stop contractions under stress. It's a curious anomaly in equidae."

"She can't just stop!" Allegra expostulated.

"She just did," Joe said dryly. "Should we leave her alone?"

"It'd be best, at this juncture. Let her settle down."

We exited the stall, closed the door, and turned out the overhead lights. Sunny rustled a little in the dimness. Then I heard her at the water bucket.

"We'll wait a bit," I said.

No one spoke for a moment. The three of them peered anxiously at Sunny through the wire mesh. I took the opportunity to contemplate aloud on the consequences of the research on Jerry Coughlin's computer. The news was of too much significance to keep to myself.

"FieldChek," I mused, "began with a simple, quite brilliant idea. What if one were able to immediately detect the presence of EIA specific antibodies in a cheap, quick, disposable testing device?"

"You mean a portable Coggins?" Allegra said after a moment.

"Yes. A portable Coggins. A Coggins a veterinarian could carry with him . . ."

". . . or her," Madeline added.

". . . of course. Could carry with him or her." I sighed. The locution was deplorable, but what was one to do? "Could have with him/her/it at a barn call. Rather than waiting weeks for the state-approved testing facility to get the results by mail or fax. And all that tests is whether the horse was infected at the time of the serum draw. It is of no help in determining the health of the horse after that time."

"You could use it at shows, too," Allegra said. "That'd be handy."

"Handy, indeed. Think of its utility at a show. All horses could be tested before entering the grounds. Do you know, there are at least two hundred cases of EIA reported each year? This would help stop the spread of the disease entirely. And it works. Coughlin used it successfully on three horses, Faraway, Hugo, and his own mare. Each successful test was marked with an upward arrow."

Madeline touched me gently. "You're waving your hands, around, sweetie. It's disturbing the mare."

We all peered through the mesh at Sunny. She peered back

at us. I turned the infrared light back on. After a moment, she relaxed under the warmth.

"Gosh!" Allegra whispered. "I think that'd be good thing, Dr. McKenzie. A portable Coggins."

"That's what Coughlin was working on?" Joe asked.

"Not just that. If it were just that, it would be, as McClellan told us at dinner, a handy product that would sell well, at a profit.

"But what if there was at-point testing for pregnancy for farm animals? Even better than that, for human diseases like cholera, flu, and pneumonia? What if physicians were able to carry a small diagnostic tool wherever they went?"

"You're talking millions of dollars," Madeline said.

"Billions of dollars, my dear. *That's* what FieldChek was all about. What's more, I'm certain of the very device Coughlin was going to adapt for its use." The diabetic glucose monitor was still in my pocket. I withdrew it.

"Can I see that?" Allegra took the monitor and examined it. "How do you get the data out of this and into the system? Does this thing have a computer hookup or something?"

"That thing doesn't," Joe said. "My grandmother used one just like this. But if you designed a computer chip that could send data over a wireless modem, you sure could. Or if you adapted it to plug into a telephone, like the cardiac monitors, it wouldn't be a problem at all."

"You realize," I said, "that this puts the case in a whole new perspective."

All three of them looked at me.

"Cui bono," Allegra said. "Who benefits? Is that what you mean?"

"Precisely. The potential here is for a fortune that would rival Mr. Gates's."

"It's hard to imagine," Joe said. "That kind of money, I mean."

"Our murderer seems to have no trouble at all imagining it."

"There she goes," Madeline said in a pleased way. She had been focused, of course, on the pregnant mare.

Sunny's contractions had begun again. This time we remained outside her stall, "giving her some space" as Allegra said, until it became clear that the birth was under way.

The mare's ears twitched. She thrust her head forward, knuckled over, and rolled to one side. I entered the stall and stood quietly at hand.

The hindquarters came first, then the long back legs, folded neatly under the belly, and the slender head and neck, resting out the outstretched front legs.

There has never been a study to verify this, but I believe it to be true: pheromones are released into the air at a birth that makes everyone attending feel drunk with joy. How else to explain the happiness that sweeps over one when a new life emerges? A new being appears as if by magic, and the world has another soul in it. I cleared my throat. Several times.

Sunny delivered a filly, dark with blood and amniotic fluid so that we weren't at first able to discern her color. But as Joe and I cleared the nose and eyes with a soft cloth, I saw a white star on the little thing's forehead, and noted four white socks on her feet. The probability was high that she would be a chestnut, like her mother.

"Come and help us, my dear. And Allegra, too. It'll do the foal good to be handled by man, first thing."

"And woman," someone whispered.

The four of us helped the foal to her feet. There is a school of thought—to which I have never subscribed—that it's best to let the baby struggle to its feet on its own. This has never made much sense to me. They are so small, so confused. And why are we human beings here, if not to help?

Sunny herself was puzzled. She peered around at her hindquarters as if marveling at what she'd done. Then she nickered, that low, chuckling sound that a mare reserves only for her young. The baby wobbled, stalky feet splayed out, and took a few tottery steps toward her dam. The mare met her halfway and began to lick her all over. This is the first of several tests a new mother undergoes and Sunny passed it with flying colors. Madeline and Ally guided the small wet nose to the mare's teats. Sunny's lower lip pulled up a bit as the foal began to nurse, but she soon relaxed.

"Sunny keeps turning around to look at her, like she can't believe the baby's there," Allegra said. "I can't believe it, either."

"Better than the movies," Joe agreed. And indeed, watching

a newborn engage in that most pedestrian of activities—wobbling—is most compelling.

"She hasn't cleansed yet," Allegra said worriedly.

"Passed the afterbirth?" Joe said. "That won't happen for an hour or two. Don't fuss."

"Can we name her, do you think?" Madeline asked. She was incandescent with feeling. "I know she doesn't belong to us, but we can't just call her 'hey, you.'"

The baby fell into the straw with a sudden bump. Sunny nosed her upright, and guided her back to the teat. It was a task Lincoln would have aided. I realized then he wasn't with us.

"Let's call her Sweetie," Allegra said. "Because she is."

I looked down the aisle to the overhead doors. Moonlight streamed beyond. The aisle was empty. Neither Pony nor Andrew was visible; undoubtedly they had gone to sleep. But the dog should be here. I walked away from the group and whistled.

"Sweetie?" Behind me, Joe made a noise like "urk." "The mare's a Trakehner. What about calling her Tracks?"

Allegra's voice was frosty. "It's sort of a tribute to Madeline."

"Thank you, darlin'," Madeline said comfortably. "Sweetie it is." She came up behind me and touched my shoulder. "What is it?"

"Have you seen the dog?"

"Lincoln? Come to think on it, I haven't. That's odd, isn't it?"

I stripped off my gloves and tossed them into the garbage can. "He's probably back at the house. I locked Juno in the pantry to keep her from harassing the puppy. She was barking fit to raise the dead. Her complaints may have raised his interest."

Madeline followed me down the gravel path. Behind us, Joe and Allegra were engaged in another squabble over the filly's name. Ahead, the sky was clear and the moon was at the full, with that clear white light that floods the world. So there was no mistaking Lincoln's body. He lay beside the steps to our back door.

Sixteen

~~~~~~

THIS has been Austin's story, until now. But I have to horn in for just a few minutes, to say what I did the day my dog was attacked. Austin never did find out about it, thank goodness. He wouldn't have approved at all.

First, I have to admit that I've never been so mad in all my life.

Austin saw Lincoln's body before I did. He reacts faster than I do. He always has. I think it's because he can push his feelings aside for a while. You have to be able to do that, when you're a vet. So by the time I got myself moving, Austin was on his knees, running his hands over that tawny head and calling his name. We didn't speak to each other. I had to let him work. I went past him to turn on the porch light, so he could see better, and then I ran back to the barn to get his carryall, where he'd left it by the mare's stall. Joe and Ally were still looking at that beautiful little foal. It was Ally who picked up on the trouble first, but Joe wasn't far behind her. She jumped up and ran straight to me.

"What *is* it, Maddy?"

"Something's happened to Linc. I need. Austin needs." I stopped. Ally put a gentle hand to my face. "The kit?" she said. "Austin needs the carryall?"

I nodded, because I couldn't speak for crying.

"Where are they?" Joe asked.

"House."

Joe grabbed the carryall and ran out of the barn. Ally dug into her jeans pocket and brought out a fistful of tissue. I mopped my face with it. "Just give me a sec. I'll be fine. It was just such a shock." I stopped mopping and pinched my lip as hard as I could. So I stopped the bawling, at least. Funny how pain steadies you. I took a breath. "There. Sorry, child. I think I'm overtired. I'm all right now. I just didn't want Austin to see me like this. We'll go back to the house now."

But as we left the main barn, we saw Joe and Austin running straight to the clinic. Lincoln was in Austin's arms. Ally sprinted ahead of them into the waiting room, switching on lights like some crazy Tinker Bell. I opened the door to the surgery and got out of the way as Austin carried the dog past me. He laid him down on the operating table and adjusted the klieg light over the table.

There was a mat of blood at the base of Lincoln's skull. It colored the white of his ruff like a disgusting eclipse.

"You'll want X-rays," Joe said.

Austin said, "Yes." The klieg lights showed every line in his face. It was past two o'clock in the morning. He was exhausted. That's all we needed. My poor darling to have a heart attack. I was so angry I couldn't breathe.

Joe wheeled the X-ray equipment to the table, plugged it in, and got out the lead blanket we use with small animals. He laid it over Linc's flanks. The dog still hadn't moved. But he wasn't dead. I knew he wasn't dead. I would have known that from the set of Austin's back.

"Austin?" I said.

"A blow to the head, my dear. He's unconscious, but I'm getting a deep flexor tendon reaction."

So he wasn't in a coma.

"I don't know anything more. Not yet." He turned his head and looked at me. "But I think he's going to be all right."

I pinched my lip again. This was just plain dumb. I never cry. And here I was, gushing away like a faucet at *good* news.

Austin turned back to our dog. And he whistled. That short, sharp whistle that always brings Lincoln at a gallop. Linc's legs twitched, the way they do when he's dreaming.

"Good sign," Austin said. I don't think he had any idea how tired he sounded. "But we need X-rays."

Joe started to put the lead apron on, then hesitated and looked at me. I smiled as best I could. "You go on and give Austin a hand. I'll go make us some hot tea. You stay here, too," I said to Ally. "As soon as you know something more, you come right up and tell me."

"You don't want any company?"

I shook my head. "You check on the mare in about half an hour. See if she's passed the placenta." I stood at the door for a bit, watching the three of them work on the best dog we'd ever had. Lincoln sneezed, bless him, and then made as if to get up. He quieted right down when Austin told him to stay.

I was over the tears. Over the shock. And I was plenty mad. Somebody'd attacked our dog. I had a pretty good idea of who. And an even better idea of why. I was so mad, I was ready to scream. I was so mad, I had no recollection of getting back to the house. I was surprised to find myself in the kitchen where Juno was barking fit to raise the dead.

The kitchen and living room were an unholy mess. It shocked the mad right out of me. The cushions were pulled off of the couch. The La-Z-Boy stood on its head. The books were tumbled off the shelves.

I'd seen hurricanes that'd left less of a jumble. I picked my way over to the living room and then picked my way back again. And there, right next to the contents of the lower drawer that held all my baking pans, was a big, fat hazelnut.

There isn't a hazelnut in my house. I don't care for hazelnuts. But I knew darn well who did. And why. That greedy guts Sullivan. And he must have figured we had the laptop. I suppose we couldn't have been more obvious, questioning him like we did.

That big, fat slob in his size-seven shoes had torn right through our home. The laptop wasn't on the table when he tramped in here, of course—Mr. Smilin' Phil Sullivan wouldn't have opened all my kitchen cupboards, trashed my couch, and turned over Austin's desk if he had found it.

So Austin must have hidden it before he'd come out to the barn. The question was, had Sullivan actually found it after he'd beaten our dog half to death, or did he make this mess because he hadn't? There were a couple of hiding places that only Austin would think of, and I stood there and thought about it some.

The puppy squirmed in her nest and made a little squeak.

Would he have put it under the puppy? No, the Lab wasn't quite housebroken, yet. He wouldn't want her to pee on it.

Juno's barks were beginning to sound a little hoarse. The pantry? I opened the door, and Juno raced out of there like a Thoroughbred at the sound of the starting bell. She skidded to a halt in the middle of the floor, then looked around as if she couldn't remember why she was in such a hurry. She caught sight of the pup, which was what the fuss had been all about in the first place, and hopped into the basket, grumbling to herself all the while.

I checked the pantry out pretty thoroughly, and there wasn't a thing out of place, which said a lot for Jerry Coughlin's training skills. "Good dog," I said to Juno. I checked the oven. Nope. The refrigerator?

Yep. There it sat. Right on top of the last of my pecan pie. I took it out, wrapped it up in Saran Wrap to keep any moisture out, and put it back. I had one more thing to do before I started to set the rooms to rights.

I picked up the phone and keyed in Lila's number.

"What!" she shrieked, when she picked up the phone. "Who is this?"

"It's me, Lila. Maddy."

"Maddy? You okay? What's wrong? It's the middle of the night."

"I'm fine," I lied. "I won't say I'm sorry to trouble you, because if I were that sorry, I wouldn't have."

She didn't say anything. Maybe she was too sleepy to work that one out.

"Lila?"

"Yeah. So what's up?"

"You know where that Phillip Sullivan is staying?"

She didn't say anything to this, either. But I think she was grinding her teeth. "Why?"

"Never mind about why." Goodness. I was more upset than I thought. Austin always says I get rude when I'm freaked out. It's not like me at all. "Lila?"

"Why should I care where that jerk is staying?"

"I don't care if you care, I just want to know."

"The Marriott on Route Fifteen. He wanted me to come over

there tonight, instead of to my place for dinner." She simmered down a bit, then said, "God, Maddy, I am a fool about men."

"We all get the stupids once in a while." I don't think she took this in quite the way I meant, because she banged the phone down, just like Austin does when he's hissy.

I took a look at my poor kitchen with the drawers upended every which way. I got mad all over again.

"That's Number One," I said aloud.

I thought of our beautiful dog with a crack on his head.

"That's Number Two."

There was my Austin, working himself into a heart attack out in the clinic.

"And that's Number Three."

Juno looked at me and barked herself silly.

"Hush, dog. I'm not mad at you."

I could take care of One right away. I sat down and thought a bit. How did a messed-up house rank on the revenge scale?

Not nuclear, but pretty damn bad.

I looked up the number of the Marriott in the Yellow Pages. I punched in the numbers and told them it was an emergency. The phone rang a couple of times, and he picked up. I pinched my nose shut and I said, "Mr. Sullivan? Mr. Phillip Sullivan."

"Who the hell is this?"

"The Tompkins County ER. This is Crystal Homburger, the ER RN."

"What?"

"We understand that you ingested a pork dinner at the home of Lila Gernsback this evening?"

"Yeah, what of it?"

"We're sorry to tell you that Mrs. Gernsback didn't make it." I rattled the call button on the phone and hollered "Sorry! We're breaking up! You need to get down here right . . ." Then I hung up.

If I wasn't going to get any sleep, neither was that ton of lard. And that was just Bomb One. I had a lot more in mind for that turkey.

Then I began to clean up.

I was amazed that it didn't take all that much time to tidy up. By the time Ally dragged herself in, you couldn't tell we'd been invaded, which was what I was after. I didn't want anybody to know about this. Not yet.

Ally smiled at me. "Lincoln's going to be fine, we think. Joe and Dr. McKenzie both decided to stay out there, in case something weird happens. But if you ask me, they're staying out there because they're too tired to move."

"Austin's a wonder, isn't he? What'd the X-ray show?"

"A hairline fracture of the . . ." A yawn interrupted her and she twirled her finger around the side of her head.

"Skull?"

"The skull." She yawned till her jaw cracked. "Sorry. But it's not—ah—subducted? Is that right?"

"It means it hasn't slipped anywhere it shouldn't."

"And Sunny cleansed. I stuck it in a bucket so Austin could check it out for tears, but it looked okay to me."

"You take her temperature?"

"Yep. One hundred three degrees. Normal-normal-normal." She swayed to a chair and sat down. "I'll set my alarm for six and check it again before I feed everybody."

That's the thing about animals. They're 24/7. No sleeping in.

I looked at my watch. Three-thirty in the morning. The baby'd been out and up for more than two hours. Chances were the placenta'd slipped out whole, with nothing left behind to sicken Sunny. I roused poor old Ally from her semi-stupor and sent her up to bed. I took the puppy out to pee. Then I took a pot of hot tea and the oatmeal cookies down to the clinic.

Joe was asleep on his cot in the back room. Austin was dead to the world on the couch. And Linc was in his crate, awake, but definitely dopey. There was a shaved patch the size of a saucer just under his skull. A neat bandage been taped over it. Austin'd stuck a drain in the wound, which meant there were at least a couple of stitches there. Poor boy. Poor old boy. That Sullivan was going to rue the day. I sneaked Linc a cookie crumb, adjusted the horse rug Austin'd thrown over himself, and took myself off to bed.

I'd think about Bomb Two and Three in the morning. And of course, I couldn't forget the computer.

* * *

"My dear," Austin said at breakfast, "the contents of my desk appear to have been rearranged."

Between not very much sleep and a mad-on at Phillip Sullivan, I was as sluggish as a catfish in August. I just looked at him, a spoonful of peaches and oatmeal halfway to my mouth.

"That's weird," Ally said. "The stuff in my duffle bag was messed up, too."

So the rat fink'd gotten up to Ally's room?

Austin looked around the table at the three of us. "Were there any other anomalies?"

"There was a laptop in the refrigerator when I came in early for coffee this morning," Joe said.

"Which is why he didn't find it," Austin said, a little smugly. The man's mind moves like lightning, I swear.

But it wasn't there now because I'd taken it away myself. Darn. I should have hidden it somewhere else before I'd gone up to bed. Kids Joe's age can survive on a couple of hours' sleep for days. I should have known he'd be up with the chickens and into the refrigerator.

"Why who didn't find what?" Ally asked.

Austin glanced at Lincoln. The dog was stretched out on the kitchen floor, asleep. There was a fresh bandage on his head. "It's a matter of simple deduction, Allegra. Last night, Joe acquired Coughlin's computer, presumably from the man who stole it from Coughlin. Subsequently, my dog was attacked. My desk has been rearranged. Your duffel bag has been searched. Hence, the house was searched." He pulled his mustache. "Since the computer is still here, I can assume that Mr. Sullivan will remain interested in acquiring it. I see I must develop a plan."

"Now, Austin," I said. "That's exactly what I don't want us to do."

Austin looked at me over his spectacles. He got up, opened the refrigerator, checked for the laptop, which I'd moved too late, and came back with the pecan pie.

"Where is it, my dear?"

I must have glanced at the puppy. Austin walked over to the basket, moved her gently out of the way, and took out the computer. "I wouldn't have thought of that," he said approvingly. "Although the puppy isn't housebroken yet."

"I wrapped it up pretty tight."

He smoothed the Saran Wrap. "So you did." He sat back down. "You clearly have a plan, my dear. What is it?"

"Well." I looked at Lincoln. "Any man that would attack a dog wouldn't think twice about bashing people. As a matter of fact, most people would sooner bash another person before they attacked a dog."

"True."

"I don't," I said firmly, "want any more bashing. I know that the research Jerry Coughlin was in the middle of is important. So I copied his hard drive onto this." I pulled out a flash drive from my caftan pocket and set it on the table. We all stared it for a minute. "And I was going to give the laptop back to that stinker Sullivan today. Most likely he'll be at Ben Grazley's funeral. I'd decided to give it to him then."

"Just give it back?" Joe said, startled. "Just walk up to him and give it back?"

"Why not? He wanted it badly enough to half kill Linc."

"But he couldn't have killed Jerry Coughlin," Austin said. "He seems to have a verifiable alibi for all of yesterday morning. And I can tell you with certainty that Coughlin had been dead for more than three hours when I found him just after two o'clock."

"The fact that he didn't kill Coughlin doesn't mean the man isn't dangerous. I know you, Austin Oliver McKenzie. You wouldn't sit still half a minute if Sullivan showed up here threatening us. I just didn't want a shoot-out." I didn't mention my plans for Bombs Two and Three. Time enough for that after it was all over.

"It's plain enough why he wants it," Joe said. "The stuff that's on the hard drive is worth billions."

Austin kept on looking at me. "So you just planned on handing the computer over to him? Just like that?"

"Don't pull your mustache, dear."

"You," Austin said, "are planning something else. I know you, my dear. You are fierce in the defense of your own."

I took the pecan pie away from him, just as he was about to stick his fork into it. There was about half left. I cut myself a little piece and stuck the rest in front of Joe. Then I said, "Nothing really illegal, Austin."

Joe coughed into his oatmeal. Ally bent down and retied her sneakers. Austin took all this in for a bit and said, "Will it affect the course of the investigation? Do you plan, for example, to put Sullivan out of commission?"

"Not so's you'd notice."

"Interesting."

So that was all right.

Seventeen

REVENGE is a dish best served cold. I was astonished that Madeline, usually the warmest of women, was capable of contemplating it. Whatever it was, it was bound to be spectacular, and perhaps actionable. Regarding the female of the species, Kipling had it in one. I would leave her to it. But I was prepared to post bail, if necessary.

I finished my oatmeal in a state of mild envy vis-à-vis Joe and the pecan pie. It was Saturday, the fourth day in the Case of the Roasted Onion. I was fatigued, but not unduly so. A great deal remained to be done.

I cleared my throat. "I intend to bring this case to a successful conclusion. And soon."

That certainly got their attention.

"I called Victor Bergland this morning. As I'd anticipated, the ESLA test revealed the presence of antibodies formed in reaction to the virus. Coughlin's test subject was infected with equine infectious anemia."

"What about . . ." Allegra stopped in mid-sentence and looked down at her plate.

"What about Sunny?" Joe asked. "I was wondering about that myself, doc. And Tracks, too."

"Sweetie," Allegra said. "Her name's Sweetie. You should have seen her hopping around the stall this morning."

"She *is* just the sweetest thing," Madeline said. "But Austin wouldn't have brought Sunny back here if he thought there was any chance she was infected. Would you, darling?"

"The chances of infection were remote," I said.

"But," Joe began.

"I agree. The isolation stall was attached directly to the barn.

Just like the human HIV virus, EIA is transmitted through the exchange of fluids. Unlike the HIV virus, the mosquito can act as a reservoir in equidae. So yes, transmission would have been possible." I rose to my feet and walked about the room. "Coughlin had already been testing the validity of—shall we call it the Portable Coggins? Allegra's title, and an apt one. He used Sunny as a test subject. She tested negative. As a matter of fact, I believe there were three other horses he tested the device on: Faraway, Hugo, and Beecher. All four had the nota- tion CC on the Coggins form. And Coughlin referred to his immunoassay test as the CC-ESLA. So we need have few worries on that front.

"Exactly. Now. We know that Sullivan is representing Mc- Clellan in his divorce. We know that Sullivan stole the laptop from Coughlin. And of course, Coughlin was working on a revolutionary testing device for FieldChek. And FieldChek, as we know from McClellan's own rather drunken revelations two evenings ago, was in part owned by Schumacher and Grazley."

"So McClellan's killing these guys off so he'll own the whole shebang!" Allegra said excitedly.

"It doesn't prove it, my dear. It infers it." I sat down again. It had been a short night for sleep. "Inference is not proof. It is a symptom. You may recall that my investigatory model is based on . . ."

"We *do* recall that, sweetie," Madeline said.

"And what about the horses?" Allegra said. "You think Beecher's being drugged, and Faraway's being dead, poor thing, have anything to do with that business? Why attack them, too?"

"It's not McClellan," Madeline said darkly. "It's that slob Sullivan. Anybody that'd hit a dog would kill any number of people. Or horses."

Joe rapped his knuckles on the table. "We're getting pretty far from the point here."

"Money," Allegra said. "It's always about money."

"This case seems to be about money," I agreed. "I believe the insurance scam to be a small venture of Sullivan's own. He was part owner of Faraway, and Beecher, too. And I'm sorry to say that I believe Jerry Coughlin aided him in this scheme. Among the files on Coughlin's computer is Turbo Tax. He was preparing his tax return, naturally, since that time is almost upon us. He received a substantial check from a week prior to Faraway's death last year, and a similar sum the week after. The items are listed as 'consulting fees.'"

"I'd sure like to nail the bugger for that," Joe muttered.

"As would I. We are considerably handicapped by a complete lack of evidence, however. With a little luck, Sullivan's time will come. If nothing else, we can make sure that responsible horse owners will not sell to him, by making what we know to be true known: that horses owned by him come to bad ends."

"Not much satisfaction in that," Allegra said.

"Oh, don't you worry about Sullivan." Madeline smiled with a confidence that made me quake. There was nothing to be done about that, however, except to let events unroll as they may.

I recalled them to the task at hand. "There is one curious point. The device wasn't ready for marketing. A great deal of work remained to be done. Why eliminate the researcher before profit could be made? If McClellan's intentions are to kill all the stockholders so the company remains in his control, why not wait until the research is finished?"

"Could he hire someone else to complete the work?" Joe asked.

"Certainly. But any new scientist is going to take months, if not longer, to come up to speed on this project. It's quite complicated."

"We're looking to you for some answers, my dear." Madeline said.

"I don't have them. Not yet. First, I will ask you, Allegra, to go to the county courthouse this morning to review the documents for incorporation of any of McClellan's businesses. The shareholder agreement is of particular interest to us."

"She has to ride today," Madeline said. "There's almost no time for her and Hugo to get ready for Earlsdown."

"Very true."

"I'll do it," Joe offered.

"The second part of the task is to seek out Nigel Fish. I

thought Allegra might have a better chance of coaxing information out of him."

"That wiener from the paper? I can handle him."

"Handle him with tact, if you would. See how the investigation into Grazley's and Schumacher's death is progressing. There is a remote possibility that we are on the wrong track altogether, and that a sniper is indeed among us." I turned to my beloved. "And you and I, my dear, will pay our respects to Ben Grazley at his funeral this afternoon. I expect that the McClellans will be there."

Madeline smiled, wolfishly. "And so will Sullivan."

The remainder of the morning and early afternoon passed uneventfully. I kept Lincoln on a mild sedative, to give the fracture time to begin to heal. I attended to Tracks, pleased to see that the little filly was full of spirit.

And I called the Liversedge farm to see to the disposition of Coughlin's Longhorn heifer. The family was in Houston; the farm manager was disposed to keep the heifer at my clinic rather than move it. He was not as disposed to pay the charges this would incur. The prospect of payment was moot: the youngster needed attention. I needed Lincoln's help to get her into to the stocks, but the poor fellow was still recuperating in the house. The option was a tie-down, that is, looping rope around three legs and then easing the animal to the ground. It was a tactic that young stock see as a challenge to a wrestling match. Madeline was washing her hair in preparation for our trek to the funeral; the task was mine alone. I may have mentioned that the heifer was a Longhorn; although her horns were nowhere near the nearly five-foot spread they would achieve when she was full grown, they were a significant obstacle to her immobilization. Liversedge's cattle manager had good reason to want the calf under someone else's care.

The heifer and I were contemplating one another when Joe returned from the village. He walked into the barn with a cheerful whistle.

"Can I give you a hand with that, doc?"

"You are just in time, my boy!"

Joe was a dab hand at anticipating both the tenor and direction of the heifer's objections to being tied down. His only complaint was a mild "oof!" when she kicked him in the shins and a rather panicked shout when she aimed her left horn at the zipper on his jeans. (She missed.) But we had her comfortably restrained in a few minutes, and I sluiced the infected teats with Betadine. "She had her antibiotic this morning?"

"About six o'clock."

"Good. Take her temperature again this evening."

"You're not going to the funeral after all?"

"We are."

He ran his hands through his hair.

"Allegra will prove more than competent as an assistant."

He growled.

I released the rope with a jerk, and the heifer skedaddled to her manger and grabbed a mouthful of hay. Animals are wonderful. She'd been rudely, yet painlessly handled, but she didn't sulk. Not like human beings at all.

And suddenly, it all fell into place.

The anomalies were resolved.

I knew the identity of the Summersville Sniper.

We watched the heifer for a moment, and then I said, "Was your mission to Summersville successful?"

"It was interesting." He dug into the pocket of his jeans. "McClellan has incorporated one business here. Greenplace, Inc. It's the company that's behind the development Fish talked about. The corporate officers are McClellan, Sullivan, McClellan's wife, and Ben Grazley."

"The development company has little or nothing to do with the case at hand."

"Yeah, but Greenplace is the parent company for FieldChek."

Now that got my attention. "You mean Sullivan is a partner in FieldChek, too?"

"Yep."

"That," I said, "changes things quite a bit." And indeed it did.

"I found out something else. More than a hundred thousand dollars worth of liens have been filed against Greenplace."

"Now *that*," I said, although I was unsurprised, "Is very interesting indeed. What's the nature of the debt?"

"Bills from an excavating company, preconstruction stuff, mostly."

I sat down on a bale of hay, the better to organize this information in my mind. To be fair, there could be any number of reasons why a bill remained unpaid. A dispute over the performance, disagreement over price. On the other hand, I remembered McClellan's fight with his wife over the credit card bills.

"And Nigel? Did you run into him?"

"At the Monrovian Embassy. Had to buy him a beer. I had to listen to a lot of crap about Allegra, but the guy sucks up all the gossip in the village. He's like a shop vac. Anyhow, I picked up three pieces of information about the suspects. McClellan's project has hit a snag with the EPA."

"Ah. That plus the liens may be a fairly clear indication of money problems. And?"

"Phillip Sullivan's sent a notification of intent to sue."

"To whom?"

"The Tompkins County Hospital. Nigel knows a nurse there. She was at the reception desk when Sullivan waddled in with the letter. Failure to provide due care, or something like that."

This was perplexing.

"And the third thing is the sniper murder. Nigel has it on the QT that the cops are up the creek without a paddle. Unless there's another one, they don't think the case is solvable."

"Oh, my. That's not good." Again, I was not surprised.

"Well, what are they going to do? There's no evidence. None. Just two bullets. And they're bullets like ten million other bullets out there. Sherlock Holmes himself couldn't solve a case like that."

"So they are at an impasse."

"Guess so."

I got up. I had a few more duties in the clinic, and then I needed to bathe and change for the funeral service at four o'clock. I also needed time to think how best to bring the murderer to justice. For the evidence was scant, indeed. "Thank you, Joe. Have you eaten lunch? The remainder of that meatloaf makes an excellent sandwich."

"No thanks, doc. I've got some studying to do. And I thought after evening rounds, I'd wander on over to the Monrovian Embassy. They've got a jazz group booked." He left with a cheerful wave.

I was in the clinic proper, in the process of checking the cast on the Lab puppy, when I heard the sound of a horn in the drive. A car door slammed. Footsteps crunched on the gravel.

"Hey, doc."

"Lieutenant." I didn't look up, being engaged in trimming remnants of acrylic from the puppy's leg. I was, however, mildly pleased to see him. Perhaps he had brought my badge.

"Cute little guy."

I regarded the puppy for a moment. "Her name is Blackie." I set Blackie on her feet. She immediately sat down and washed the area again with her tongue.

"Good name. Ever noticed how some people give their animals really dumb-ass names?"

"Sweetie, for example," I said.

"Or Poopsie."

I put Blackie on the floor. She bounced in a circle, apparently pleased that the cast was lightened. Then she scrambled to the lieutenant and gnawed at his shoes. I debated whether I should point out the similarities between the puppy's fur and the evidence retrieved at the scene of Schumacher's shooting now, or at the time when I revealed the murderer's identity.

"What can I do for you?"

"Wondered if you had a chance to go through those files of Coughlin's."

"I have." I wiped the examination table clean and sprayed it with disinfectant. "Have you had a chance to discover that Coughlin wasn't a diabetic?"

"How'd you know that? Autopsy said he was in pretty good shape for a guy his age. Except he was on Prozac. I told you the guy was depressed." Provost moved back a few steps. The puppy followed. It was definitely time to take her for an outing. Perhaps she could ride with us to the funeral.

"Coughlin's good health and the presence of the glucose monitor are not incompatible pieces of data." I explained the research Coughlin had been doing.

Provost heard me out. Then he gave me a sharp look. "Thought all you got from that filing cabinet was some patient files."

I was ready for that one. Madeline would be most unhappy

to have the laptop fall into official hands at this particular moment. "I also had the serum samples, Lieutenant. Victor Bergland was kind enough to run the assay tests last night in his lab."

"And he got all that from a couple of tubes of blood?"

"I have engaged in bit of inductive reasoning on my own."

"So you can't prove all this science stuff?"

"In the fullness of time, Provost. In the fullness of time. I'd be happy to turn the results of the assay over to you as soon as I myself received them. Or Victor can fax them to headquarters. At this stage of our investigation the documentation is moot, in any event."

"But you think we're looking at big bucks, here? Is that what you're telling me?"

"Yes, 'big bucks' are certainly in the picture."

"But you said the dingus wasn't ready to use."

"Not quite."

"So why would someone kill Coughlin for a dingus that isn't worth a bucket of warm spit, yet?"

"Someone else could complete the research, of course." I picked the puppy up. There was one more piece of information I needed to satisfy my theory. "You found Coughlin's personal papers in his desk?"

"Yeah. You were there."

"Did he leave a will?"

"Everything to his son, Gerald Junior. Had a heck of an insurance policy. The kid's going to be sitting pretty."

I frowned at that. "Everything? Stocks, for example?"

"Everything means everything. It was one of those forms you can pick up at the office supply store. Poor bastard didn't have two nickels to rub together. Guess he couldn't afford a lawyer."

"Did you happen to find a partnership agreement in the papers?"

Provost sighed. "Does all this have anything to do with anything, doc? Or are you just talking to hear yourself talk? There was a folder with some business documents in it."

"Did you happen to notice the partnership agreement?"

"I looked at it, yeah. I looked at all of it. I did call the Feds, you know, after you explained about the horse AIDS, and when those guys come onto a case, it's good-bye to the small-town guys like me. So I read everything I had while I was waiting for them."

"Did you take notes?"

"Sure. I always take notes."

"Turn to the portion of your notes regarding the partner-ship agreement."

Provost sighed. "What can that have to do with the price of bananas in Brazil?"

"Humor me, Lieutenant."

He pulled the steno pad from his jacket pocket and thumb through it with a few totally unnecessary flourishes. "Okay. What's your question?"

"Share distribution. To whom do the shares go if one of the shareholders dies?"

"The company was called FieldChek, Inc." He smacked his forehead with his open palm. "Well, hell. That's the company for the dingus, right?" He read through his notes. "The shares go back to the company, it looks like."

"Good," I said, pleased. "Provost, you're a thorough man. I like a thorough man. However, I'd like to see those documents myself, if I could."

"Tough bounce. Once the Feds came in, they grabbed everything and took it off somewhere." He dug into his pocket, took out a piece of gum and popped it into his mouth. "'Course, they think it's a suicide, too. They'd walk away from it, except for the guy from the Department of Agriculture. This morning, he got all hot under the collar about the dead horse and the horse AIDS."

"It is not 'horse AIDS,'" I said somewhat intemperately. "It is equine infectious anemia."

"Whatever." Provost chewed his gum a little faster, and gazed at a spot somewhere beyond my left shoulder. "There's a reason I came out here, doc. Thing is, to everybody but you, this case is a no-brainer. Coughlin offed himself. There just isn't much question about it. One thing I'll say about the Feds, they get results a lot faster than the Tompkins County PD. And Coughlin's fingerprints were all over the plastic hose he stuck in his mouth, the duct tape, the whole bit."

"It was murder," I said flatly.

"Sorry. We're closing it out as a suicide."

I regarded him steadily. "You are making a mistake."

"Yeah, well. The other thing I dropped by is to tell you is we found Coughlin's son."

Sunny and Tracks. Oh, my. "And he'll want to retrieve his father's property, I should imagine."

"All of it," Provost said, with a slight stress on the word "all." "So if you have any other stuff of his you aren't telling me about . . ."

"Of course," I said blandly. I glanced at my watch. "Goodness. Madeline and I have to get to Ben Grazley's funeral. I have just a few moments. That mare of Coughlin's foaled last night."

"No kidding!"

"Would you like to see them?"

"Sure would."

I led the way into the barn proper. Andrew and Pony were out at pasture, but Sunny stood quietly in her stall. The filly nursed. At our approach, Sunny shifted away from the youngster and came up to the mesh opening. She was searching for a treat. I prevented Provost from giving her a piece of gum. Nonhorse people are idiots.

"Well, isn't that the darndest thing," Provost said. The filly squealed, kicked her heels and raced around the perimeter of the stall. "Amazing that they run around like that, doc. How old is she?"

"About twelve hours." I sighed. Madeline would miss Tracks. "You'll let Gerald Junior know? The mare and the filly undoubtedly belong to him."

"We got hold of him last night. Lives in Chicago. He'll be in this afternoon. Sure, I'll let him know."

A cowbell hangs outside our back door. It rang twice. "That will be Madeline. I'm afraid we must be getting on to the funeral, Provost." We walked together out of the barn and into the April sun. "Any progress on the sniper front?"

He shook his head. "Dammit, no. Heck of a thing, doc, two murders in Tompkins County within a week. This sniper thing's a bugger. We haven't been able to find a bit of evidence. Nothing. Even if I knew who pulled the trigger, I couldn't convict him. I just hope like hell we don't get another one."

Did he? Which was better—two unsolved homicides, or three, with the murderer apprehended?

Neither.

And what was worse, there might be another one.

So I finally told Provost what I suspected.

GRAZLEY had been a noted contributor to the world of equine veterinary medicine, and his funeral was well attended. The nature of his death attracted a few members of the media. I was glad to see that his widow was attended by two burly men who kept the more intrusive members of that pack in abeyance. In the receiving line after the modest service, Mrs. Grazley introduced them as her brothers.

"It was so good of you to come, Dr. McKenzie," she said in a soft, weary voice. "Ben thought highly of your work."

Madeline clasped the widow's hands warmly and said, "I'm so sorry. It's so hard. Are you going to be all right?"

"Oh, Ben was well insured," she said bitterly. "I won't want for a thing. Except the company of the best man that ever lived."

Tears came to Madeline's eyes. "It's so unfair."

Mrs. Grazley bent her head and bit her lip. She was a small, neat woman, with brown hair drawn back with a simple barrette. Her two half-grown children hovered by her, bewildered. She murmured something we didn't catch. Madeline leaned forward. The widow raised her head, her teeth drawn back, her eyes glittering. "The only thing keeping me going," she hissed, "is that they'll catch him. They will catch him, won't they?"

Madeline looked at me.

"I hope so," I said.

We had been invited to the gathering that is usual after a funeral service. It was to be held at Grazley's Canandaigua clinic, due, I believe, to the fact that were so many who had come to pay their respects. It was a forty-five-minute drive from the church in Covert to the site. The afternoon was warm, and the air filled with the scent of spring.

"It's a shame we're on such a sad errand," Madeline said wistfully. She slowed the Prius to forty-five miles an hour. Blackie, who was in the backseat, was much appreciating the outing. "It's such a beautiful afternoon. It seems a long while since we've had time to take a drive."

"We are on more than an errand of respect, my dear. We are on a errand of justice."

"Justice," she repeated.

"You realize that both Coughlin's and Grazley's murders are about to go unavenged?"

"It doesn't sound good," she said. "Do you know who did it, sweetie?"

"I'm reasonably sure."

"Do you know why?"

"I believe so."

"Who is it?"

"My first thought was Brewster McClellan, of course. I've thought so all along. He's in financial trouble. He's divorcing his wife. He's the kind of scumbag that thinks one veterinarian can substitute for another, and that any fool can finish the research. Worst of all, he's the kind of man who would happily see his own child hang instead of himself. 'Kids can get away with anything nowadays,' remember? Now, with the added incentive of share ownership, I'm certain of it. For days the issue hadn't been who, but how do we prove it?"

"Damn. I did want it to be Phillip Sullivan. Even though I knew it can't be." She almost drove off the road. She righted the car and waved apologetically to the sedan behind us that had been forced to brake rather suddenly. "So it's not that rat Sullivan? Didn't I tell you I wanted it to be that rat Sullivan?"

"You knew it couldn't be Sullivan. He had an alibi for Coughlin's murder, and the same person murdered Coughlin who murdered Larky and Ben. As a matter of fact, I fear he might be next."

Then she asked, "Why?"

"Ownership of FieldChek. The shares in the company revert to the company."

"So the heirs to the estates are compensated for the value of the stock, and the stock stays with the remaining shareholders."

She shook her head. "What a creep. Why couldn't he just wait for it to be a big hit? He'll be rolling in it when it hits the market. All of them would."

"He appears to be in financial trouble now. Joe found a number of liens against the property development this afternoon. I should imagine those liens are only representative of the total indebtedness."

"And the horses? What about the horses? What about Faraway's death? And that goofy price for Hugo? And the drug issue with Beecher?"

"Sullivan appears to be behind all that. It is unrelated to the murders."

"Nuts," Madeline said. "Rats. How are we going to catch McClellan, Austin? I refuse to believe that either of those two is clever enough to outsmart the both of us."

"Perhaps they are. But . . ."

"Hang on a second. I almost missed the turn."

The long white buildings of the Grazley clinic loomed in the near distance. We had overshot the drive. Madeline swung a U-turn, to the consternation of the vehicles behind us, and turned back into the drive. A large sign had been posted at the head of the drive. CLOSED 5:00 TO 7:00. The sign lost the dispute with our bumper. I nipped out of the car and forced it upright again. I hopped back in.

"You suppose McClellan's going to be there, blatting away, big as life and twice as natural? At the funeral of the man he killed? It's disgusting."

"It is, indeed. But, Madeline . . ."

Madeline interrupted me, her eyes fierce. "You have to catch the murderer, Austin. You just have to."

I wasn't at all confident of my ability to do so. And in her current state, Madeline was not going to listen. So I sat back and contemplated the probability of the success of my plan. It was not high.

There were a fair number of vehicles in the large parking lot. The flag of the State of New York hung at half-mast. A large canvas awning, of the type that one sees at horse shows all over the Northeast had been erected on the acreage adjacent to the clinic buildings. A young girl with a black band around the sleeve of her blouse directed us to a parking spot and Madeline came to a stop at the end of a long line of vehicles.

We disembarked. I am farsighted. Our quarries stood just outside the entrance to the tent. There was no mistaking the red-haired fat man who stood in the group—Sullivan. Standing a little apart from the group, sipping a glass of wine, was the unfortunate Marina. Her fate was dismal: to be married to a man like McClellan. If the gods were at all just, we would find a way to bring him to justice.

Stephanie was nowhere in sight.

McClellan turned. He saw us. He waved and stepped away from the group. A red dot appeared in the center of his forehead.

He jerked suddenly. Blood blossomed on his face. He fell back and lay still.

"My god," I said. "The man is dead."

Eighteen

~~~~~

ANOTHER death. I was well served for my arrogance. Even though this one was, perhaps, deserved.

The moment McClellan flew backward, I thrust Madeline unceremoniously into the driver's seat and leaned against the door so she couldn't get out. She immediately complained I was blocking her view. A few people screamed. About half the crowd dropped flat on their bellies. The other half either ran for their cars or the clinic building. By and large there was little panic. Horse people are tough. Sullivan lumbered for the nearest car as fast as his dog-bashing little feet could carry him, shoved the man who was sitting there out of the driver's seat, and locked himself in.

Marina threw herself over her husband's body and screamed for help.

Madeline shoved herself to the passenger side of the car, let herself out, and came around to stand by me.

"Please get back in the car," I said.

"Not on your life."

"It's your life I'm worried about, my dear."

"I'll get in if you'll get in."

After twenty years of close companionship, I knew when to give up. She settled herself against my shoulder.

"There's nothing we can do to help?"

I sighed. "I doubt it. You hear the sirens?"

"I do."

"The bullet hit him squarely in the center of the forehead. I'll go and see what's to be done. You get back in the car."

"As if," Madeline said.

Then Greg D'Andrea appeared out of the confusion and

knelt by the body. He lifted Marina to her feet and hurried her away to the clinic building.

"That was brave," Madeline said, "and to think I took against the poor boy because he chewed toothpicks."

I opened my mouth and closed it again.

It was quiet, except for the sounds of the sirens in the distance. Brewster McClellan lay staring into the setting sun.

So we returned to the car and waited for the police to come. I pulled Blackie onto my lap. The ambulance arrived just after the police. Both the medical technicians and the police raced onto the field with no thought for their own safety. In a short space of time, the area was roped off, and the police were crawling all over the clinic roof. After a long while, the police led those people out of the building who had sought refuge there, and everyone returned to the tent. A well-spoken young policeman came up to us and asked us very politely to go give our names and addresses to the "guy with the sergeant's badge." So we got out and sat at one of the tables and waited our turn. Blackie alone was unaffected by the atmosphere. She romped at our feet, tail wagging with delight at being out in the fresh air.

Marina sat with Greg a little apart from everyone else. Stephanie had surfaced. She sat at distance from her mother, staring into space. Someone had draped a blanket around Marina's shoulders. Sullivan lumbered up and laid a consoling hand on her shoulder. He looked jumpy. And when he sat down, it was behind Marina, so that she was between him and the clinic building. I thought about sneaking up behind him and yelling "Bang!" into his fat red ear.

Finally Simon Provost arrived. He looked exhausted. He avoided my gaze. He spoke quietly to Marina. She had her face buried in her hands, but she nodded a couple of times.

"They found the gun," somebody behind me said. We looked up. Two policemen on the clinic roof waved at the men on the ground. One of them held up a long skinny gun with a scope on it. It was encased in a large plastic bag.

"I'm going to get you something to eat, sweetie." Madeline eased herself off the bench. "There's all that food that's been set out for the funeral, going to waste."

I straightened my shoulders in surprise. It seemed an odd time to eat. "I'm fine, my dear. Would you like me to get you something?"

"Nope. They have rumaki over there, and I wouldn't mind a bite of that. Then I want to stretch my legs a bit. Why don't you walk around with me?"

Then she leaned over and whispered in my ear.

I leaned back. "That, my dear, is far better than the plan I had in mind."

There is no question in my mind that Madeline is the brain of our family. The woman is brilliant. If I'd had the wit to see what she'd seen . . . well, she had a point. No matter what, we both knew that this particular murder could not have been prevented. It would have happened at some other time, in some other place.

We each took a piece of the rumaki. I fed mine to Blackie, who wriggled with delight at the unexpected delight. We drew Provost aside and spoke to him. He listened intently for long minutes.

"Hell," he said, "I don't mind looking like a fool. Not my jurisdiction anyhow." He grabbed a friend from the Canandaigua Police Department and asked him to give him a hand.

Then we approached Marina and Greg D'Andrea. The puppy took one look at Marina and began to howl in fear. The heartrending sound stilled the tumult in the tent.

"She remembers, you see," I said. "Did you use a baseball bat?"

Provost had stashed the chewed toothpick from the rumaki in the evidence bag. He held it up and said, "Jig's up, D'Andrea. Found this where you hid on the roof with the rifle."

Then, with a facility I truly admired, he and the other policeman pulled their guns and trained them on D'Andrea's chest, as quick as a flash. D'Andrea put his hands up, his face wary.

I turned to him. "You're a scientist," I said conversationally. "Certainly good enough to pick up where Coughlin left off. And as a scientist you know more than most about trace evidence. The DNA on the toothpick will be proof positive of your presence on the roof."

"Marina," Madeline said. "It was dumber than dumb to get mixed up with a guy like that. As soon as you got married, he'd probably kill you, too."

As my wife had predicted, it was Marina who broke.

Epilogue

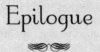

"At first, I was suspicious because she just flung herself on Brewster's body," Madeline said to Lila Gernsback. "They purely hated each other. Why would she all of a sudden risk her own tail to cover up a husband she wanted deader than a doornail anyhow?"

"Makes sense," Lila said.

"And, of course, what Austin had been trying to tell me finally sank in. You know how he likes to start a story from the very beginning . . ."

"You mean how he blabs on and on and on?"

"I wouldn't," Madeline said with an injured air, "call it blabbing, exactly. But he was in the middle of telling me that McClellan *wasn't* the murderer, and I cut him right off."

It was the first day of the Earlsdown event. We were assembled in the committee tent, waiting for the opening ceremonies to begin. The day was a brilliant blue. The air was crisp and dry. The show pennants snapped in the breeze, a tuneful accompaniment to the scents and sights of a major horse show.

My Veterinary Commission had been deployed and the equine entrants had been tested and approved as fit to ride. The Berglands, Lila, Madeline, and I sat at a large round table with drinks in hand. Lincoln, Juno, and Blackie were sprawled at my feet. The air was alive with expectation.

"I would have been scared out of my *mind*," Lila said. She and Allegra had been so busy with the last of Hugo's interval training she was starving for news of the arrest. "And then what happened?" She leaned forward. She was wearing some sort of scarlet thing that displayed generous amounts of bosom. Beside me, Victor cleared his throat and leaned forward, too. Thelma scowled at the both of us.

Madeline was magnificent in a sapphire caftan. Her auburn hair was freshly washed and piled in luxuriant curls on the top of her head. I caught the scent of freesia from her hair. "Well, *then*, when everyone else was crammed together in that tent worried that the sniper was still out there, Marina and Greg sat right out in the open, with their backs to the roof. Now, I ask you, Lila. Would you sit out in the open with a sniper on the loose?"

"If it were a male sniper, she would," Thelma snarled.

"Of course you wouldn't," Madeline continued. "Marina's not dumb. And she's not brave. She didn't even have the gumption to go help her own daughter out of the fix she was in when Beecher dumped her. Austin told me all about it. Why would a woman like that be brave all of a sudden with a husband she didn't like?"

"I just can't believe it," Lila said. "What a mess. What a mess."

"It's still a mess," I offered. "The physical evidence is tenuous, at best. The physical evidence has been our problem all along. A good lawyer can make mincemeat of the prosecution."

"At least they'll try to put the pair of them in jail," Madeline said.

"I think the toothpick idea was brilliant," Victor said. The man was in heaven. Between Madeline's creamy effulgence and Lila's extraordinary mammary display, he was surrounded by an aesthetic he didn't find at home. I poked him in the ribs with my finger.

"What the hell, Austin."

"Stop staring at my wife."

"I do think the toothpick was brilliant," he said in a tone of injury.

"Not all that brilliant," Thelma said sourly. "Get me another gin and tonic, Victor."

"Very well, dear."

"Austin says it was the heifer that put him on to her," Madeline said.

Lila blinked. "The heifer?"

I cleared my throat. "Despite the manhandling we put animals through, they generally always forgive us. Unlike human beings. There was more than greed behind Marina's plan. She hated Brewster for his abuse."

"And that rat Sullivan is behind an insurance scam for killing horses?" Lila's bosom heaved.

"We knew *that* because of the hazelnut," Madeline said. "It just goes to show that a little tiny nail can bring down the whole shooting match."

"I don't get it about the hazelnut."

And she probably never would. We had indeed, returned Jerry Coughlin's laptop computer to Phillip Sullivan, who had accepted it with a surliness beyond belief. We had left it at that. I'd had my doubts about prosecuting the man for breaking, entering, and attacking my dog after we had broken, entered, and engaged in theft first. Although I would not admit it to Madeline, I doubted that my charter as a Summersville deputy extended that far. Lila must have caught the drift of my thoughts by some telepathic means, because she said, "I couldn't believe that you proposed that jerk Sullivan as a jump monitor, Maddy. I thought you would have been glad to see the last of him. I sure was. And you never did tell me why you wanted to know where he was staying that night."

"I told him volunteering would go a long way toward having folks forgive him for tryin' to sue the hospital," Maddy said. "Gave him few tips about how to handle the monitor job, and that was it."

"Well, just tell me where he is standing, so I can stay away from him," Lila groused.

"The water jump," Maddy said.

"I can't believe that I almost sold him my horse."

"No, he's not a man you want to have in the horse community," Madeline said.

Lila drained her iced tea and jumped up. "I'm going to go check on him and Ally. Want to come with me?"

Madeline nodded. "I've got the camcorder. I want to get as much as I can on tape. Thelma, you come with us, too. You don't want to sit here with these boring men."

Thelma blushed. "You really want me to come?" Lila rolled her eyes. Madeline gave her a nudge. "Yeah, yeah, yeah," Lila said. "You know how to scrub tack?"

"I'm a very good housekeeper," Thelma said. "I'd probably be able to learn."

Victor and I watched them leave. "About that FieldChek," Victor said.

"I know. Unfortunately, the whole of the company now belongs to Phillip Sullivan and Marina McClellan."

"Marina may need to sell her shares to pay for her defense," Victor said thoughtfully. "Sullivan's a problem, though. The man's a walking monument to greed."

I adjusted my spectacles. "At the moment, FieldChek's worth is all potential, not actual. And the agreement stipulates quite a cheap buyout. You might be able to pull some university funds together and buy him out."

"How's that?"

I wished, once again, that I had not been forced to give up my pipe. It adds a certain je ne sais quoi to the summation of a case. "The current cheap buyout was one of the reasons for the timing of the murders. The device was not complete. The partnership agreement would be up for renegotiation upon the divorce. And of course, the couple was out of money." I smoothed my mustache. "It is a very valuable process, Victor. If it can be made to work."

"You don't need to tell me that. As you say, if it can be made to work."

"And it'll do enormous good in the agricultural community. Imagine being able to test for pregnancy in the barn! It would considerably lower costs. And if the process can be made available to humans . . ." I shook my head at the immensity of the potential.

"Comparable to getting rid of smallpox." Victor said, with a considerable degree of self-importance.

"Hardly that," I responded, annoyed.

"Well," Victor said reluctantly, "I suppose I can make some

inquiries about buying the research from Sullivan. You said it's not complete?"

"By no means. It requires a substantial investment in continued development. By scientists. It would be an ideal project for one of your young PhD candidates. And who knows if the device can be actually manufactured? There are a lot of 'ifs' in the equation at the moment. That's one of the reasons McClellan was short of investors. It's a hard idea to sell to those outside the agricultural community."

"You know what the money situation is like at the school. And Sullivan's the kind of creep that'd demand an arm and a leg."

"It may be less costly than you think. You remember Faraway?"

"Of course I do."

"There is some evidence—not enough to carry us much further—of insurance fraud. Sullivan was peripheral to that, if not involved directly. At best, he had what is called, I believe, guilty knowledge."

Victor grunted in distaste.

"Precisely. But he needs the resources of the scientific community if the project is to go further. You are good at negotiation, Victor. I would suggest that you confront the man as soon as may be, and see what sort of deal can be struck."

"I get all the dirty jobs, Austin."

"You are uniquely suited to handle them."

Our attention was diverted from what was shaping up to be quite a satisfying squabble by a rumpus at the entry to the tent. Rita Santelli blew in, her digital camera held aloft, her face pink with laughter. I waved at her. She waved back at me, and proceeded to wind her way through the crowd. She stopped at intervals, apparently to display an image on the tiny screen that such devices carry, to anyone within the reach of her arm. She was followed by laughter, and an exodus to the outside.

"Hey, Austin," she said. She sat down at the table and sighed happily. "Great day for a horse show."

"It is indeed."

"What's all the hoo-ha?" Victor asked.

Rita looked at the camera and began giggling. "You know, I think I can sell this to the nationals. Look."

She thrust the camera at me. I adjusted my spectacles. There, at the water jump, was Phillip Sullivan, naked as the day he was born except for a Speedo bathing suit.

"Somebody told him the recommended attire for the water jump monitors is *always* a Speedo bathing suit. Do you see who that is? It's that awful divorce lawyer, Phillip Sullivan. And he has to stay there *all day*. Everybody's going out to look. I told them to take their cameras."

"Bombs two and three," I said.

AND a final word from Madeline:

AND that's how my Austin solved the Case of the Roasted Onion.

The Earlsdown event was just a fabulous show. Ally and Hugo didn't take a blue, of course. They'd started working together too late in the day for that. But they came in a respectable twenty-second, and a couple from Poughkeepsie made an offer for Hugo that'll keep Lila in alfalfa for months. And Austin said that Victor had found a way to get the Field-Chek research going at the veterinary school, and that was all right. And Simon Provost brought Austin's deputy papers to the farm himself, along with an official letter of thanks from the Summersville mayor. It was a shame, as Ally pointed out, that it wasn't a badge. Maybe I'll laminate something up for him.

So we came home to triumph. Ally sat down and talked to us about bringing Harker home to stay with us. So we started to talk about that.

The only sad thing was that Sunny and Sweetie had been shipped off to Jerry Coughlin Junior's farm. I'd loved having that little filly hopping around the place. And Jerry Junior decided to call the filly Tracks.

Some men just don't have a sentimental bone in their body.

CLAUDIA BISHOP is the author of fourteen Hemlock Falls mysteries featuring Meg and Sarah Quilliam. She is at work on the second in The Casebooks of Dr. McKenzie series.

As Mary Stanton, she is the author of eleven novels for middle-grade readers and two adult novels. She divides her time between a farm in upstate New York and a small home in West Palm Beach. She can be reached at claudiabishop.com.